C.W. Biggs, Country Detective

By Doc Underwood

Featuring Patsy Cline is Crazy and Bright Lights, Biggs' City

ISBN: 9780989984109

ISBN-13:97809899841-0-2

Docwoodproductions

Printing by CreateSpace

BISAC IDENTIFIERS: Primary: Fiction Mystery

And Detective-General

Secondary: Fiction-General

ACKNOWLEDGMENTS

I have no doubt that I will forget some of the wonderful people who have helped me with this endeavor but I want to try. First, I'd like to thank Susan Snow and Neil MacDonald who graciously took time to review my material for grammar and composition errors. I'd like to thank Alisa, Sarah, Brianne, Lloyd and Dudley, my writer's circle, for their help and suggestions. In addition, I wish to thank Al, Michele and the Social Studies Department at Lee County High School (both past and present) for their early encouragements. I also am appreciative of the prompt response of the CreateSpace team to all my questions. Thanks also to Adrienne Bashista for helping steer me through the labyrinth of self-publishing. I am particularly grateful to my instructors from CCCC, Marjorie and Melissa. They are, despite their protestations, singled out in the book. However, if they disclaim any knowledge of this I will understand.

I want to thank my entire family including its newest additions for their support and enthusiasm for the project when enthusiasm on the part of the author lagged. I want to single out the staff at Vest Water Plant in Charlotte for their help in taking a stranger around to see their historical facility. I also am so appreciative of Jared Terrell who stepped up at the last moment and created a wonderful cover illustration. Lastly, I want to thank my best editor, friend and wife, Melanie.

Any errors in this manuscript are solely the mistakes of the author despite the incredible efforts of all of the above contributors.

Table of Contents

HOW I BECAME A DETECTIVE
By

C.W. Biggs, Aspiring Writer

In Partial Completion of Writing Requirements

For

Creative Writing 102

Instructor: Dr. Marjorie Dellbridge

North Central Carolina Community College

I am writing this autobiographical account because of our illustrious instructor's prompt to write something we know about that's important to us. It turns out that would be me and how I came to be the best detective in Boger County. It all started when I discovered I could make money finding dogs for a living. Some were actually lost. It became the path of least resistance, especially after my success in solving the case of the Barrington Stooge Poisonings. Perhaps I should start at the beginning before this gets too confusing.

I made the move to become a detective after an intensive study program with at least eleven colleges and several others that didn't know I was attending. I later learned this is called "auditing". This decision was also thrust upon me after several important, yet intermediate, occupations such as grocery clerk, video store impresario and traffic counter for the DOT. After eighteen years of modest success, I was influenced by media perceptions to pursue a certification in private investigation. I may also have moved on after my mother threatened to kick me out of the house if I didn't start producing income. She was instrumental, some might say maniacal, helping me get my first assignment.

After receiving my certificate from the Shamus Institute for Private Investigation or SI PI to its alumni, I returned to my hometown of Green Top, a metropolis of 5,000, to make my fortune. I was the only detective in town. I soon found out why. Everybody in Green Top knew everything about everybody which makes being a detective kind of superfluous. Fortunately, my mother ran a successful cosmetics business out of the trunk of her car and one of her most consistent customers was this old widow woman up in Branch County. This woman was older than Aunt Hester's snuff. She had a reputation for being ornery and loving only one thing–her dozen yapping, yipping Pekinese. But her dogs had begun to disappear at an alarming rate, despite living next door to the Sheriff. Soon she was only left with the three meanest of the bunch misnamed, given their disposition, Curly, Moe and Larry. Well, maybe not Moe.

My reputation, such as it was, rested on my ability to recover lost pets. Based on these strong credentials and my mother giving the widow a twenty five percent discount on her next cosmetics purchase, I got my first real investigative assignment. It would seem that the dogs, led by the three stooges were creating all sorts of crap both literally and figuratively, on her neighbor's yard, the aforementioned Sheriff. I went up with a friend of mine, set up two or three video cameras, loaded up with video tapes (yes, I am that old) and began what we in the detective business call "a stake-out".

Nothing happened for a few days, until I got a shot of the good Sheriff feeding Curly and Moe a hot dog. It seemed harmless enough, but the two dogs got very sick and were soon headed to doggie heaven. Now, I have to tell you they were both over 11 years old, which is pretty old by dog standards. It could be seen as mere coincidence, but I smelled a rat or in this case a dirty cop.

I felt like I had enough tape evidence to pull the trigger on most everyone except a well–connected Sheriff. I needed more evidence before I went to the District Attorney to ask for a dog autopsy. I mulled going to see the old lady after the doggie funeral out at the Barrington Animal Cemetery. But, events moved faster than I could.

Determined to get extra evidence, I had returned to the scene of the crime and was sitting in my semi-duck blind on the old lady's property when Larry ended his mourning period for his comrades with another present for the Sheriff. The Sheriff showed up with another hot dog, but Larry must have decided that the hot dog might lead to him being a dead dog and high tailed it to his own property. The frustrated Sheriff stared in disgust and went back into his house for his trusty squirrel rifle. He only had to wait until twilight when Larry showed back up and crossed the Mason-Dixon Line.

The Sheriff's reputation as a crack shot was well deserved that night, and Larry was no more. Now I had the evidence that would seal the deal. Unfortunately, I let out a loud gasp, and the Sheriff knew he had been seen. By the time I got to my old Dodge parked on the main road, blue lights were coming towards me. I knew I couldn't outrun the sheriff's LTD, so I had to think fast. A scheme presented itself that was quite fortunate for me, but not so for the widow.

You see, killing dogs down south is political suicide. You remember the Congressman who got into election trouble when he grabbed that reporter who stuck a mike right into his nose? Well, that's nothing compared to what people would think if you killed dogs, even Pekinese. The Democrats would think the Sheriff was horrendously cruel and the Republicans would claim he was cowardly for using poison and not shooting all three of the dogs from the start. So I knew I was holding a winning hand, if the Sheriff didn't shoot me first. I think that crossed his mind for just a few seconds.

When the Sheriff stopped me, I got out with the video camera in hand and made sure he saw the red recording button on the little camera. I quickly introduced myself and asked how his re-election campaign was going. He stared at me in disgust, but the sheriff was a smart Democrat, who had been elected in a county that leaned Republican. He caught on very fast where my conversation was going. We quickly came to terms. I would tell the old woman that the other dogs had gotten into some bad hamburger, providing a made up autopsy from the famed veterinarian Dr. Werner Von Schlossburg who conveniently had moved out of state and therefore would be hard to contact. The Sheriff would bury Larry and I would hold onto the videos until hell froze over or he lost an election. The Sheriff quickly agreed. I smoothed things over with the widow by getting her a mongrel from the local animal shelter and having her invest in a cheap electronic dog fencing wire. I even taught the dog myself, ironically using hog dogs and shock therapy.

The Sheriff gratefully tossed some cases my way every so often and told some of his fellow sheriffs that I was willing to take contract jobs. You wouldn't think there would be much for me to do, but you have to understand that in these small counties, the Sheriff's Department would get strange calls from strange people (who also happen to be voters) that have to be investigated. Especially in election years. You know–things like alien abductions and wayward wives or husbands. By the way I am hoping to publish a paper of mine that shows a direct correlation between reports of alien abduction and reports of straying husbands or wives. There's no way the sheriff is going to pull a deputy off a speed trap for stuff like that, so the locals would contact me either directly or indirectly. Business boomed for me. (Boomed being relative when your asking price is $35 an hour plus expenses). And my lucky benefactor, the Sheriff, kept getting elected.

A few years later the Sheriff would set me up to solve my most famous case to date, the infamous "murder" of Patsy Cline. And that's how I became the best detective in Boger County.

Patsy Cline Is Crazy

This is the almost true story of the murder of Patsy Cline. No, not that Patsy Cline. This Patsy Cline worked as a personnel director out at the mill on the Highway 32 Bypass in Barrington. If you know anything about the recent economic history of the South and in particular North Carolina, you know it was once dominated by textile mills. Every town had two or three big ones and a half dozen little ones and Patsy's town of Barrington was no different. But now? Let's just say, the personnel director is the busiest person in the plant and one's liable to make enemies every other Friday when a few more would get pink slips. And Patsy's demeanor didn't help any. In fact she could act–let's get this out of the way—crazy! Yeah, like most everybody, I know that was one of the other Patsy Cline's greatest hits. So, every time this Patsy was introduced, someone would start whistling or singing "Crazy". Now I have to warn you, this is going to be a continuous theme in this story so you might as well get used to it. In fact, it might help to check your old CDs and see if you've got the song somewhere and put it on. It will help you get through the slower passages.

I got into this mess with Patsy because I'm a private eye, the best shamus in all of Boger County. The fact that I am the only detective in the county has very little to do with that title. If you haven't read my autobiography, my name is C.W. Biggs, a name that rested well with me until this network that nobody watches came along and started billing itself as the new CW. Now everybody gets a real kick out of calling me the 'Old' C.W. No matter what the situation, "friends" can't wait to say "Here comes Old C.W.," even though I'm on the near side of 40 and within twenty five pounds of what I weighed when I played college baseball, maybe thirty. I have all my hair (except that little spot on the back), I only wear glasses when I'm reading. . . everything, but my hearing is almost as good as before I went to hear POISON and had front row seats in

Charlotte (or was it Raleigh?). Anyway, my mind is as sharp as a steel trap. (Maybe it was Norfolk.)

It doesn't matter. I need to get on with how I came to be the chief detective and principal investigator in the disappearance of Patsy Cline. Actually I had known Patsy since high school. She was a few years ahead of me and at the time was known as Darla Jean Patricia McRorie. Now, again, if you're from the South, that name is not going to shock you. If you're not, just know that if you say it with a drawl, it doesn't sound nearly as bad as it does if you're from Boston or New York. But Patsy didn't like her first two names and when she left our poor tobacco dominated county for the big city of Barrington two counties to the north, she began using her middle name. She became a secretary in what was the biggest mill in town, Cline's Textile. Still is the biggest, though that doesn't mean as much as it once did. It was there she met the son of the owner, Frank Lee Cline.

Now I'm not one to cast aspersions but Frank was a bit of a cold fish and Patsy was one of the first women who had paid much attention to his acne marred face.   Patsy was no beauty queen but she did have a fantastic figure and she knew how to use it. Before too long it became common knowledge that Patsy's rise through the administrative ranks seemed to match Frank's hand marching northward toward Patsy's, um, unmentionables. Soon a marriage became inevitable.

Neither of the betrothed's mothers was happy about the gathering nuptials. Frank's mom seemed convinced that Patsy was a gold digger and Patsy's mom was just as convinced that the Clines were Carpetbaggers. You see, the Clines were originally from up north and their name was spelled "Klein." Some said it was really Kleinschmidt, and others said they went to church on Saturday. Despite the fact that the family could trace a heritage in Barrington back as far as World War I, there was a feeling among some of the

Daughters of the Confederacy, in which the McRories could claim membership as least as far back as their Klan membership, that something wasn't kosher about the Klein's.

Nevertheless, the two families merged twenty two years ago and have rarely spoken since. As is the case with many marriages, there were ups and downs, which gets me into the picture, after a bit of a detour. About a dozen years ago, after my ten years of college and trying my hand at movie video sales and other high paying jobs, I noticed that my town, Green Top, lacked a private eye. I filled the niche by receiving a certificate in investigative science from SI PI University. Too late I discovered business was very sparse because everybody knew everything about everybody. There was no need for a private eye. Luckily, I got a big break by saving the Sheriff of Branch County from a doggone scandal which could have ended his political career.

The Sheriff would send some cases my way and told some of his fellow sheriffs that I was willing to take contract jobs. He kept getting elected and I got cases like finding crazy Patsy Cline.

About five years ago, Patsy went out one weekend and didn't show up at work on Monday. Now, she already had a reputation for flightiness so the only person who seemed concerned was her husband. But the Cline family was big enough that the Sheriff couldn't ignore them like he did some calls. It wasn't even an election year and the Cline's were willing to pay expenses, but the Sheriff considered it not worth his time. After a perfunctory search, he called me to see if I could find Patsy. This led to my taking a trip to Edenton. As an added bonus I would have more money to work with than usual (not the sheriff's money, of course).

How I Met Her Mother

The Sheriff didn't have much to go on, and he said he didn't have enough time to go chasing after a woman who might be on a ten day drunk. I could tell he wasn't real fond of Patsy, so I decided to start with her husband, Frank, for information. I headed for the pseudo-mansion. The heads of both families truly did have mansions by my standards, but Frank's job as assistant manager of the main mill had them living in a 1950s 4 bedroom, 2 bath ranch split-level at the country club development just outside the city limits. It was nothing to sneeze at, but it seemed underwhelming knowing this was one of the richest families in the county. Frank was genuinely concerned, or did a good job acting when I went to see him. Frank said that he had seen Patsy a week ago Saturday and she was in a good mood. He had no reason to believe she had any reason to leave. After a few more questions, his concern was replaced by some taciturn, perhaps even suspicious answers. It quickly became obvious I wasn't going to get anything more than "yep" and "nope" from Frank, so I decided to pursue another lead.

I remembered that when Patsy was still Darla Jean she used to hang around with a girl named Etta Mae Winstead, a distant cousin, who had also moved to Barrington. She had never married, in part because, well, Etta Mae was skinny as a rail. Actually she was skinnier than a rail and she had a buck tooth smile than was pleasant until she opened her mouth. I had been warned that Etta Mae was not a spinster and enjoyed the company of men. So much so that some guys claimed that they had spent a weekend at her house and didn't remember a thing. Will Buckles, a friend of mine, warn me not to drink any tea, sweet, hot or flavored with strawberries.

Forewarned but wishing to appear as friendly as possible, I approached her front porch with trepidation. Etta Mae lived in a small bungalow just a few blocks off Barrington's Main Street. I introduced myself and she vaguely remembered me from high school and definitely remembered my older brother. (I asked him about that later and he claimed he didn't recall). I politely took a cup of the tea, but was quite careful to make a large sound of sipping without drinking anything. When she turned her head or checked her watch I would pour as much as I could into a potted lily. Thinking I was hooked, the scarecrow shaped siren turned into quite a conversationalist and gave me some valuable information. This took several hours so I'll give you the summary.

She claimed that Patsy was not happy in her marriage despite Frank's protestations to the contrary. She said I should check out a gentleman named Don Rivera, the yarn mill supervisor at Cline. Etta Mae also told me Patsy's relationship with her mother was not good, and had grown worse since her mother had divorced Patsy's father and moved into Barrington by marrying into another FFB (first families of Barrington), the Worshams, who could claim membership in the DOC, the DAR, and half a dozen other organizations that looked with disdain at some of us poor peasants.

You remember I said that the families didn't talk and the Worshams saw the Clines as carpetbaggers of the worst kind. Patsy's attempts to mend fences with her mother had led to more broken fences. Etta Mae said that Patsy had a hard time ignoring her mother's admonitions that she had married beneath her. I decided to call an end to the conversation since I was getting light-headed from the fumes of the tea. I also was afraid she would notice the lily was already drooping. So, I sprang up which startled Etta Mae who was already plumping up the pillows on the couch. I gave her a quick wave and a thank-you before she could react, and headed to the Worsham's mansion.

The mansion was a real one this time, right in the center of town with the columns and balcony and everything. The yards were immaculate with the ivy evenly trimmed but I knew I was in trouble when I drove up to the house. It was a warm September day but there was frost on the windows. It was a Victorian two story painted blue which added to the frosty feeling.

I knocked on the door and saw the first maid I had seen in twenty years. She asked my name and business and said she would let Miz Eurydice know I was here. Now, I have a standing rule that if a woman's name starts with a Eu, you should do everything you can to get away as fast as possible. It went back to a great aunt named Eudora who liked to grab my ears and drag me around her house showing relics of the Ice Age. I waited in the frosty foyer blowing in my hands to get some warmth wondering how the house stayed so cold without the hum of air conditioning. I thought about turning around and getting in the old Dodge but I needed the money. A door opened and an austere relic motioned me to the room, a Victorian style library. The maid closed the door behind us and I stood facing a formidable woman dressed in a high collar blue dress that almost reached the floor.

I began with a standard opening, "Mrs. Worsham, my name is C. W. Biggs, I'm a detective and I've been hired to check into the disappearance of your daughter, Patsy."

"Darla Jean has not disappeared," she haughtily stated, "and that husband of hers knows it."

"Well, perhaps 'lost,' is more accurate." I tried to recover the initiative on what was becoming an icy slope.

With a frozen stare, Mrs. Worsham replied, "Nor is she lost. She knows exactly where she is and when she's ready to tell that nitwit husband of hers where that is, she will."

I wasn't exactly sure how to proceed, and there was a pregnant pause before the Ice Queen spoke. "Biggs," she said as the icicles began to grow on the mantle. "I'm not familiar with any Biggs in Branch County."

Ah, a chance to warm up the conversation, "No ma'am, I'm from Green Top." Instead, the room turned fifteen degrees colder and I knew I had misstepped as soon as the words left my mouth. I swear she hissed as she renewed the conversation. "Green Top? I have not been to Green Top in eighteen years. Is it still as rustic and rundown as ever?"

Now I know Green Top isn't New York City or Raleigh, hell it's not even Siler City, but you defend your hometown. It's a matter of Southern honor, so I tried to deflect the canard with a bit of humor.

"Well, Ma'am, we do have a new Super Wal-Mart." There was no sound except for the icicles on the mantle falling and plinking on the hearth. I had never seen a woman's eyebrows arch that high as the silence continued for what seemed an eon. Finally she broke the silence, "As you may know, my family was NOT from Green Top. My family was from Edenton and I was a Hewes."

Again, an awkward silence followed as I watched the icicles on the hearth reconstitute themselves into an iceberg. I knew I was supposed to say something but I could think of nothing. As the berg moved closer to my feet I began to feel like the Captain of the Titanic.

The Ice Witch finally spoke, "You do know your North Carolina history, don't you Mr. Biggs."

Not remembering a thing from my Seventh Grade North Carolina history class, I once again tried the familiarity approach. "Oh, you can call me C.W., Mrs. Worsham."

"Why?" she interjected.

"Why what, Ma'am?" I noticed the berg becoming a glacier.

"Why would I want to call you C.W., Mr. Biggs?"

Silence again, I began to feel like the mouse who knows the cat is through playing with him. I asked if we could sit down. She motioned me to a sofa and unfolded herself in a red velvet chair.

Eurydice stared at me for a long moment. "Hewes," the ice oracle returned to her family history, "Mr. Biggs, Joseph Hewes, one of North Carolina's signers of the Declaration of Independence!"

"Oh, yes, yes, of course," scrambling to recover while I wondered if she had been present for the signing.

"He was a relative and my family is related on both my mother and father's side." Her face had briefly broken into something nearing a smile. A glimmer of incest crossed my mind, but my lips were frozen tight out of fear as much as the buildup of the glacier.

I decided this was going nowhere and I needed to get to a lifeboat before they all filled up. A strategic retreat seemed appropriate, actually a strategic rout was more accurate. I manage to chatter out, "Th-th-thank you, Mrs. Worsham for your time. I think I have all the information I need," and stumbled out the door before the avalanche overwhelmed me. As I drove off, I tried to think of anything useful I had gotten besides just avoiding frostbite. At first I came up with nothing. Two things finally stirred from my frozen neurons–Mrs. Worsham's comment that Patsy had not disappeared and was not lost and her references to Edenton. Was she trying to give me a clue or was it a red herring? I had never been to Edenton and it meant travel expenses I could charge to the county, so what the hell. I went to the Sheriff on a court day which can always be very busy with all the traffic violations he could conjure up. I hoped he would be too busy with the miscreants to pay much attention to my request. I was partly correct, he signed off on the voucher as he grumbled about the lack of deputies for finding jurors but he made sure there was a limit of $200 dollars on my entire venture, not exactly enough to live it up even in the staid town of Edenton. The next morning, after getting a battery jump from a friendly stranger, I got the old Dodge started. I gassed up and began the two hour trip to Edenton.

My Trip to Edenton

Now Edenton is one of the oldest and most historically prominent towns in North Carolina. It has a history that dates before the Revolution and, indeed, one of the more important events in our history took place there with the Edenton Tea Party, an event that was famous for ladies of the town refusing to drink British tea. It was one of the opening salvos of the Revolution and left the town as a historical landmark, one that the citizens of the town were loath to let anyone forget.

I began my investigation at the Edenton Police Station and asked the police chief if there had been any reports of mysterious women in town. He smiled and said Edenton was full of mysterious women. I would have found that more credible if I hadn't notice his secretary was giving him a salacious smile as she unbuttoned and buttoned back the first button on an already low cut blouse. I changed tactics and asked what he could tell me about the Hewes family. His back suddenly stiffened and his voice turned icy (what is it about that name and ice?). He said there were several members of the Hewes family but he had very little to do with them. I pressed him as to why, since they were one of the more prominent families in the community. He snickered and said he was Methodist and they all were Episcopalian. Now I could have believed there was a rift if he was a Baptist, but everybody knows the Methodists are High Church wannabes so I knew he was feeding me a line. That was as much as I got from him as the saucy secretary interrupted us and said that he had an important call. He did wish me luck and as I got up to leave he said to try the local library. He didn't give me directions but I saw a library sign when I walked out to the car.

The library was small and cozy and very quiet. It looked like I was the only person in there until a small woman rose up behind the main desk and asked if she could help me.

The librarian, Ms. Faversham, was much more helpful, though both her verbal and physical movements made men moving in molasses seem like Olympian runners by comparison. I asked her what she could tell me about the Hewes family.

"Yes," she began and three minutes later, "there are a number of Hewes still in the Chowan County area." Another long pause, "Now would you be interested in the upper river Hewes, the in-town Hewes or the cross river Hewes, of course they're not really in Chowan, but they were originally."

How the hell was I to know? A Hewes was a Hewes was a Hewes to me. But she was trying to be helpful, so I thought about it a minute, which didn't seem more than a second to her. I said, "May I be honest with you Ms. Faversham?" "Of course, young man," she quietly replied.

"Which of those are the most haughty?"

She giggled, at least I think she giggled, it could have been a death rattle, but she still seemed able to move, "That would be the in-town Hewes, young man, the in-town Hewes, and if you want to know anything about that family you need to talk to Euphonia Hewes on Second Street."

I gasped "Oh, God," and thought to myself, not another Eu. "What is the matter with you, young man?" croaked Ms. Faversham.

"Nothing, nothing, ma'am, I was just thinking how much more fun I can now have in Edenton."

Missing my sarcasm, Ms. Faversham said, "Don't be too excited. Mrs. Hewes can be somewhat temperamental." Somehow that did not surprise me. "If you would like," she whispered, "I could call her for you and set up an appointment." I was truly impressed by her kindness to a stranger and told her that would be wonderful. Thirty minutes later she returned and stated that Mrs. Hewes would see me at 2:00 sharp and advised me not to be late.

I thanked her profusely. It didn't take long to find Second Street. The town wasn't much bigger than Green Top. I parked my car at 1:30 and waited there rather than take the risk of missing what I hoped would be a useful interview.

Staring at the house, I was reminded of that famous quote Yogi Bear said to his little buddy. "BooBoo," he said, "It looks like déjà vu all over again." The house could have been an exact match to the Worsham's in Barrington. As I walked up the driveway, it looked like the panes were already frosting over. There wasn't a maid, but I was met at the door by an elderly gentleman who I discovered served as chauffeur, gardener and butler. I would have loved to converse with him. I had a feeling he could have told me where all the bodies were buried. But he said nothing and led me into the parlor (yes, a real parlor) to meet Mrs. Euphonia Hewes. She was larger in girth, if not height, than Mrs. Worsham and a bit more elegantly dressed, but her voice was even more powerful. In that small parlor her voice seemed to echo in my ears with each stressed syllable. I began the conversation with the usual introductions and was hopeful for answers before I got another history lesson.

It was worse. "I am afraid I do not know any Worsham," declared Mrs. Hewes, "and certainly none from Branch County," she finished with haughty disdain. So, I tried to see if there was a connection by going through some of the genealogy of Patsy's family. It was going nowhere until I mentioned that Eurydice had married a McRorie in Green Top.

"Oh," she sniffed, "Highlanders." Now I had no idea what that meant until I got back home. It would seem that many Highland Scots supported the King in that recent revolution 230 years ago. Apparently, at least with the Hewes, old feuds die hard. She continued, "The family you are referring to are not real Hewes, they actually lived in Bertie County across the river."

"Not really Hewes?"

"No, Mr. Biggs, those Hewes's claim to be related to Joseph Hewes has been rejected by our local DAR chapter. I cannot answer for Bertie County, but I'm sure they would agree." She answered with a smugness that reminded me of my fifth grade teacher, Mrs. Finger, who once kept me out of recess because I had misspelled "oxygen." (Who knew you could use a "y" for an "e" or an "i"?)

"You do know who Joseph Hewes was, don't you Mr. Biggs." Praise be for Eurydice.

"Yes, ma'am, I think every native Tar Heel knows about Mr. Hewes." I proceeded to give out my newly found historical knowledge. She seemed suitably impressed so I felt I could get back to the investigation. "What I wasn't clear on was how you could know that the ones across the river Hewes were not related."

"Mr. Biggs," she lectured, "has your family ever done any genealogical research into your family?" Good Lord no, the Biggs were always worried about finding out they were related to drunks, murderers and horse thieves, but that's not what I answered.

"No, ma'am," I sputtered, "not to my knowledge."

"Well, Mr. Biggs," I swear she was almost warming up to me, "The DAR carries out a quite rigorous review of the family's history and I just happened to have been on the committee that checked on that group. It turns out . . ." and she leaned over to me as if to whisper, "that it's very possible these particular Hewes could have been illegitimate."

"No!" I gasped as much to cover up my need to laugh as anything else. The Biggs have so little legitimacy in our family tree, our family Bible list only three church weddings in 150 years.

"Oh yes, and it gets worse." She was on a roll, "It's possible they originally were . . ." she leaned over so far, I thought she was going to fall into my lap, "servants." Now it didn't take a genius to know that "servant" was a code word for something else, and she related that Eurydice's family quashed any further research when it became obvious where this might lead and explains why she 'fled' back to Green Top and the McRories.

"And that's about as much information as I can give you, Mr. Biggs." She said with a flourish.

Talk about your dead ends–though I could hardly wait to see Eurydice and deflate her trumped up ego. But it did nothing to help find Patsy. I was now wondering if the sheriff would even honor the vouchers. I started back for Barrington with my tail between my legs but, with a fortunate stop, my luck changed.

The Road Back From Edenton with a Very Fortuitous Detour

I started back for home, hungry. I had passed on lunch for fear of missing my appointment and the possibility I was going to earn my commission from the Sheriff. I had dreamed of giving myself a surf and turf dinner at a well know restaurant on the river. I now wondered if he would even pay for a soda pop. As I headed out of town, I noticed a little diner called Mary Lou's Café that looked cheap and not too seedy. Walking in, I decided the cheap part was right but I may have been too kind on the seedy reference. It had two booths, both severely ripped and repaired with duct tape, and about seven tables. The stapled paper that served as a menu was plain and down home.

I sat down at a booth in an empty café at about 3:15 in the afternoon anticipating the agony of the drive home if I ate anything more than crackers at this bistro, and then she showed up, an angel disguised as a waitress called Mabel. Even with the grease stains on her apron she was gorgeous. She was short and curvaceous with dark hair and even darker eyes and a personality that sparkled.

I got a BLT special for $3 which included potato chips and coffee and the coffee was fresh brewed. Mabel told me it was the first made since the lunch crowd had left. I must've looked really depressed as I stirred my coffee over and over and over (plus there was no one else in the restaurant) because the angel came to the booth and said in the most sympathetic voice I had heard since this investigation started except for Etta Mae's desperate attempts at sexual conquest.

"What's the matter, hon?" Now it's possible she showed such empathy for every customer who ever visited that hole in the wall, but it was all I needed to open up and tell whoever would listen to the pathetic story of Patsy Cline. She listened intently and occasionally asked a penetrating question or made a sympathetic comment and the story poured out of me. I know it was only fifteen minutes or so but it was so cathartic and I felt so much better even before she dropped the bombshell.

"Listen, hon, you're looking in the wrong place," she said matter of factly. "I've only been here a couple of years while I try to finish my degree at ECU but everybody knows if you're looking for a woman in trouble in Chowan County, you start at Mrs. Beasley's Home for Wayward Women."

"Huh," I muttered, "the what for whom??"

"Mrs. Beasley's Home for Wayward Women. Well that's what the locals call it," she said soothingly. "I don't know what it's called in the telephone book but it's been around for generations. Every mother worth her salt who's got a wild child knows Mrs. Beasley, although the original Mrs. Beasley's been dead for decades. It's where you hide certain situations, pregnancies, broken engagements, temporary insanity, for the girls of the more prominent families who want things to remain hush-hush," she continued. "Although everybody knows about it, they all pretend it doesn't exist, and if you don't know where it is, you can get lost pretty fast."

"You're kidding me, I didn't think anything like that still existed," I interjected.

"Maybe not in big cities like Barrington and so close to Dix Asylum, but out here, there are a few still in existence," whispered Mabel with almost a sweetheart's voice. She continued to tell me a story or two of the strange comings and goings of Edenton's worse kept secret.

I was enraptured and could have sat there for hours looking at those big eyes but duty calls, so I asked for directions. I promised to stop back by and give her the low down on another Edenton scandal when I returned.

"You better," she replied, "you're the first interesting thing that's come into this restaurant in six months." I was blushing deep red and falling in love by the time I got to the door.

Mabel wasn't kidding. Mrs. Beasley's was one of those places where you can't get there from here. It was about a dozen miles north of Edenton as the crow flies, but it took me about an hour and three wrong turns before I finally found the dirt road that led to this out of the way little piece of nostalgia. It was fifteen or so cabins arranged around a pond with only one way in and one way out. There was a small guardhouse with an elderly gentleman who made Methuselah look like a young whipper snapper.

I got out of the car and said, "Excuse me, sir, is there a Patsy Cline at this facility?

"Eh," he replied and I repeated myself and continued to do this for about ten more minutes before I finally got an answer. "They're at dinner, sir, but you can wait here until they finish," he ultimately replied. Well, by now it was closing in on 6:00 and sure enough, a few ladies began to emerge from a facility right next to the guardhouse. Within just a few minutes, a sandy blonde haired woman with an outstanding figure and weary face appeared and I knew it was the one and only Patsy Cline. She looked over at me and I waved. Patsy responded with a matter of fact statement that made my jaw drop. "Wait a minute," she said, "I'm already packed. I'll get my things and join you in just a second."

I was flabbergasted, after all the runarounds and innuendos I had found her without any fireworks, so I responded in the only way I knew how, "Well, okay." As I walked back to my car to wait on Patsy, all I could think was "What the hell?" I mean, I've put in some real leg work and now it seems I might have been no more than a cheap chauffeur. What in the world was going on? It was now obvious that her mother had known all along where she was.

So why not come out and tell me and why couldn't Frank have just come to pick her up?

Waiting in the car, it dawned on me that Frank had no idea about Mrs. Beasley's home for wild and crazy women and that Patsy had used this little oasis before. It was an idyllic location in some respects, a nice place to get your mind together. I had no doubt that Patsy had found solace at Mrs. Beasley's in the past. The only difference was that she had stayed here a bit longer this time and may have not dropped the word to the right associates that she needed a little time to get her life back together. But what was my role in this affair? Was I being used and if so, by whom?

By now Patsy was heading back to the car with a small suitcase pulled behind her and her first words to me were unintentionally revealing. "I wasn't expecting you until later," she said without a hint of sarcasm. "Patsy," I said, "you don't recognize me, but I'm C.W. Biggs. I was a few years behind you in high school. I think you know my brother, Phil. I wasn't sent by your mother or anyone else. I was given a job by your husband and the Sheriff of Branch County to see if I could locate you."

She looked as if I had hit her with a ton of bricks and at first was at a loss for words. It took her a few minutes to respond as the two of us put the suitcase in the trunk of the car, but when we settled into the front seat, she finally spoke again and said, "I remember you C.W. It just took me a little time to place you. You've changed a bit, put on a little weight." Not exactly the friendliest of greetings, so I responded in kind, "Tell me what's going on, Patsy," I said gruffly.

She stared at me sweetly; at least I think it was her version of sweetly and said, "C.W., let's head back home." When we passed Mary Lou's I tried to pull in, but she said she wasn't hungry and wanted to get back to her husband. I gritted my teeth wondering if I would ever have the opportunity to see Mabel again. For the next two hours I tried a new angle every fifteen minutes to pry some information out of her. I got very little. I told her that Frank was missing her and got no response. I told her that her friends were worried and she turned her head and sighed. I did get a small response when I said that Etta Mae was especially worried. It sounded like "Yeah, I bet."

She did agree to call home and tell Frank she was fine and heading home. We pulled off the road just west of Windsor and she borrowed my old cell phone and stepped out of the car. I caught little of the conversation, she talked almost in whispers, but I thought I caught a terse "Love you, too" and then she was back in the car and we were on the road again.

Thirty miles from Barrington she finally asked me a question, "You said some of my friends were concerned about me, do you remember who?" I couldn't come up with any names immediately until I said, "I think Etta Mae mentioned a Don Rivera." For the first time I sensed a change in her disposition and I thought I saw a hint of a smile, but it faded quickly and she ended the little conversation with a request. "C.W., I'm tired. Can we stop the questions and turn on the radio. I think I just need to relax."

Since my psychology classes at three different colleges had all ended in low 'C's', I responded with a Freudian "Sure." I don't think she said more than three words the rest of the trip but she fiddled constantly with the radio dial and only stopped for a few minutes on an Hispanic radio station that was playing a song called "*Besame mucho.*" At least I think that's what was playing. It seemed to soothe her.

We arrived at the house at Barrington about 11 and Frank had managed to arrange a group of friends to greet her. A banner had been hung across the driveway that said "Welcome Back, Patsy". She saw it and seemed ready to cry, but quickly regained her composure as she got out of the car. Frank gave her a hug that was sort of reciprocated, shook my hand and thanked me. About that time the sheriff drove up, walked over to me and thanked me. No one else seemed to notice, I guess you don't pay any attention to the taxi driver. Two days later, I got a visit from him and he handed me an expense voucher for over $200 and a check from Frank, or rather his father according to the signature, for $500. He told me there would be another check for $500 in three months if nothing appeared in the media about the case. For that amount, I could pretend I never met Patsy. Still, I had a lot of questions that I wish had answers. You know that phrase "Be careful what you wish for". It was about to be fulfilled the next time I heard of Patsy Cline.

Edenton: There and Back Again

It was last fall, almost five years to the day from my last sighting of Patsy Cline when I got involved with the Cline Family Tree again. The phone rang in my "office" and it was the Sheriff of Branch County. "Well, if it isn't Old C.W.," he began, immediately endearing himself to me. "I understand you're still working out of your mother's basement," he chortled. I went from endearment to heated passion (to shoot him). I wasn't overly in the mood to discuss my situation with him. The money I had received for originally "finding" Patsy had allowed me to briefly have a small office at a dying strip mall in Green Top. Then the Bush recession hit and continued through Obama. Toss in the yearly fees to the state to keep my license up to date and the amount I paid for continuing education and before you knew it, I was back in my mom's basement, often staying the night on our old day bed just to avoid utility charges at my meager apartment.

"What do you want, Sheriff?" hoping he would pick up on the pent up anger in the conversation.

"Thought I might give you a job, if you want it," he continued, "Guess who's missing again."

Now I knew who it had to be, but I didn't want to disappoint the Sheriff's opinion of me, so I questioningly said, "Who?"

"Patsy Cline, who else, you dolt!" the Sheriff shouted.

Duh, damn, I wish I wasn't so desperate for money, so I meekly said, "You don't say."

"Yeah, and it looks like the same kind of situation. Her and Frank may have had a row and now she's been missing for a weekend and the Clines are willing to pay expenses again. You'll probably find her in Edenton again. Up for a little trip?" His voice had changed from sarcasm to business-like.

No, not really, I thought, but suddenly my idealized vision of Mabel that had only increased over the years crossed my mind and I said sure, but the old Dodge was in the shop so I'd have to wait a day or two before I could head for the coast. "No problem," said the Sheriff prophetically, "I doubt she's going anywhere."

Two days later, after a $250 bill for fixing the transmission on the relic of Chrysler's heyday, I set off for Edenton. I wondered once again whether I was being paid to be a cheap chauffeur. I doubted Frank had ever found out about Mrs. Beasley's Home for Wayward Women. I speculated on how the rest of the Cline family felt about those events. I wondered about a lot of things as I headed down the road. Mainly I wondered about Mabel, who, in my mind, had now converted into a black haired Angelina Jolie and decided that the first thing I would do was go to Mary Lou's Café for another cup of coffee, and other things. I was almost sweating as I crossed into Chowan County and began to look for that run-down old diner . . . that was now shuttered up!

Why was I not surprised? The old Biggs luck when it comes to romance was staying consistent. I pulled into the little parking lot and just sat there uttering one expletive after another. I got out of the car and went to the front door and shook it-like that was going to make a difference, walked around, kicked an old trash can, near 'bout broke my toe, and moaned. I got back into the car, turned on an oldies radio station from somewhere just in time to hear the start of "Dream Lover". I kicked the radio and I knew my toe was broken.

Well, this was setting up to be a nice day. I arrived at the police station and gingerly ambled up the sidewalk hoping that my trip might end early. No such luck. But the chief had changed and was much nicer. I faced an imposing lady with the intriguing name of Raquel Wambgass. I knew she was not from around these parts and the lilt of a Bahamian or Jamaican accent simply confirmed that. Ms. Wambgass spent nearly thirty minutes with me comparing my description of Patsy with anyone who had come through town and aroused suspicion over the last five days. We talked about Mrs. Beasley's.

"Yes," she chuckled, "it's still open, but it has very few residents these days. Sorry for laughing but when I came here, I thought the veterans were kidding me when they told me it existed. I was wondering if they were sending me on a wild goose chase, as you mainlanders call it, when I went out on patrol to visit it. I could not believe such a place existed in this day and age, but there it was, and I must admit it is a pretty little place."

She filled me in on my other reminisces. Mrs. Faversham had just retired last year at the age of 80 and moved to Swan Quarter. Mrs. Hewes had died on Halloween of last year, no surprise there. And lastly, I quietly mentioned that I had found some information from a waitress named Mabel and wondered if I could have her address. She didn't recognize the name and turned to a burly older officer and said, "Sergeant, do you know what happened to the waitress that used to work at Mary Lou's?"

"Yeah," he said, "I think she married some porn star and moved to Las Vegas." *MABEL, not Mabel, she can't be*, I thought, though the image from the Eagles lyric on the 'Devil's Daughter and Angel in White' made me reconsider some possibilities. My face must have looked like a whipped dog's because the Sergeant immediately tried to shore me up. "I'm just joshing you kid, but she did move and I think she did get married."

Chief Wambgass gave him a baleful stare and broke into a wide grin. "Sergeant Cook, if you don't start behaving, I'm going to tell your wife about last year's Christmas party."

It looked like Edenton's police force might be a fun place to work, but it did nothing for my mood and disposition. I drove out to Mrs. Beasley's Home for Wayward Women without a lot of enthusiasm and, of course, I was rewarded. The place looked a bit run down and there wasn't an old security guard. In fact, there

28

were only four cabins occupied and none of them had heard of Patsy Cline either the singer or the missing woman. I bid a fond farewell to Edenton after a brief stop at the shuttered Broken Heart Café, I mean Mary Lou's, to drink a Sun Drop and eat a Moon pie. Empty handed and disgusted, I set off for Barrington.

I arrived about four in the afternoon and saw the Sheriff walking out. I quickly gave him a report and offered my expense voucher, but he told me to put it away. Great, I thought, I'm not even going to get expense money. "Listen, C.W.," he started, "my budget has gotten really tight since those damn Tea Party Republicans began to snoop around cutting my deputies right and left. But if the Clines are willing to pay, and they will be if they aren't told this is a dead end, I might be able to get a bit more for you and a little for the department–if we do things quietly, you get my drift."

I got it alright, but I wasn't overly enthusiastic, still there was nothing cooking on the old telex at home (actually I do have an old telex and I did cook a pop tart on it once, but that's another story). The Sheriff didn't exactly give me carte blanche, but he said as long as my expenses stayed at my going rate, I could see what I could find out and keep him out of what might not be more than another Patsy tantrum. My search for Patsy Cline was now in high, well maybe medium gear, considering my car's transmission.

Frankly Speaking

I thought that I'd start like the last time with a conversation with Frank Lee Cline, but I decided to do a little research on Frank to see if I could shake him from that dull turtle shell of his. I headed to the local library to see what I could dig up. It turned out to be very little. You know how you can Google up information on almost anybody these days. Well, with Frank almost all you got was connected to Cline Industries and even there he wasn't listed as high as you might think, considering he was the owner's son. He had risen very slowly and had been one of four assistant managers at the company for the past ten years. Interestingly, one of the other assistants was Don Rivera. He definitely was going to be the next interviewee if I got nothing from Frank. Frank was cited in a couple of local clubs, but never as an officer. He would just appear as a part of a picture in the local newspaper, the Barrington Stars and Bars as part of a group picture. So, armed with one note card of information, I headed for the Cline Mills headquarters in Barrington.

Frank seemed to recognize me as I walked in and as I began to strike up a conversation with his secretary, he ran over and said quietly, "Is this in regard to that matter I spoke to you about?" I hadn't spoken to him at all, but I could tell by the smirk on the secretary's face that it was common knowledge that Patsy had gone to pieces once again and Frank didn't care to share his dirty laundry with most of the Cline's staff. He asked me if I could meet him in about an hour at his house and escorted me out of the plant. I got a bit lost getting to the house. It had been five years and my version of a GPS, a local map and a service station attendant, were both on the fritz, so I didn't beat him by much in getting to the house and the interview.

Frank invited me in, which was more than he had done last time, when our talk had started and ended in the driveway. I immediately noticed the shrine to Patsy. There were pictures of her sometimes-smiling face all over the living room, the kitchen and, as I found out in a visit to the facilities, even in the bathroom.

"Mr. Cline," I began, "as you know I have been retained to see if I can locate Patsy. I have yet to duplicate my success from five years ago, so I thought I might ask you a couple of questions to see where it might lead us." Frank gave me his usual taciturn nod and I continued, "Now some of these questions may be a bit personal, I hope you don't mind." He nodded again. I was beginning to think I was talking to the Pep Boys bobble heads. I began gingerly, "Tell me about your relationship with Patsy."

"Patsy wa . . . is the love of my life. I have adored every atom of her for our 19 years of marriage. She is a wonderful woman. Do you remember the lady in *Gone with the Wind*?"

"Scarlett?" I said.

"No, the other one," he said, "the saintly one, Melanie." Now from what I knew about Patsy, the only connection with Melanie was that they were both women, but I decided to keep my mouth shut and just listen for a while. That may have been a mistake. For the next fifteen minutes, Frank waxed poetically on his angel. I know he compared her to Mother Teresa, Roslyn Carter, Joan of Arc and Nancy Reagan. I'm not sure how he got the comparisons with those disparate ladies, but he was on a roll and I could only listen as my lids got heavier and heavier. I had to do something to shake this guy up, so I interrupted and said, "Mr. Cline, tell me about her relationship with Don Rivera."

He seemed unfazed as if he had been expecting the question and began with the same kind of litany for Don. "Don is a gifted and talented employee at Cline's," he began, "his work with the Hispanic employees has been exemplary."

"But what about his relationship with your wife," I snapped.

Frank took just a second to catch his composure and began again as if there were cue cards signaling him somewhere behind me. "Patsy and Don worked well together and often attended personnel seminars together. I trust them implicitly; their relationship is business like and highly professional." Yeah, I thought, and I'm the King of Siam. "I consider Don to be my closest friend, next to Patsy, of course."

This guy was either in never-never land or else he was as crazy as Patsy, which led me to try that tact. "Mr. Cline, there are some who believe Patsy, um, suffered bouts of depression. Do you know if she was on any medication?"

He sighed again, "Patsy did take some medication, she had some tough times and it sometimes led her to be a little . . ."

"Crazy?" I interjected."

"Absolutely not," he stridently said, "and I resent the implication, Mr. Biggs. Patsy has had a tough time with her mother and with our failure to have children and sometimes she needs a little pick–me–up." *And I bet that pick–me–up was Don Rivera*, I speculated, but not out loud.

He began again with his songs of praise for both Patsy and Don. I had to do something to shake this cold fish if I was going to get any relevant information. I remembered that in the research last time I had stumbled on the gossip about the Cline's heritage. Perhaps I could shake him with a snappy reference to the possibly questionable family tree. I decided I'd try that tact, just as soon as I could get a word in edgewise, for a guy who didn't speak much he was becoming quite verbose. I waited for another homage to Don to spring my trap.

"Don is the salt of the earth, he works for the Boy's and Girl's Club, he's happily married, he's . . ."

I suddenly sprang up and using the only German I knew shouted "FRANK LEE, MEIN HERR, I DON'T GIVE A DAMN." I figured that would shake him up but Frank looked at me and did something amazing, for him. He laughed, not just a chuckle but for the first time since I had known him he actually guffawed.

"That's a good one" he spluttered, "Frankly, mein herr, that was quite clever."

What the hell was he talking about? This guy was a tough cookie, I was beginning to believe even the CIA couldn't break him down. He was still chuckling, "I don't give a damn, I'm going to have to tell that to my father, even that old sourpuss might get a laugh out of that!"

I had no idea what this man was talking about and I was running out of bullets to break down his façade. I could think of only one thing more that might ruffle this stone cold assassin.

"Mr. Cline, do you love your wife?" I said confrontationally.

"Yes, Mr. Biggs, I love my wife," he answered coolly.

"Cline, do you love your wife?" I was going to keep up the pressure just like they do in real cop shows.

"Yes," he said emphatically.

"Are you telling me the truth?" I pushed.

"Yes," he laconically replied.

"I want the truth, Mr. Cline," I probed.

"I am telling you the truth, Mr. Biggs," he countered. There wasn't even a bead of sweat.

"Are you? I think you're lying."

"No, I am not," he said, but he sounded a little more deflated. I decided to go in for the kill. "Mr. Cline, I want the truth, I deserve to know the truth, tell me the truth, do you or do you not love your wife?" I had him squirming.

He took a deep breath and said, "Yes, Mr. Biggs, I love my wife and I have to tell you, your Clark Gable is much better than your Tom Cruise."

Now I was stumped. Here I was trying to shake an answer out of "Stone Face" and all I get from him is irrelevant movie trivia.

I stuttered out the same refrain again, but by now my heart wasn't in it. This guy's resume must have left out he was a Ranger or a Marine or something. God, he was tough hearted. Maybe Cheney was right, maybe there is a place for waterboarding. That looked like the only way I was going to get anything from this guy. Now all I had to do was convince everybody Frank's real name was Frank Al-Clida. Nope, it would never work. I might as well cut my losses and head on, especially after he got up to shake my hand and said, "This has been most enjoyable, Mr. Biggs. Do you like Turner Classics? I usually watch them in the evenings with Patsy. Would you like to join me this weekend? I'm not sure I should be alone. They're doing a Clark Gable retrospective." He ended with a look that suggested that should be the clincher for our "date".

"No, thanks," I replied. "I have to find out what happened one night."

"Yes, that's one of them with Claudette Colbert and Gable. I didn't realize you were such a renaissance man."

All right, that did it, suspect or no suspect, if he made another movie reference, I was going to bust him up good. I got up abruptly and said as I went out the door. "I'll be back."

He hollered something back about the termites, but I had already got to my car. Maybe my techniques would be more effective on the other part of this menagerie a tres, (that's French you know), and headed off to see Don Rivera.

Don Juan Rivera?

Now, Don Rivera's name had popped up more than a few times with this investigation, but I really knew very little about him. So, I decided to see what I could find out from the gossip queen of Barrington, Etta Mae Winstead. I almost went to see her. You see, I had not been in a serious relationship (heck, any kind of relationship) for two years and my hormones were getting desperate. I had a dream the night before I called and Etta Mae appeared as some kind of angelic vision (which for Etta Mae meant 31-22-32) and in the state I was in I was fearful that her buck tooth smile might make me think I was seeing Megan Fox, so I phoned.

"Etta Mae, this is C.W. Biggs, remember me?"

"Of course, C.W., how can I help you?" she said in a most melodious voice.

Ignoring the suggestive nature of the question, I said, "I guess you've heard that Patsy has gone again."

"Yes, isn't it terrible?"

"Etta Mae, she's been gone long enough that this is starting to get serious. You mentioned Don Rivera one time and his name has popped up in some other conversations. What can you tell me about him?"

Now I'm going to skip a huge part of this because, as usual, Etta Mae was full of so much information that, well, remember that book *War and Peace*? I once read about seven pages in it. Over the few hours, Etta Mae would have filled up two of those tomes. So, here's the gist.

Diego Rivera, aka Don or Don Diego, was an exchange student from Spain who came to the U.S. about twenty five years ago to Tarboro. He liked it so much he convinced his father, who was a textile magnate in Seville or Cordoba, to pay for his education to college here and he attended N.C. State in, wait for it, Textiles. While in college he met a little lassie from Denver (North Carolina, not Colorado) who fell for him in a big way. Don Diego was a classic Spanish conquistador with jet black hair, a swarthy complexion, built reasonably well and an elegance that would remind you of those paintings from the Spanish golden age. The girl, who Etta Mae told me was named Candace, or Candi to her friends, was so in love, she converted to Catholicism. Now, that may not sound like much to you, but twenty five years ago in this part of the state that would lead to some mild "eyebrow raisin". Candi and he settled down and quickly began to raise a family.

Don found a job almost immediately after college, in part, because the Clines thought it would be great to add a person who could speak Spanish to their already burgeoning Hispanic work force. What they didn't realize was that Castilian Spanish has a very different dialect from Mexican Spanish. Most of the workers couldn't understand a thing he was saying. It was like me trying to explain something to somebody from Flatbush. The New Yorkers hear the words but it doesn't make any sense. Also, the workers had a bit of disdain for Don Diego. They called him "hidalgo" or "gacupines" which I understand are not necessarily nice words. However, Don was good at textile engineering and he soon learned this new kind of Spanish. Before you know it, Don Diego was just Don and one of the most valuable "players" at the Cline Mill. Indeed both Frank and Don were Assistant Managers, yet nearly everyone knew which hidalgo was higher in the pecking order.

Now you notice how I had the word players with the italics, that's another literary device I learned. It's called foreshadowing because Don was a player right from the start of his career. His romantic conquests were almost legendary. Every Valentine's Day when the unsigned flowers began to arrive for loved ones at the plant, it was automatically assumed the flowers were from Don, even if there were a half-dozen anonymous cards. At one time, Patsy was just one of the harem, but somewhere along the line as both parties matured, she seemed to have developed into the Queen Consort. Yet, Frank seemed to show no jealousy. Indeed, the threesome was seen at lunch together almost every day.

Etta Mae said Patsy's acting skills were never better during those luncheons, alternately reminding Frank to use his napkin and asking about Don's family. More interestingly, Etta Mae said that Patsy and Don would attend seminars on personnel matters together where they would find time for, um, personal matters. They were clever, though. They would stay at different motels, but Patsy or Don's car would be seen at the other's motel. Etta Mae knew this because she was always searching for some vicarious thrill, even if it meant following a couple like a dime store detective. You can't imagine how difficult it was to write that down.

Even more clever or diabolical, Patsy would often go to visit an aunt on her father's side that lived in Raleigh and Don would have Knights of Columbus meetings in the same city during the same time. Once again, leave it to Etta Mae to dig up the dirt. She said she went to the old lady's funeral (this is where Etta Mae and Patsy were somehow related) and the relatives said they had not seen Patsy since she was a teenager. And yet, Frank never suspected, Candi was another story according to Etta Mae. She suspected a lot but had chosen to play the role of the docile wife, if for no other reason than the children.

As she wound down, Etta Mae did sound sympathetic towards Frank. She was convinced he was still in love with Patsy and Patsy still had a great deal of affection for Frank. "It's sad, you know, C.W., Patsy was crazy for trying to keep this going."

"Tell me about it," I said

"Yes, she was crazy for lying, and crazy for crying." Uh-Oh, I knew where this was headed. "Crazy for feeling so lonely, crazy for feeling so blue," she continued.

"Uh, yeah, Etta Mae, I think there's another call coming in," as I tried to stop the madness. It didn't help that I could barely afford a telephone, much less one with multiple lines, but it was the only thing I could think of. She continued, "Someday, he'd leave her for somebody new."

"Yeah, uh, Etta Mae are we talking about Frank or Don?"

"Neither, I was just thinking of an old song," she whispered. I had to end this soon. I half expected another invitation for an iced tea afternoon.

"Yep, that's the other line buzzing." I tried to imitate a phone with little success, so I simply finished. "Bye, Etta Mae. Thanks for the information. You were a great help" and hung up.

With a regular encyclopedia of information on Diego Rivera, I set off for the mill to talk to my Spanish Romeo. This time I was determined to get off to a good start. When the secretary issued me into his office, I knew exactly how to start off.

"Hola, Senor Rivera, como esta usted?" I would have to thank my Spanish instructor from the local community college for having nailed it.

"I am fine, and how are you?" he said laconically.

"Muy bien, e tu?" as I kept up my Spanish patter.

"I've already said I'm fine," he said sarcastically.

"Oh," I think he was trying to keep me off my game, but I wouldn't let him. "Me llamo es C.W. Biggs." I continued.

"Yes, Mr. Biggs, I know who you are," he said somewhat quickly. I refused to be put off, "Conoces Patsy Cline?"

"Yes, I know Patsy, and may I add Mr. Biggs, I have been in the United States for twenty five years and probably speak English better than you, if you don't mind, I wish you'd stick with English and stop mangling my native language," he replied.

Well, I thought, there's no need to get snippy, I was just trying to make him feel at home, unless he feared he would give away something in his native language. But since I was running out of my favorite Spanish conversational phrases, I said, "Alright, Mr. Rivera, we'll play in your ballpark. I need to know about your relationship with Patsy Cline. As you may be aware she has not made contact with her husband or other members of her family for nearly a week now."

About the end of that sentence, Don looked around me at the open door at the secretary's desk outside. I looked too, and, yeah, she was trying to listen in. He replied. "Mr. Biggs, it's getting close to lunch. How would you like to go out and eat with me? I'll pay."

It was actually a little past 10:30, but a free meal was more than tempting. On my income it was a blessing from heaven. I said, "Sure."

"I have a few things to clear up here at work. Are you familiar with the Bypass Grill out on 32?" he said. Yeah, I knew it and it wasn't the Golden Corral which happened to be on the same street with a huge buffet, but beggars can't be choosers, so I agreed and headed out the door.

The Bypass Grill had a bar with a few stools and ten or twelve booths and tables. It also had one of those old juke boxes though it didn't look like it worked. It was only open for lunch and breakfast so they really put on the spread for lunch. You could have sandwiches, soups and the blue plate specials. I didn't know how generous my host was going to be so I ordered sweet tea and sat and thought about what I had gotten myself into. I knew I had to visit the Ice Queen, Patsy's mother, and the confrontation had me considering ordering something a lot stronger than iced tea but I was afraid that once I started I wouldn't be able to stop. This was looking more and more like a serious investigation, the kind that a sheriff ought to be doing, not some P.I. from Podunk.

My paranoia kicked in. I got to wondering whether I was being set up for something, but what? And the only things that crossed my mind were murder or kidnapping. If that was the case, even that old video tape wouldn't save me. I was just about ready to cry in my beer, er, tea, when Don walked in. He certainly had charisma or machismo. Every woman's head and even a few men, in the café turned towards Don Diego and watched him until he got to my booth.

He came over and got ready to sit down when he looked more closely and questioned, "Did you do this on purpose, Mr. Biggs? Is it one of your detective tricks?"

I looked at him with a dumbstruck face and asked what was he talking about?

"This is the booth where Patsy, uh, Mrs. Cline and I always sat right next to the juke box and we'd usually play one of our favorite tunes." I hadn't asked anything and he had basically admitted to all I suspected was happening between the two, so I struck hard and fast, "So you and Patsy were having an affair."

It had the effect I thought I was going to get from Frank.

Haltingly, he began, "I love my wife, Mr. Biggs, I love her dearly. But Patsy was special. She lit up the room when she walked in. She had charisma, and she made life worth living. I adored every part of her, her hair, her nose, her mouth, her lips."

"Okay, Okay," I said, "I get the picture," although the lips allusion somehow led me to think of Mabel for a second. "I'm guessing that you knew Mrs. Cline, in the biblical sense."

He hemmed and hawed over that. "Can anyone say they really know someone? Can anyone explain the human heart? Can anyone truly understand human emotion?" I felt like I was standing in the aisle at the Hallmark Shop on Valentine's Day. I pressed on, "How long has this liaison been going on and how did you keep it from your spouses?

"We have tried, Mr. Biggs, many times in the past dozen years to break it off, and for a while it would work, but always we were drawn back to each other. She is my soul mate," he said in almost a whisper.

"And your spouses, what were their responses?" I asked.

Slowly, he stated, "I think Candace knew, I can't speak for Frank but Patsy said he was okay with it." *And you believed that*, I thought. Both these guys must have fallen off the potato wagon more than once or else love is blind and deaf and dumb, too. I knew sooner or later I was going to have to interview Candace and I was not looking forward to it, but for now, I needed to stay with the plan.

"Can you tell me when you last saw Patsy?" I queried.

He leaned back against the booth seat. "It was last Friday, I saw her at lunch, she seemed reasonably happy. I told her I would try to see her that weekend but she said she had to go to see her mother about some important matters."

I leaned forward to counter his casual demeanor. "Did she talk about Frank?"

"Not that I remember, we actually were sitting right here next to the juke box, I remember after our conversation she put on a Frank and Nancy Sinatra song."

"No country and western? I parried.

"No, she didn't like country and western, especially female singers." *Interesting*, I thought. "She liked old standards, that song meant something to her, but I'm not sure what," he finished.

"But you can't remember the song?"

"No, except it had something to do with love. Patsy was a true romantic." *Yeah*, I thought, *with someone else's husband.* I remembered Frank had said that they couldn't have children and implied it was something with Patsy. I decided to follow up.

"Do you know if Patsy ever wanted children?" I asked.

"Yes, she did, almost desperately, but something was wrong with Frank and he never wanted to adopt. Frank was more of a company man than most. I really believe he worried that children might make it more difficult to stay on top of things at the mill. He is a dedicated man and we have had some hard times." Don seemed to empathize with Frank. It had been a hard ten years and the mill's employment and future as an independent company weighed more on Frank than Don. But I was drawn to the statement that it was Frank's problem. It didn't jibe with what Frank had told me, though I hadn't followed it up. Maybe something had happened to cause Frank to suddenly change his mind about Patsy and Don's relationship, a pregnancy perhaps? I wondered if I had any chance of getting any information from Patsy's gynecologist. Not likely unless this turned into a murder investigation and if that happened, I would no longer be on the case.

I finished my conversation with Don by asking if anybody might have wanted to do bodily harm to Patsy. He sat straight up, looked me in the eyes and said, "No, not a soul Mr. Biggs, she was the salt of the earth with everyone she came in contact with." I hoped that comment about salt and earth would not turn out to be prophetic. He continued, "What are you implying C.W.? Do you really suspect foul play, what is going on here?"

I quickly moved to amend the situation, "No, No," I said, "that's just a standard question that every detective asks at the deposition or interview or whatever you call it." I hoped I had recovered when Don made a curious statement.

Turning his head as if he meant to say it under his breath, he muttered, "There's only one person who could dare harm her, but I can't believe that one of her own would cause something to happen to Patsy." He shut up realizing he might have said too much and looked toward the juke box. That stirred up an old memory from my last visit with Patsy. "Don, can I ask you to translate something for me?" He nodded. "What does *besame mucho* mean? He looked at me strangely and said, "Basically it means kiss me a lot or kiss me more."

I posed a couple more questions to him but he had clammed up after I mentioned that song. It obviously meant something to him but he said he needed to get back to work. I thought back to the last statement of "one of her own" harming her. Was he referring to Frank or was he accusing Patsy's mother? Could a mother harm her only child? It seemed improbable. My next visit to the Worsham house was very likely to be very tense.

The lunch crowd was starting to really filter in now as I finished my hamburger steak Don had paid for. I saw a couple of people go over to the juke box, though only one played anything, laughing with their colleagues at the ancient tunes on the old machine. I doubted it had been changed for years. I had a thought, shocking I know, maybe I could locate the song Patsy played the last time. I looked and looked and finally found a Sinatra duet. It was called *Something Stupid.* It had some interesting lyrics about someone so in love she could constantly forgive her lover. Two lines particularly stood out to me as I listen. *"I could see it in your eyes that you despise the same old lines you heard the night before . . . and then I go and spoil it all by saying something stupid like I love you."*

Paired together with that other song Don had translated for me, it made me wonder, Had Patsy reached the end of the road? Was she trying to tell Don that it was time to put up or shut up and, if he ignored or didn't catch the method to her, um, madness, could it have caused, what? It could be a suicide or a confrontation that led to murder or just a runaway wife. It was the question I needed answered and it could lead back to Frank or Don or Mrs. Eurydice Worsham. As I walked out the door of the Bypass, I thought about how much I hated women whose name started with Eu, and how I absolutely had to go see a that old lady. Etta Mae had once told me that Mrs. Worsham's husband and her few very close friends nicknamed her Dice, which I understand is a slight mispronunciation of her name, but I thought it was appropriate. I was not looking forward to those "snake eyes."

Worse-ham for Wear

The Sheriff had told me that the past few years had not been kind to Mrs. Worsham. She was a widow now and her husband had left a mountain of debts with very little equity. She had been forced to sell most of the family's assets and he thought Frank and Patsy were sending her some money each month. Nonetheless, I was unprepared for the obvious changes as I drove up the driveway to the mansion early in the afternoon. The broken hedges looked like they hadn't been cut in years and the ivy ran long tendrils all across the drive, with some being big enough to cause the Dodge to jump slightly though that could have been due to the twenty year old shocks. Even the window panes didn't look nearly as frosty. They now looked more like my apartment, dingy with a film of dirt. I even saw cobwebs on the front porch portico. I had an image of Dice with her whip in one hand and shaking a finger in the face of the maid with the other demanding she clean them up.

But when I arrived at the door, I didn't find a maid this time. After a couple of buzzes on the doorbell, I was astonished when Mrs. Worsham answered the door. She was just as tall as I remembered but thinner and grayer. She reminded me of an actor from some spooky movie but I couldn't come up with a name. The house seemed run down and Mrs. Worsham was wearing a badly frayed shawl and a faded dress that certainly suggested tougher times. Her only companion was a dog, a feisty little cock-a-poo that kept trying to nip my legs. She pushed the dog aside and said "Let me put my dog up and I'll be right back. Come on, Mac, behave yourself," and picked up the dog to take him into another room.

I found the name interesting. Her dead husband was named Mackenzie Worsham, but everybody who knew him called him "Mac". She had named her newest companion after her dead husband; somehow I was not surprised but I was surprised by what happened next.

"Mr. Biggs," she began, "it's good to see you. I thought you would be around to ask about Darla Jean." It was a genuinely warm welcome and I wanted to walk back outside and see if I had the right address. "Thank you," I said and I'm sure she had to notice the astonished look on my face. "What can you tell me about Patsy's, uh, Darla Jean's, disappearance?"

She didn't object to Patsy this time and began to tell me the last time she thought she was going to see Patsy. Dice motioned me towards the small library we had met in before. It was much warmer. "She was supposed to have lunch with me last Sunday," Eurydice began. "We have had a regular brunch date ever since Mr. Worsham passed away. We were going to the new fish house out near the lake, but she never showed up." She seemed to sniff as if holding back a sob. I was trying to take all this in. It was all I could do to keep from laughing when she really threw a pitch I couldn't handle.

"I know Frank must be really worried," she continued, "he truly adored her."

My Scooby Doo senses were on high alert, something was definitely fishy about this and I wasn't talking about the menu at the new fish house. She recognized the skepticism written all over my face and addressed it.

"I see you're puzzled, Mr. Biggs, but Frank and I have made our peace. I have been very impressed with the way he has handled himself and how he has treated Patsy since the last time we met."

There was a silence for a moment as I tried to digest this, but it wasn't intimidation this time, it was curiosity. I decided to tell her what I knew. "She isn't in Edenton this time Mrs. Worsham, I've already been there and nobody has seen her in town or at Mrs. Beasley's."

"Yes, I know, I called Mrs. Beasley's on Monday and they told me. I am becoming very worried for her safety."

This time my eyebrows arched, "Do you think anyone could do harm to Patsy?"

"I can think of no one, although Frank and I have had a conversation or two about one individual, but I hesitate to mention him. I don't want to cast aspersions," she said quietly.

Why not, I thought, *it's what you do best.* But knowing I wasn't going to get anywhere with sarcasm, I leaned over to say, "I don't suppose that person could be named Don Rivera." She stared sternly at me, thought a minute and carefully said, "I know there have been rumors about Patsy and Mr. Rivera. Frank seems to think there is nothing to them, but I am not sure. However, I must say Patsy has never mentioned this gentleman in my presence." She said the last part with a near sneer, ah, that was the Ice Queen I knew.

"If that's so," I countered, "how did you hear about the rumors?"

Now it was her turn to lean in, "I know that you are quite aware, Mr. Biggs, rumors can move very quickly in a small town. There were whispers at our book club circle last month that I wasn't supposed to hear, but I have very sharp ears, Mr. Biggs, very sharp," she emphasized. About that time there was a loud noise like a radiator starting up. It startled me in the quiet of that run down mansion, but Mrs. Worsham seemed to take it in stride with not even the slightest turn towards the area behind us where the noise had emanated. I wondered if the sharp ears meant like Mr. Spock instead of an acuteness of hearing. Maybe it was the dog getting into something in the other room, though it sounded like it was coming from below me.

Continuing, I asked why Frank didn't seem upset about those rumors. She smiled, at least I think it was a smile, though it could have been the way a vampire looks when it's ready to take its first bite. "Frank is an intelligent young man, but I am afraid he may be a little naïve about the affairs of the heart, though I think Patsy considers that one of his most endearing charms."

You ever had those moments when you wish you had done something. I had one, I wished I had recorded that conversation five years ago and could play it back to her. Nobody could believe this was the same woman. There were three possibilities: a) she was lying to me and still playing me for a fool, b) she had a brain tumor that was affecting her personality, or c) she had found Jesus and was trying to make amends before she met her maker. I had this vision of her down at the Evangelical Baptist church at the baptismal font being dunked and spluttering as she came up, "Yes, Yes, I'll change my wicked ways, only don't drown me." Now that I looked around I did notice a couple of bibles and one of those omnipresent pictures of Jesus that is in almost every home in the southern part of the United States.

Once again, I was somewhat stymied. My instincts were having a hard time believing that Eurydice had 'a come to Jesus' meeting. But I had no evidence to suggest that Eurydice was anything other than a loving mother. I had to admit that although I had been put off last time by her disdain for Frank, she had not said anything bad about Patsy and even seemed to possess a quiet confidence, almost bragging, on Patsy's abilities to get through tough times. Maybe I could find out more about how she felt about Don Diego.

"What can you tell me about Diego Rivera?" I asked gently.

"I have been asking around Mr. Biggs, ever since I heard of this gentleman. I had hoped the rumors were false, but it seems Mr. Rivera may be a home wrecker and Darla Jean is not the first woman to fall into his web," she said stridently. "His string of conquests are almost legendary according to my book club circle," she continued. Intriguing, I thought she was just listening at the meetings not actively participating. "I can give you at least three names if you're interested."

I hemmed and hawed about that but finally decided it might come in handy as she went to get a note pad to write down the names of three gentlemen who would like to catch Mr. Rivera in a dark alley. While she was gone, I looked around at the bric-a brac in the old Victorian. There were very few pictures of Patsy but there was a huge painting of Mrs. Worsham. She was posed like some president's wife with the pearls, the matronly blue dress and the high collar. It was quite imposing. She came back and saw me looking at the painting.

"Do you like it, Mr. Biggs? It was painted by the famous artist from Lexington." I knew this was to impress me, but I hadn't the slightest idea who she was talking about, but I wasn't going to play the dumb foil again. "Oh, yes," I said, "how interesting. I've always been impressed how he used colors." Thank God it was a man because she smiled, yes actually smiled, and said she agreed. She sat down at a desk and copied the names on a piece of paper using a left handed scrawl. She handed me the names and I decided to leave for now while we were still on good terms. But as I got ready to leave, a question did cross my mind. "Do you know what Darla Jean wanted to talk to you about last Sunday?"

She seemed taken aback for a second and replied, "No, not really, I thought it was just to talk. Darla Jean has been so good at checking on me since Mr. Worsham died. I think she just wanted to see how I was doing. It didn't occur to me that it might have any other meaning. Why, do you suspect something, Mr. Biggs?"

"No, it's just that Mr. Rivera knew she was coming here on Sunday," I said matter of factly.

She gave me a stern look, "Mr. Biggs, you need to check that man out more carefully. Don't be fooled by that so called magnetic personality. There is something unseemly about that

man. Why I wouldn't be surprised if the man didn't have a record."
Hmm, I hadn't thought about that and the Sheriff hadn't mentioned
anything, but he was still convinced that Patsy was at a rehab facility
somewhere.

I sensed there was more. "In fact, Mr. Rivera told me that
Patsy wanted to talk to you about some important matters."

"How intriguing," she responded, "I can't think what she
would be referring to, unless, yes, yes I bet that was it. Mr.
Worsham's estate is still in testate. He had children by an earlier
marriage and they are contesting my part of the will. It has been
quite drawn out and I have had to dip into my savings quite a bit to
keep up app . . . maintain the house. It's really quite unfortunate. I
truly like his children."

"Would any of his children still be around the area?" I asked.

"No, they've scattered. There are four of them and I think
the closest lives in Arlington," she countered.

"Texas?" I questioned. "No, Virginia," she replied, "I think
he works for the federal government." Dice had said that with a
quality in her voice that suggested she was not fond of government
officials. That probably meant the Sheriff but I wondered if it also
included the minions that worked for him.

She changed the subject with what seemed an earnest
plea, "Mr. Biggs, bring my baby back, she's all I have in the world,"
and tears formed in the old gal's eyes.

I was touched and told her I would do everything I possibly
could to find her. She thanked me and hobbled along towards my
car, looked at it and said, "Is this an antique, Mr. Biggs?" "No,
ma'am," I replied. "Oh, I thought you might be involved in some
kind of renovation project to make it look more like it did in the
1950s." Actually it was an Aspen from the '80s, but I didn't want to
go into further details. Back to her old self she finished with a
flourish, "Well, perhaps you can find some parts at the local junk

yard or maybe even another wre . . . er, replacement." Just when I was starting to like the old broad, she returned to her old ways. Oh well, glaciers, I thought, often take thousands of years to move just a few feet.

As I walked down the driveway I passed the rather large garage off to the right and a thought occurred to me–cars (you can see by now I depend on visual cues). I sprinted (ok, jogged) back up the driveway and called to Mrs. Worsham as she started in the door.

"Mrs. Worsham, Mrs. Worsham!" I shouted. She turned, as I panted up to the front door. Out of breath, I managed to wheeze, "Mrs. Wor-wor-worsham, how did Patsy get to Edenton five years ago."

"Oh, she rode with a friend, now don't give me that suspicious look, Mr. Biggs. As you now know Darla Jean had visited Mrs. Beasley's before and had made a friend with one of the psychologists there." There were psychologists at Mrs. Beasley's? I thought they only had expert electricians for the shock treatment room. She continued, "The psychologist's family lived in Raleigh and the young lady would visit them. Every now and then, Darla Jean would find out about her visits to her family and catch a ride back to Mrs. Beasley's to renew her energy. Darla Jean said the ride was worth at least as much as the visit to the facility. They became quite good friends."

"Do you remember her name?" I asked.

"I believe it was Rhoda, Dr. Rhoda Morganstern," she stated. That name seemed awfully familiar to me but I couldn't quite place it. I did think that it was highly unlikely that girl was born around here.

"Does she still work in Edenton," I questioned.

"No, I believe she moved back to Raleigh to be close to her family, particularly her mother, if I remember correctly," she continued.   "It's kind of interesting but after everything was straightened out we found out that the Clines were good friends with the Morgansterns. Small world, isn't it?"

Yes, I thought, and full of coincidences, strange coincidences. I had one more question before I left. "Did Patsy mean to drive over here last Sunday?"

"Um-hmm," said Mrs. Worsham, a bit reluctantly.

"Do you know what kind of car she drives?" She thought a second and said "I believe it's a Chevrolet or maybe a Ford, I'm not good with identifying cars, Mr. Biggs, I usually am in the back seat, but Frank could tell you," she finished.   "Well, good night, Mr. Biggs."

Curiouser and curioser, I thought. Suddenly I had several new tasks to ahead of me. I needed to talk to this Morganstern lady and Archibald Cline.   And why, for Pete's sake, couldn't Frank volunteer any of that information?   Did I have to think of everything?   What did they think I was—an oracle or a detective? Hmm, don't answer that, I'm trying to maintain the high opinion you have of me if you've read this book this far.

By now it was mid-afternoon, probably too late to get to Raleigh, I'd give this Doctor psychologist a call tomorrow morning, but I could see Mr. Cline today. After calling the Sheriff and passing along the new information, I called the patriarch of the Cline family. He was gracious on the phone and told me he'd be glad to see me around seven.

It dawned on me that I hadn't said anything to Mrs. Worsham about what I had found out about the Hewes family tree in Edenton and that it didn't seem to include her branch (or twig might be more appropriate). Oh well, the old gal had been through a lot in the last few days, no use heaping on the bad news. I know you're thinking, that I'm too nice a guy to be a private investigator but I knew I was never going to make much money working in Green Top, so why not settle for that niche. No use burning any bridges if the detective business doesn't work out. And I still had that little genealogy history in my back pocket should I ever need it in another meeting with Mrs. Worsham.

Eine 'Clina' Nacht Muzik

Before I rang Mr. Cline's doorbell, I thought I'd give Frank a call. He was at his Elk's Club meeting which seemed strange to me all things considered, but Frank always seemed a little strange. It was hard to hear him. I don't know whether that was because of my sorry cell phone or the Elks. I got through to him long enough to ask what kind of car was Patsy driving when she left the house. He said he didn't know because he wasn't there, but her green Ford LTD was missing. Frank took everything literally. I asked him why he didn't think to tell me that in the earlier conversation. He said I didn't ask. True, but suspicious. I said there were some things that I would have thought he would want to tell me straight out without waiting for the question and I tried to sound steamed, though I'm not sure he could discern that with the noise in the background. The Elks were having quite a meeting.

OK, I said, could he think of anything else I needed to know. He said he couldn't think of anything. Man, this was like pulling teeth. "What was she wearing, Frank?" He said he didn't know, he wasn't . . . *There*!" I finished. Geez, I was surprised he could remember her name.

"I know she wasn't wearing her Sunday clothes," he stammered. Now, that was curious, I wondered how he knew that. "She might have been wearing casual clothes. She and her mother were going to that new fish house which is very relaxed. Have you been there, Mr. Biggs? They say it is very nice." "No," I said. Frank was starting to make me nervous. Could he really be this cool about what was happening or was there a more sinister motive? I tried an easy question, "What kind of car do you drive, Frank?" "An old white Mercedes."

"And is it in the garage?"

"Of course not, Mr. Biggs, it's here with me at the Elks Club." Like I said, literal minded. I knew I wasn't going to get more out of

Frank. I thanked him and asked him to contact me if he thought of anything else.

Driving up to the Cline's house, I was impressed with the Victorian house and setting. It was only one story, but it had one of those wide wrap around porches and that made it seem larger than the Worsham's two story. Unlike that house, the yard and the hedges were kept in immaculate condition; the grass was still green and matched the paint job. The driveway seemed long but I think that had more to do with me being anxious. Despite Mr. Cline's name on the checks I received when I had found Patsy, I had never met the man. Everything I had heard was impressive. The economic times had been tough, but Archibald Cline had closed only two mills in the past ten years, and none in Barrington. He had done it with ruthless efficiency, a willingness to computerize most aspects of the factory, and, of course, the use of immigrant labor that often was being paid less than minimum wage.

I knocked on the door and was met by a man of medium stature, clear eyes and, as I quickly found out, a strong handshake. He was eighty two years old but he looked mid-sixties to me. He cut an imposing figure, especially considering he had battled two heart attacks and a bout with cancer in the ten years preceding our meeting.

"Mr. Biggs," he began, "it's so nice to finally get to meet you in person and thank you for the work you did for us five years ago." My ears were burning, all I could think to say was "You can call me C.W."

He laughed and said, "And you can call me Arch." What a change in demeanor a few blocks in geography can make. He escorted me into the hallway and asked if I had eaten yet. I said I hadn't and he replied "Good, I hate to eat alone which has happened all too often since my wife, Genie, died." From what I knew that had been more than a few years. "I sent the staff home," he continued, "but I had my chef cook us up a beef burgundy and noodle dish, something nice and hearty." It sounded delicious. "Would you like a glass of wine before we eat?" I thought one glass wouldn't hurt me and readily agreed.

We walked into a large parlor and, as if by magic, there was a wine bottle and two glasses sitting on a small table. He walked over and uncorked the bottle, handed me the cork and said, "This is a Cabernet Sauvignon from California, it's only six years old, but the reviewers say it's quite tasty," and waited for my response. I stood with the cork in my hand and wondered what I was supposed to do, re-cork the thing? How would I know if it's any good unless I tasted it? He smiled, took the cork from my hand and poured out a glass for both of us. He startled me by sniffing his wine. I never sniffed Mad Dog, my wine of choice, just drank it as fast I could. He said, "The wine has a scent of blackberry with just hints of oak and a touch of spice." Ah, I thought, a wine cooler, but he worried me with that thing about oak. I looked real closely but I didn't spot one sliver.

Finally, he drank, or should I say, sipped. I, on the other hand, did drink and came up coughing. This was better than any 'three buck chuck' but it was strong. He chuckled and covered my embarrassment by saying, "I like a man who drinks hearty." I was really starting to like this old fellow. We walked into another room that was dominated by four larger than life paintings, one was of his wife. I guessed it was painted more than a few years back when she was a striking beauty but I noticed little resemblance to Frank. The other three were of his sons. I found that intriguing. My mother had three boys, too.

He pointed to the paintings and began. "This is my first, Mike. He is a corporate lawyer in Greensboro and has done quite well for himself. Here's my second son, Don. He is a surgeon at UNC hospitals, and, of course, you recognize Frank."

I was struck by the coincidences with my family. My oldest brother was the richest of us, chief mechanic over at the Tool and Die in Asheboro. My second brother, Phil, the one who knew Patsy, was a carpenter for Stewart's Remodeling over in Sterling. Both he and Arch's son had to be good with their hands and there was me and Frank. It just goes to show that families from two different backgrounds can grow up to be remarkably similar. Yep, Mr. Cline and I had a lot in common, apart from the money . . . and the large house . . . and the prestige.

I commented on our family's similarities when we sat down for dinner in a room that was as big as my apartment. "I know you are proud of the success of all your sons, Mr. Cline. It is a remarkable family." I was kinda fishing for a compliment for my family. It didn't come.

He did smile and say, "I must admit I was most impressed with Mike and Don's willingness to abandon the family business and strike out on their own. I guess I wasn't too surprised when Frank decided to stay with the company. He always seemed happier to stay in the shadows of his big brothers. I wonder if his mother pampered him too much as the youngest."

I sensed an opening to find out more on his enigma of a son. I began "Frank has a little less self-confidence than his brothers? I'm sure he's done a fine job at the mill."

Arch took another sip of his wine before commenting, "Just between you and me, C.W., I have had to cover for some of Frank's 'lack of self-confidence' over the years. Oh, I'm not saying I'm disappointed, I love Frank dearly, but he just never seemed to have the drive or the smarts of the others. That's why I was so excited when he married Patsy, as opposed to his mother who believed she married him just for the money. Patsy, I thought, was going to be the spark that set him up for the future. She seemed so full of life, such joie de vivre, but I was wrong." He stopped to dig into his beef

57

and noodles, possibly because he saw I was well on my way to finishing. This meal was a lot better than what Don had treated me to at the Diner. I would try not to let that influence my opinion.

"Well, I know he is in love with her. It's obvious every time I speak to him."

He leaned back a bit from the dining room table and said, "Yes, perhaps a little too much. I thought she would give him energy, but instead she seemed to suck the energy right out of him." I had an image of Patsy at that moment, hovering like a vampire over Frank. I shook my head to try and clear that picture. He took it as a sign I didn't believe it.

"You disagree, Mr. Biggs?"

"No, not necessarily," I said trying to recover. "I'm not sure I really know Patsy well enough to make such a judgment. She was a few years ahead of me in high school and my only real contact with her since was on the trip home from Edenton and she had very little energy that day. Indeed, she seemed rather tame."

He chuckled, "Patsy is anything but tame, she's something of a wild child, and I must admit that at first I was taken by her energy and her charm." *Charm*, I thought, *more like witchcraft.* I needed to change the subject.

"Tell me what you know of Don Rivera," I commanded, well sort of; I said it in a high squeaky voice which I blamed on a hot noodle.

"Ah, you've come to that moment, have you? Well, I like a man who is direct and to the point," he said forcefully. "Don is probably the most valuable person at the mill now. His engineering and people skills are as good as anyone I have in management and my ability to keep the mill open owes a great deal to him. Indeed, he probably could have moved on to something bigger and better a long time ago. Luckily, we've managed to keep him happy here." A strange thought crossed my mind but it was too outrageous to pursue so I kept quiet.

He continued, "I've known about Don's reputation as a ladies man almost from the moment he started with the company, but he was always discreet and I didn't think it was any of my business. Then Patsy came along and I thought this might lead Frank to fight for what was his, but he didn't. I was disappointed but I kept quiet."

I leaned forward, listening intently to every word Arch said. "At first," he continued. "I believed he was a coward, but through some careful questioning and a little investigating of my own, I came to believe that Frank didn't know and truly didn't want to know. It seemed to work until his mother died two and a half years ago. I believe that Frank worshiped his mother and I think he transferred some of that idolizing to Patsy, especially after Genie died"

I looked over the old man's shoulder at the matriarch's visage. She seemed to be frowning, though I could have sworn that she had a smile when I had sat down at the dinner table. "Do you think it is still worshipful, Mr. Cline?" I asked.

He shrugged his shoulders, stared at Frank's picture and said, "I think so, but C.W., I am very worried about what my son would do if the idealistic illusion he has of Patsy is ever broken. I know he's a good man, but even good men can do bad things. " A silence fell between us that seemed to last for an eternity. I wasn't sure what to say to a man who may have done everything but name his son a suspect in the disappearance of his wife. I turned to the last few noodles in my bowl and tried to look squarely at them and not the man.

He came to the rescue, "But I know Frank is tenderhearted, he wouldn't hurt a fly. I guess I'm more worried of what he would do to himself."

"Does he have a gun?"

Mr. Cline laughed and said, "You're not going to believe this but the only gun I know he has is a little two-shot Derringer, you know, the kind that women used to keep in their pocketbooks. He got it from his mother and it has to be fifty years old."

Yeah, but even a Derringer put right at the temple can do some serious damage. "Do you know Don's wife well?" I countered.

He seemed caught off guard. He played with his beef noodles for a while before looking up. "If there's one person in this situation I'm more worried about than Frank, it's Candi. She's a tenderhearted woman and I know she's smart enough to figure out what's going on. I don't know her well enough to know how she will respond to Don or has responded to Don. I have never seen any scars on that handsome face, for what it's worth."

"What about Patsy?" I tried to bring the conversation back to something that more closely resembled my task.

He leaned forward, the timbre in his voice strengthening, "What about her? Patsy, I think, has the uncanny ability to land on her feet. It wouldn't surprise me if she shows up in a day or two smelling like a rose."

I wish I was as confident. "If that's the case, why are you financing this investigation?"

He cocked his head and said "You're smarter than you look, C.W. I have to confess that I agreed to the Sheriff's little arrangement because I thought it would end the same way and I was impressed with the way you had kept your mouth shut the last time. The company does not need more bad publicity. Soon, I am probably going to have to let another fifty workers go and if it came out that I was paying considerable amounts for covering up other things, it might make things rather sticky in old Barrington."

Be careful, I don't need to lose this 'bigg' contract, "I hope I can continue to have your confidence."

"For a few more days, Mr. Biggs, for a few more days."

We paused for dessert which had mysteriously appeared, but I was not in detective mode. It was strawberries with real cream. I didn't want to ask anything for fear of him hearing me slurp. This was beginning to be the best meal I had eaten since my high school prom night.

After dinner, he took me into the library and once again the invisible servant laid out dainty cups and sat a pot of coffee on a table at the entrance. We talked about business and history and small towns. For a moment Patsy's disappearance had moved to the back burner and I felt like I was talking to an esteemed father figure. Eventually, I returned the conversation to my investigation. "Do you know a Rhoda Morganstern, Mr. Cline?"

He gave me a puzzled look, "Well, yes, yes I do. She was in school with my second son and, yes, I know she counseled Patsy. She is a very sharp lady, but I doubt you'll get much information from her." I asked why. "It's her profession, Mr. Biggs. She's trained to listen but to tell very little. I doubt you'll get more than three words out of her. Indeed, she'll be obligated to say nothing." Sounded like a dead end but I thought I'd still try anyway. He yawned and I took that as a sign to end tonight's meeting. He saw me look at the clock on the wall overhead and said, "Well, I think its past my bedtime, but keep me informed Mr. Biggs, let me give you my business card." He got up and walked to a small desk near the doorway, got out a card from a big stack, returned and handed it to me.

I got up to leave but as I did I finally saw the figure who had been keeping us in food and drink all night. I was astonished I hadn't noticed him. He was a huge man, easily six and a half feet tall and built like a pro basketball power forward. Mr. Cline noticed my jaw dropping and spoke, "That's my butler, chauffeur, nurse, etc. He is my most constant companion. His name is Robert Truelove and he's of Indian heritage. Navaho, I think. Isn't that right

Robert?" Robert seemed to nod slightly. "I helped Robert get out of some trouble with the state some years ago and he has been a friend since. I think he would do anything I asked of him. I'd like to think I have many friends like that, Mr. Biggs, perhaps . . ." The thought drifted off either because I was not worthy of that honor or because he thought he had said too much.

I must confess upon hearing what Mr. Cline had said and seeing the size of Robert, my nefarious mind began to spin several things out on what this giant of a man could do. I knew Cline was one of the most powerful men in this part of the state. For all of our friendly banter, it occurred to me that he had the resources to make people disappear. If he thought Frank might not do anything after being cuckold, would he be willing to settle scores? And would that consist of paying off Patsy, or something more sinister? Did this old man's smile hide a "Godfather" complex? Yikes, suddenly I wondered if I was the guy at the spaghetti parlor. I decided to ask no more questions and began looking all around to see if I could spot Robert hiding in the shadows, holding a strand of piano wire.

I walked backwards to my car pretending that I was just being friendly by constantly saying how much I enjoyed the dinner and how I appreciated his help, but all the time I kept moving my head around looking for any more of Mr. Cline's friends among the well-manicured bushes, and praying my car would start on the first turn of the ignition. For once it did, and I scooted out of the driveway with a last wave goodbye. As I took one last look in the rear view mirror I saw he had been joined by the hulking Indian. Robert was leaning over to hear something Arch was saying to him. I drove back to Green Top wondering if that conversation had anything to do with me. That thought and the richness of the incredible dessert kept me awake the whole night.

Help Me, Rhoda

I began the next day with a visit to the Sheriff. I wanted out of this mess, but I knew I was in too deep. Still, I tried, "Sheriff, I think I'm in over my head."

"Yeah, you're probably right, C.W." Thanks for the words of encouragement, what was even more distressing was the way he said "C.W.". He didn't use "old C.W." The way he said it made me think it was the late C.W. Pushing ahead, I filled him in on what had happened and mentioned the hulking figure of Robert, the Navaho. He did nothing to calm my fears when he said, "That is one bad red man. They call him Indian Bert. It used to be Big Bert, but that nickname led some folks to call him Big Bird by mistake. That would get him upset and he'd bash someone's head in. He's been in prison for clearing out a bar with just his hands and a knife. He was up for first degree murder in Saxapaw County, but somehow he walked. I hope you didn't say anything to upset him." I assured him I had said nothing that could upset the giant, indeed I had said nothing, period. But now I wanted to know how he got connected with Mr. Cline.

"Do you remember the attempt to unionize the Cline Mills?"

"Only vaguely," I answered, which was more than true, I didn't even know there was an attempt.

The Sheriff leaned back in his chair placing his feet up on his large desk. "Well, a lot of people think the attempt failed because of Arch Cline's sudden generosity. He raised the hourly wage for over two-thirds of the employees, but what very few people know about is the visit by Indian Bert to a number of the more prominent union supporters. Many left the county after the union petition failed and others, hmm, acquiesced. You don't want to mess with Indian Bert." I said I would keep that in mind.

"Do you think Arch Cline is capable of eliminating, umm, threats to his company?"

"I'm not sure you want to know the answer to that, C.W." But he could tell from my look, I did. I asked, "Sheriff, what have you gotten me into?"

"Now C.W., don't panic. Arch has to know that if anything happened to you, I would be suspicious and he would be first on the list." Somehow that did not reassure me. He continued, "Listen, C.W., if nothing breaks over the next two or three days, I'm going to have to take over anyway. There's this nosy reporter with the Stars and Bars who is snooping around and I think she has enough sources to go to press in next week's edition. You see, there's this real gossip queen by the name of Etta Mae Winstead and I'm pretty sure she's been giving the reporter information. You haven't heard of her have you?"

"Uh, no, Sheriff, I hardly know a soul in Barrington. Should I check her out?" I said innocently and hoped he didn't notice I was sweating.

"Good God, no! Don't go anywhere near her, there are stories that guys who visit her are never the same afterwards and look out for that reporter, too, C.W. Her name is Rita Worthington and she can be a pain in the ass. She's a stringer for WRAL and the News & Observer. All I need is for the cameras to start rolling on this story and my tenure as Sheriff will come to a quick end. No, I need this story settled as fast and as quiet as possible, but I already got an angle if we don't solve something soon."

"Oh, can I ask what that angle could be?"

"Now don't worry, C.W., I got it handled, but let's see if we can tie up some loose ends before then. So tell me, who do you intend to talk to next?" I told him about the psychologist and that I needed to talk to Candi. I asked him if Don had any kind of criminal record. He said he didn't know of any but he would check it out. He wished me luck and told me to keep him informed and whisked me out the back door at the jail. Man, did I feel alone. I needed a psychologist at least as badly as Patsy.

I called Rhoda Morganstern from home on my mom's phone hoping she might pay the long distance charges without realizing it was business. Mom kept dreaming I was going to find the right woman, actually any woman, marry and move on. So she just might think one of my many attempts at computer dating had panned out. I got a recording and left a message. Sometime after lunch, Dr. Morganstern called. Mom answered and gave me thumbs up as she handed me the phone. I headed out to the patio and hoped she couldn't hear me.

I exchanged pleasantries with the good doctor and quickly caught an accent that was definitely not southern, though she would sometimes use a colloquialism or two that showed me she had spent more than a few years in the Piedmont. I gave her the gist of what I knew and needed to know. She began to give me the spiel about counselor-client confidentiality. Despite that caution, she got very chatty, one might even say verbose, and it all began with a relatively innocent question. "Dr. Morganstern," I started, "is Patsy capable of harming herself?"

"Oh no, I don't think so. Patsy is a strong woman. She's been through a lot in her life and I don't think she would take her own life under any circumstances."

"Why all the visits to Mrs. Beasley's?" I parried.

"I'm sure you've done your research and know that Mrs. Beasley's is not really a clinic for distressed people. It's more of a quiet getaway to let women who have faced difficult times recharge their batteries. Some women do it by going shopping, some go to Vegas, but others just want to get away and enjoy some tranquility and believe me Patsy could use some tranquility."

"Meaning," I quickly interjected.

She sighed, "You know I can't get in to much of that, but surely you've uncovered enough to know that Patsy's marriage and relationship with her mother were not ideal."

"Yeah, but who's fault was that," I countered.

She paused again and said, "You don't like Patsy do you, Mr. Biggs?"

The question caught me off guard, but no, I didn't think too much of her. She seemed a lying and arrogant manipulator who may have left a string of broken hearts in her wake. I had never considered her otherwise. I hadn't known her well in high school, but it was a small school and I remembered how she treated me. She was four years ahead of me, I was a puny ninth grader when she was a super cool senior, but she knew my brother, Phil, who was an 11th grader and already a star athlete, handsome, too. He could have dated any of the best looking girls at school but Patsy was just below that list and wanted desperately to be in the elite. Grabbing Phil would have been a star in her crown, kind of like Frank, I imagined. Phil would basically ignore her, so she took it out on me.

If I saw her in the halls and I was alone or with my buddies, she would ignore me. But if I was with Phil, she would always say, "I see you're babysitting again, Phil." Phil would smile slightly and walk on, but I was embarrassed particularly if 9th grade girls would be around. I would turn red faced for fifteen minutes. No, I didn't like her, but I didn't want her dead.

However, my reply to the doctor was a bit more circumspect. "I don't have any feeling one way or another. It's just a job but one I want to succeed at. She's been gone over a week this time and there are more than a few people interested in her whereabouts."

"I appreciate your honesty, Mr. Biggs, but she's my friend too. Listening to you has made me a bit worried myself, but she's a big girl, a tough woman and can take care of herself."

"Oh? Do I take it you mean she had something for protection, a gun perhaps?"

"No, I don't mean to imply that, though I know she took a couple of self-defense classes. It's just that I think she has the ability to size up a situation and handle it," she said in an assuring voice.

"Would she pick up a stranger?" It was an angle that was beginning to worry me.

"No, I can't imagine it. No, if anyone would do her bodily harm, it would have to be someone who caught her off guard, someone she trusted." Well, that only eliminated one name on my suspect list. Robert Truelove was someone whose appearance was enough to catch someone off guard. She continued, "Patsy had inured herself to keep her emotions contained and be on the alert. She learned at an early age to be tough, especially after the death of her sister."

Now there was a stunner. Why didn't someone think to tell the private eye important facts like that, did they think I was supposed to do all the research? But I wasn't about to let the good doctor know how little I know.

"Oh, yes," I tried to sound informed, "the sister, Ma . . ."

She interrupted me, "Barbara Jean." "Yes, Barbara Jean," made sense I thought. "And she passed away when Patsy was . . ."

"Eight, Mr. Biggs. She died when Patsy was eight. Are you sure you have this information?" she asked. I lied I knew about it, but had placed it at the back of my mind. She continued, "Well, you can imagine the trauma on an eight year old when her younger sister died. And, there was her mother."

"Her mother? Now that part I'm not familiar with." I hoped I had recovered, but the doctor squashed that and much more information by saying she wasn't at liberty to talk about that. Yet again, despite her protestations, she turned chatty. She told me the old lady worshiped the younger girl and Patsy never matched up to the idealized version of the younger McRorie. That explained a lot and I waited to see if Rhoda would say more, but she abruptly ended the conversation with "I think I've said too much." The Doctor wished me well and told me to keep her informed, and interestingly, "Mr. Biggs, I'd like to send you my card, I think I can help you." Wow, I had impressed her so much the poor girl was looking for a hookup, must be my sexy southern voice. "Yeah," I said and gave her my address and phone number. "I'll include my rates on the back of the card, I might be able to give you a discount considering the nature of your work." Crap, she saw me as a client not a stud. But intentionally or unintentionally she had given me a lot to think on.

Not more than three minutes after I hung up with the good doctor, the Sheriff called. "Well, if it's not old C.W." He was so original. "I've got some bad news for you. Don didn't show up at work today and didn't leave word with anyone. I called the wife and she said he didn't come home last night. There's something else, C.W., I checked on Don: he has a record with two assault charges, both were dropped."

Interesting, I thought, "So Candi had stood up for herself."

"No, C.W., the person who filed the assault charges was Patsy. Both were dropped before they went to trial, actually before anyone had to post bail. The Cline family again. You know what I said about giving you two or three more days, C.W., well, it's two, tops, now. If we don't have this wrapped up by Sunday, we're going to have to go public." I had the rest of Friday and the weekend to end this. I headed out to see Don's wife feeling there was no way this was going to be settled that soon. I turned on the radio and hit search on the dial. A country and western station popped up and believe it or not, it was Patsy Cline on the radio, the real one, but when it got to the lyrics about "crazy for lying and crazy for trying",

I turned it off. I was beginning to get a very bad feeling that for the Patsy I knew, "lying or trying" may have been replaced with "dying".

Lucky Rita and Candid Candi

You may have guessed by now I'm not exactly a hard-boiled detective, and a good reason for that was I couldn't handle spying on spouses, especially if kids were involved. Now, don't get me wrong, I've done a few cheater cases, but except for the ugly confrontations, they're not like the ones on TV. In small towns, it's more like the cheating spouse has to go out of town, far out of town, and the track down takes longer than the confrontation. I also had a hard time asking questions to either spouse. This one was not going to be easy and from all accounts Candi seemed like a very nice lady.

The Rivera's lived in Wake County, somewhere between Cary and Apex, but since those towns run together, I'm not exactly sure whether I was in Cary or Apex. From what I could gather, the family wanted their kids educated in Wake, which meant a fairly long commute for Don, but a perfect cover for being tardy on certain nights when he and Patsy worked late. I arrived at about 3:30, but my rendezvous with the aggrieved wife was put off for a few moments. When I turned the corner in a subdivision cul-de-sac, I saw someone waiting on the curb at the Rivera's house. It didn't take a genius to figure out it was Rita Worthington. That plus the fact her car had a big placard on the side that said Barrington Stars and Bars.

There wasn't any place to run, so I parked the car and approached her. She didn't look like the harpy the Sheriff had suggested. She did look kind of nerdy, mid 20s, hair in a bun, glasses, white blouse and dark skirt, very little makeup. Still, she wasn't ugly either, a little bit of this and a little bit of that and she could be an early morning anchor on a third class TV station.

She moved toward me, "You must be C.W. Biggs, the famous detective." *Sharp cookie*, I thought, not catching the sarcasm in her voice. "How did you know?" I asked. "Oh, the

Sheriff tries to hide his little secrets but I am a Carolina graduate," she said haughtily, "Let's talk."

"Wait just a doggone minute, first tell me what you're doing here."

"Same as you, C.W., I want to talk to Candi Rivera about a certain missing lady, and a husband that likes to 'play' with his employees."

"Who's missing?"

She wagged her finger in my face. "Now don't play games, C.W., you know as well as I do, Patsy Cline is missing."

"No she isn't, she knows exactly where she is." Oh God, I was sounding like Eurydice Worsham.

"Are you saying that Patsy Cline is not missing?" she asked as she pulled a pad out from her pocketbook and a pen out of her hair.

"No, I'm just saying she knows where she is." This was kind of fun. Maybe Eurydice was on to something.

Exasperated, Rita tried a different tact. "Ok, C.W., give me something to go on or I'm going to march right up to that door and knock again for the tenth time this afternoon."

"Come on, Rita, leave that lady alone, she has nothing to do with this."

"Oh, so you know my name. Did you get that from the Sheriff? Why should I leave her alone, my readers need to know this sordid story."

"Oh, the Stars and Bars has readers? I thought they printed those papers for cat litter liners." I said. The snippy comment seemed to work. She reddened briefly.

"Look C.W., this is the biggest story to hit Barrington since I've been here and my ticket to join a real newspaper like the News & Observer. So I intend to stay here until I get some information, I have a deadline to meet."

"Y'all only print two days a week. The deadline can't be that close."

"Three days a week," she spat out, "and besides we have to farm out the actual publication. I need something by Monday morning."

So do I, I thought. "Ok, you tell me what you know and I tell you what you know."

"That doesn't make any sense C.W. What are you saying? Do you know something or not?"

"Listen Rita, I can be what you call a primary source, but you got to lay off Candi, at least for twenty four hours."

"What do I get in return?"

"Ok, you ask me questions and I will confirm what I can."

"Hmm, let's see. Alright, is Patsy Cline missing?"

"I've already told you the answer to that, stick to other things."

"Is Patsy Cline at her home in Barrington?" she countered.

"No." "Is she at her mother's?" "No," and I repeated that answer about ten more times, getting her more and more frustrated and flustered.

She moved closer and I thought she might throw a punch at me. "This is ridiculous," she finally said. "I'm going to march in right now and demand to see Mrs. Rivera." She turned around and headed for the front door. I knew she was grandstanding and couldn't see Candace without permission, but I needed to get in there, quick, with as little interference as possible.

"Ok, Ok," I said, "I'll give you one big bit of information, if you give up something to me I don't know."

"Go on, I'm listening," she challenged. I had to think fast, but I really didn't want her talking to Candi for a number of reasons, not the least of which was me wanting to talk to her first.

"Listen, Rita, if you want to find out something about Patsy, you need to go to Edenton and ask for a Mrs. Beasley."

She gave me a long stare and said "Edenton, huh, what am I going to find there?"

"I promise you Rita, it's worth the trip, you will get a lot of background, and did you know her family was from there? You need to ask about the Hewes."

"The Hewes?"

"Yeah, the Hewes family. Don't you know your North Carolina history?" I said pedantically. It's amazing how a little arcane knowledge can help you look smarter than you actually are. The Hewes thing seemed to catch her off guard and I could see the cogs turning in that brain of hers, I decided to go in for the kill. "Ok, I've given you something, now how about providing me with some info."

There was a pause and she tried to come up with something that would arouse my curiosity the way my Hewes reference got her intrigued. "Alright, did you know that Diego Rivera was charged with assault?" "Yeah, Yeah, I know, and Patsy dropped the charges both times. It was a probably a setup by Patsy."

She smiled triumphantly and spoke, "No, C.W. but thanks for confirming that bit of information." Damn, I thought, this girl is getting the best of me. "I'm talking about an old assault charge at ECU by a Diego Rivera against a Candace Alridge of Denver, North Carolina." Ouch, I thought, Don's penchant to violence went back a long way. It was looking bad for old Don Diego. She knew she had me on the ropes. She finished, "And did you know that Frank and Patsy have had to renegotiate their mortgage or they were going to have their loan called in? The only reason it wasn't called in already is the fact he's a Cline!"

I was starting to get a good deal of respect for this girl. A couple more bits of information and she'd be ahead of me, if she wasn't already. I sat there mutely and hoped she would add some more, but she took a good look at me and realized I wasn't much of a source. "C.W., if this thing in Edenton turns out to be a wild goose chase, I'm going to be writing an exposé of your detective ability or lack thereof!"

A wild goose chase! I thought how appropriate and effective, particularly on a weekend. By the time she got down there, almost everything would be closed and trying to find Mrs. Beasley's little house for misplaced women in the dark would be a near impossible task.

"I swear to you, Rita, you go to Edenton, and a lot of this situation will be cleared up for you. In fact, it might even lead to a whole string of stories - human interest stories - the kind that could impress a big city newspaper."

She seemed to lose focus for a minute and stared off in the distance. The chance for a human interest story had her reaching for a new job or a Pulitzer Prize. In fact it looked to me like she was clutching her notepad as if it were a substitute. "Maybe so," she whispered, "maybe so. Okay, C.W., I'm going to clear out of here and head for Edenton, but you better not be lying to me. Besides, I've knocked on that door until my hand is sore and I haven't seen anyone move toward it, even though the car is in the garage."

"I promise you, you won't be disappointed. And on the way back, you might want to stop at a little café called Mary Lou's and ask for a waitress called Mabel. She knows everything about that town. 'Course it could close early on Sunday, you know how that is in small towns."

"Tell me about it, Barrington rolls up the streets at 6:00, God, how I miss Chapel Hill. Thanks, C.W., you've almost been a help." I smiled and waved her on her way. I figured it might be difficult to find a room. With a little luck, say a flat tire and getting lost trying to find Mrs. Beasley and it would be Sunday before you knew it. And if I hadn't figured out this situation by Sunday evening, I probably wasn't going to. Now I had another reason for solving this mystery by Monday.

The answer to one mystery was quickly solved. As I was sitting in my car hoping Rita would have bad luck, a school bus drove up and let out several children, two of whom headed for the Rivera's house. Rita didn't count on Candi being such a protective mother. She didn't answer the door because she was afraid the kids might arrive as she was talking to a nosy reporter who might not care what she said in the presence of the children. The question that remained, would she treat me any differently? As I got out of the car, Mr. Cline's card dropped out of my shirt pocket. Maybe that was my ace in the hole.

I walked up to the door and gave it several good hard knocks, with no reply. I decided to try the card, slid it under the door and said as loud as I dared, "Mrs. Rivera, Mr. Cline sent me over to see how you were doing and if you needed anything." Ok, that wasn't exactly true but I was running out of time and options. I heard nothing and knocked again. I had just about given up when I heard someone moving around in the front room. A few seconds later, I caught the sound of the door unlocking and saw Candi's face through the storm door screen.

"Mr. Cline sent you?" she asked, while holding the card in her hand.

"Yes, yes, he's quite worried and I've been asked to investigate what's been going on."

"Investigate or help cover up?" she stated with a quiet, but remarkably strong voice.

"Perhaps, Mrs. Rivera, it might be better if we continue this conversation inside the house. There's been a rather snooty newspaper reporter around here. I may have run her off but she might return at any moment."

That seemed to be the charm. She opened the door wider and unlatched the screen. I stepped in to a small foyer and she motioned me over to a nicely decorated living room. I now had a chance to look at Candi for the first time and 'weathered beauty' crossed my mind. It was obvious that this lady had a style and a sense of purpose that cut across the depth of years of raising a house full of children and a husband who was away from home, in more than one sense. Whatever Don saw now, I could tell that Candi once was a radiant woman who was far prettier than Patsy ever was. There were several pictures on the wall that confirmed that opinion. I particularly noticed one that showed a smiling raven haired beauty in a summer smock tossing a young child up in the air. I tried to take in more of my surroundings but she snapped me back to the present with a harsh "Who are you and what exactly do you want?"

"Uh, my name is C.W. Biggs and I'm a private investigator hired to find a Mrs. Patsy Cline. Unfortunately your husband's name has come up more than once in the investigation."

"Biggs, huh? Don said something about you. You had a meeting with him earlier this week, didn't you?"

"Well, yes ma'am I did."

She looked at me intently. "I remember he said he hoped you weren't as dumb as you looked."

Great, I thought, another ringing endorsement, but I kept my cool and asked if I could sit down. She motioned me to a nice sofa and sat down across from me in an elegant high back chair.

I hoped to win a little favor by asking if the children were where they couldn't hear us. It seemed to work, she gave a small nod and said they were in the back yard playing. "Good," I said, "I'm not sure how much they are aware of what's happening and I'm not interested in bringing them in on my investigation." She thanked me briefly and sighed, "I really know very little, Mr. Biggs, I don't know why you bothered to come here."

I rushed in before she could go on, "But it is true that Don didn't come home last night nor did he show up at work." Tears briefly formed in her eyes and I felt like a heartless grouch, but she confirmed what I had already heard. Like I said, I had never cared for these kinds of cases.

"Mrs. Rivera, I really need to find Don and in a hurry. The situation is getting out of hand and he needs to get in touch with the authorities."

"Explain yourself, Mr. Biggs."

I took a deep breath and decided I needed to cut to the chase regardless of the circumstances. "Mrs. Rivera, there is a very real chance that this case could become a murder investigation. The Sheriff of Branch County has given me until Monday to find some real evidence of where Patsy is, dead or alive, or he may charge your husband with at least kidnapping, if not something much worse."

She gasped, "Mr. Biggs, I have been married to Don for twenty-six years and he is incapable of either murder or kidnapping."

"Yet, isn't it true you once took out papers on him for assault?"

"How did you find that out?" she hissed. "That was a long time ago and a misunderstanding. Don is very strong and he doesn't realize his own strength. I was at fault. I tried to hit him and he held my arms back until it left bruises on them. The police only charged him because my roommate had called the police and I was the only one with any injuries so they assumed Don was at fault. He was the perfect gentleman and was willing to accept the charges rather than tell them he had done it to protect himself."

She took a deep breath and finished, "I think I found out how much I truly loved him that night."

I stared at her and tried to think. There was some kind of psychological concept to describe what I had just listened to but, like I said, I didn't make any higher than C's in the psychology courses I took, so I couldn't come up with a word. It did cross my mind that Frank's utter devotion to Patsy, and Candi's blind obedience to Don, were similar.

I snapped out of it and used a rather standard line, "If you love him, you have to help him and you can help him most by either telling me where he is or getting in touch with him and having him contact the Sheriff of Branch County."

"But I don't know where he is. He didn't leave a note or a contact number and he hasn't answered his cell phone all day." Changing the subject, she asked "Do you really believe that something has happened to Patsy?"

"I can't be sure, but I am getting more worried by the minute, everyone I talk to says she can take care of herself." Candi interrupted "That's for sure!" "But I'm not," I continued. "This seems different than the last time, particularly the fact that both Mr. Cline and Mrs. Worsham are nervous about what's happened."

"I can answer that," she said emphatically, "reputations, reputations. Both of them are much more worried about the fallout if something has happened to Patsy and Don than they are about them personally."

"Oh, do you think Mr. Rivera could be in danger, too?"

"Absolutely. He's taken some phone calls recently that he would only answer after going outside, nor would he say anything about them after he came back in, but he looked worried."

"Could any of those calls have been from Patsy?"

That straightened her up and she flung out, "No, I don't think so," and clammed up. The conversation had turned chilly and there were a couple of quiet moments before I changed the subject. Looking at the mantle over the fireplace, I saw her children in various pictures and poses and made the standard (and self-serving) statement, "You have a lovely family, Mrs. Rivera." Candi relaxed and a small smile eased the furrows from her brow and the creases at the corner of her mouth. Her natural beauty returned as she began to discuss her five children.

"Thank you, Mr. Biggs, they are wonderful. This is my oldest, Ricardo, his friends call him Rick, but he prefers Card, that's what his dad calls him. He's a tax accountant at Burlington Mills. It's an entry level job but with this economy, I think he's done nicely. This is my oldest daughter, Mariel. She is in grad school at ECU." I looked at the picture of a black haired beauty, taller than Candi, but otherwise a near carbon copy. "She's engaged to be married to a young man from Edenton."

"Edenton!" I said a little too loudly. She looked at me with a quizzical expression and asked, "Yes, do you know that town well?"

"Um, yes," as I tried to recover, "he wouldn't be a Hewes, would he?"

"No, his name is John Martin." *Thank God*, I thought. "She's truly in love. In fact, there's a bit of irony in their wedding. She has told me that she is willing to change to his church because of her love for him, just as I gave up my church to marry Don.

"Methodist?" I asked. "No, Episcopalian," she answered. For Edenton that was close enough, in fact if the Episcopal rector wasn't married, she probably wouldn't notice a difference.

She continued, "This is my second son, Mark, he should be home soon. He's trying out for the basketball team. He barely made it last year and saw very little action. He hopes to play more this year and impress his father." "And he attends Apex?" I asked slyly. "No, Holly Springs." Holly Springs? Great! I really was lost. "And here are my two youngest, Esteban Bernardo, we call him E.B., he's eleven and my precious Emmaline, we call her Emma, she's eight. Which reminds me, it's starting to get dark, and the kids may be coming inside soon. I appreciate your consideration earlier, but I think we may need to end this conversation soon."

"I've got just a couple of more questions, Mrs. Rivera. I don't know how to say this nicely so I'll just be frank. You knew about the affair with Patsy, why did you stay with him?"

She caught her breath and said, "I truly do love him, Mr. Biggs. I have since I first met him. You know I said I gave up my church to switch to his, I think it was easier for me because I found so much spiritual power in the Catholic Church's ideas on divorce. I meant to make a commitment that would last forever." She saw my eyebrows arch, but continued, "I know it sounds old fashioned, and I know there's nothing to really stop me from divorcing him, but I can't. Partly because of the children, they still love him, and partly because I do, too."

See what I mean about these kinds of cases. I was at a loss for words. I thought she was foolish and I wondered how long she could keep playing this game without causing an emotional breakdown, but I admired this very strong woman. It was Don Diego I had problems with. *Enough with the soul searching!* I told myself it's time to move on. "I may never understand that kind of love, but I admire you, Mrs. Rivera, even if I wonder if your devotion is well placed."

She smiled quietly, "Thank you, Mr. Biggs. That means a lot."

"I still have to find him, Mrs. Rivera." "Call me, Candi," she said, "I think I'm beginning to like you, Mr. Biggs, and I'm a bit surprised at myself."

Thanks, I think. "Candi, what kind of car is he driving?"

"He's driving a gray Audi, 2005. He left the Buick and the van for us." *How sweet,* I thought, *but it might make it easy to spot if I could remember what the Audi symbol was.* I continued, "Does Don have any guns?"

"He used to. He liked to do skeet shooting and had several rifles and shotguns, but I made him give them up as the kids began to get older and into everything. He might still have a revolver in his car, but that's speculation. He sometimes goes into some tough neighborhoods." *Like Patsy's,* I thought.

"Can you give me any help on where to look and maybe a recent photo?"

She thought long and hard, "There used to be a restaurant in Raleigh, near N.C. State he would visit often. I think it was called Armadi's. It was where he and Patsy would rendezvous. I could always tell when he had been there with her; he would come home with a piece of cheesecake for me. I think it was his idea of a peace offering. Do you know it, C.W.?" I knew it well; it was a favorite spot for Wolfpack fans. "Yes, I know exactly where it was located."

She continued, "He would bring it home and head for a shower and I would sit in the kitchen eating cheesecake and crying. Silly, I know, but sometimes it was enough to keep me from going crazy." She stopped as if unsure whether she had shown too much of her inner self, sighed, and said, "I'll go get a photo." I thought to myself how I wish I could find a woman that was so loyal to me, or at least one that could be bought off by a piece of cheesecake.

The back door opened and two youngsters flew in, but came to a sudden stop when they saw me and their mother in the living room. She turned to them and said, "Children, I would like you to meet a friend of your father, Mr. Biggs." I certainly hoped I could be a friend of their dad, for their sake and mine. I greeted the kids and headed for the front door with some excuse about needing to get on the road. She thanked me and walked me outside. In the dim light of a setting sun, she looked at me and suddenly gave me a hug, a hug that seemed to be genuinely felt and one I would remember for a very long time. She looked up at me and ended our evening by saying, perhaps begging, "Bring my husband back to me, Mr. Biggs, please bring him back." I turned quickly because I was starting to get a bit emotional and thought to myself, *Why is everyone asking me, the ineffective P.I., to bring back their loved ones*? I had a very real feeling that if I was lucky enough to bring them home, it might not be the way they hoped.

On The Road Again

Early Saturday morning I cranked up the old Dodge and headed for NC State. Now State is one of my seven favorite universities I have attended. I spent an enjoyable three semesters there in the mid-90s, two of which included going to class, and Armadi's was one of my favorite hangouts. It was an Italian restaurant run by Greeks. It had wood paneling covered with memorabilia from State's athletic achievements. I didn't stick around long enough to really know too many of the names, so I often used long bull sessions with real students to stare at the walls and try to remember names and feats of old. It saved me the embarrassment of commenting about philosophy or biochemistry or some other subject I had no knowledge of. It was a beautiful fall day with the red and orange leaves shimmering in the morning light. The kind of Carolina day that makes the tourist brochure, so I daydreamed and enjoyed the ride to Raleigh.

I knew it would be a long shot to find Don at Armadi's but I remembered they had great lasagna. I began my quest there. I ran into a huge traffic jam just as I hit the city limits and suddenly remembered that State had a home game today. I was stuck in traffic and crowds for an hour or more but it began to thin out about the time I got to the restaurant. I got into a cozy corner booth about the time the TV showed the kickoff. Soon all the patrons left in the eatery were watching the game which gave me an opportunity to talk to a pony–tailed waitress with no apparent interest in the contest.

"Miss," I began in my usual inquisitorial style (pleading) "can you help me?"

She gave me a look like "you dirty old man". It was obvious enough that I had to respond, "No, nothing like that. You see I'm looking for a friend of mine who's in trouble with the law and I need to find him before they do."

"This isn't like a murder deal, is it?" she responded.

"Uh, no," I said, hoping I was right. "He's just got a couple of traffic tickets and I need to see him before they do."

"Oh, so you're like a lawyer or something."

"Yeah, or something." Ahh, the innocence of youth. No use disillusioning her of her idealism. Plus, I was taking it as quite a compliment that she took me for a lawyer, particularly since I was wearing a knit shirt and faded jeans.

"Sure," she said. Most of the crowd had headed to Carter-Finley Stadium so she slipped into the other side of the booth. "How can I help?"

She was a blonde with freckles and kind of cute. Watch it Biggs, I thought, you're old enough to be an older brother, much older. Snapping out of my daydream I said, "I understand he frequents this restaurant pretty often, sometimes by himself and sometimes with a blonde. Here, let me show you his picture."

She took a close look at it and shook her head, "No, I don't think I recognize him. Wait a minute, could he have been here real recently, like maybe last night? I was working the pickup corner and I think he came in to get a pizza. He was ticked off, too, said he had called in the order an hour earlier for a delivery and hadn't gotten anything yet. You see we don't deliver often, only got one driver, and nothing beyond a five mile radius. Most of our deliveries are on campus."

"Uh, yeah, but what about the guy?" I hated to interrupt her soliloquy, but this sounded like a private eye's dream. This could limit my search area by a lot and then it got better.

"Oh, yeah. Boy, did he have a fit. Thought we were going to have to call the cops. You know it's just possible he didn't take the ticket with him. I think Julio may have kept it in case we had problems with him again." I was getting excited. This girl just might replace Mabel as the woman of my dreams, "but he's not here yet, he works the night shift, though on Saturday..." She got up and said "Wait here." Where the hell was I going? In just a couple of minutes she was back and smiling. "This is your lucky day, mister, here's the delivery ticket. They had stuck it on the bulletin board to remind everybody about our delivery area. He's at the Sleep-Easy Inn way out on I-40. It's about a mile beyond where we deliver." I almost grabbed the ticket from her, but she pulled back and said, "I need this, but you can write it down on something." I had a pen but hadn't brought anything to write on, I looked around frantically. Then she said, "Use a napkin, we got plenty," and handed me her felt pen.

I looked at the note and was astonished to see Don Rivera, Room 122, Sleep-Easy Inn, 555-5122. This didn't sound like a guy who was trying to hide, or if he was, he was incredibly inept. No, it was more like a lost soul who didn't know what he was doing or maybe didn't care. I looked at the waitress again, and asked her name. She told me it was Cindy and I wanted to kiss her, but I settled for giving her a ten dollar tip. "But you haven't eaten anything," she said. Innocence again, I said thanks but told her I wanted to see my friend first, but maybe I can come back later, maybe with Don. "He really is a nice guy," I said, "but he does have a temper. If we come back, I'll make sure he apologizes."

"Don't worry about it. We're constantly getting bad asses, especially if State's had a bad game. It's why I don't like football. I remember one time . . ." I interrupted, "Uh, yeah, Cindy, I guess I need to be going, he might not have checked out yet. Sleep-Easy Inn, you said, would you know where that is?"

"Well, it's off of I-40, I think it's at the exit just before you get to the turnoff for the beach, I think." "Great," I said, and got up gave her a hug which happily she accepted and headed to the door. This day was definitely looking beautiful. That all changed when I got lost.

It wasn't anybody's fault, really. The Sleep-Easy Inn was off I-40, kind of, but it was two exits from the road to Wilmington, not one and it's really more accessible from US 70. Every convenience store clerk I talked to would send me to a Sleep Inn, a national chain of motels. Very nice, I might add, I saw at least three of them and they were all pretty and none of them had a Don Rivera. Finally, about 3:30, I found the Sleep-Easy Inn. It was a left over from the pre-Interstate days. It was a brick building and v-shaped with the office in the middle and at least twenty rooms, some more on the back side. I drove down the entrance lane and quickly spotted Room 122. It was three doors down from the office and right in front was parked an Audi, the only car like it in the upper parking lot. I felt like I would be embarrassing the Audi Car Company if I parked next to him in my old Dodge so I moved back to the very end of the lot and hid my car behind a big pickup.

I walked back to Room 122 and heard a TV, so I knew he was in there. I knocked loudly on the door and said my name. Nobody came to the door and the sound on the TV suddenly disappeared. I called out again and again got no answer. "Come on," I said, "Don, I know you're in there. We need to talk." Still nothing. This continued for about five more minutes until the motel manager came out and asked me what was going on. I said my friend was in trouble with the law and I was here to take him home. He said Don was paid up through Sunday and that's all he needed to know unless I had a warrant. "You got a warrant, buddy?"

"No, I haven't got a warrant but I might get one."

"Then go get it, 'cause you ain't getting in otherwise," he cackled.

Now I knew that Don had heard all that and wasn't coming out anytime soon. I decided to try the same strategy I had used on his wife, the Cline gambit. I didn't have a business card but I thought I might still be able to use the idea. I retrieved a note pad out of my car and wrote out a quick message. It read, *Don, your wife misses you and wants you back home. Mr. Cline sent me before the police pick you up. The cops want to talk to you and now that I know where you are I'm obligated to let them know. I need to talk to you and see if we can clear this up. I'm going to give you one more chance. Meet me at Armadi's at 7:30. If I don't see you by 7:45, I'm calling the Sheriff and he will probably issue an APB for your arrest. Please, be there. C.W.*

Pretty good, huh. Well, the thing about Mr. Cline might have been an exaggeration but it was close to being the truth. I slipped it under his door, gave one last knock and backed off to my car. I could just see his door through the pickup's window and I was pretty sure he wouldn't be able to see me unless he walked down to the end of the motel. Within five minutes, he opened up his door and looked right and left, but he didn't take off. Twice more he came outside and looked, but by now I felt pretty safe that he didn't know where I was. I didn't trust him and stayed right at my post. About 7:00, Don came out of his room, got in the Audi and pulled out without looking around for anyone. I left a few minutes later, in part because with all the turns and twists on my trip to the Sleep-Easy Inn, I wasn't sure I could find my way back to Armadi's. But Don knew exactly where he was going and within twenty minutes we were pulling into the parking lot. But he worried me when he drove to a back parking lot I didn't know existed. I didn't feel comfortable going back there because I wasn't sure he couldn't spot me right away, so I gave him the benefit of the doubt and about a five minute lead and walked in to the restaurant.

Armadi's has an interesting seating pattern with all sorts of nooks and crannies, in part because it allows them to put up more sports memorabilia but it also makes it difficult for a smart private eye to watch every section. I found a booth that allowed me to watch the front door and the pay station. I was carefully monitoring it when Don suddenly walked out of the kitchen and straight to my booth without me seeing him, until he spoke in a loud, clear voice. "What do you want, C.W.? And why are you following me?"

Caught a little bit off guard by his sudden appearance, I countered "Whoa, there, mister, I told you in the note why I'm here and where did you come from?"

He eased off somewhat as his body relaxed and said, "I've been here many times. Most of the staff knows me, but last night I got into an argument with one of the newer employees and I came through the kitchen to apologize. I made a bit of ass of myself."

"Well, you're making an ass of yourself now. People are looking, why don't you sit down and let's talk"

Reluctantly, he slipped into the booth across from me and said, "Alright, but I still don't believe Mr. Cline sent you."

"Well, he didn't exactly." Don interrupted and said "I thought so!" He started to get up again. "Wait a minute," I countered, "I said he didn't send me to look for you exactly. He sent me to look for Patsy, and all those roads, buddy, keep leading back to you."

That seemed to slow him. He sat down again, saying "Look Mr. Biggs, we've already been over this before. I don't know what's happened to Patsy."

"Why did you take off without even telling your wife? And why didn't you mention Armadi's and the Sleep-Easy were main stops on your and Patsy's romance express? It looks mighty suspicious, Don. The Sheriff is ready to call this a murder-kidnapping investigation and I got to Monday to find out something to change his mind. Otherwise, he's going to issue an all-points bulletin and ready to name you Suspect Numero Uno. I need something, Don, and I need it soon."

"Madre de Dios," he said, using the first Spanish I had heard him speak since I met him. "Do they really think it's that serious?"

"What did you think would happen when you took off?"

He gripped the table "I'm not sure I was thinking, I just needed to get away from everything. I just needed to find some place where I could figure out what was happening to me."

"You?" I nearly shouted, "What about Patsy? What about your wife and children? And why, for Pete's sake did you pick the same spot that you and Patsy used as a rendezvous? Not overly bright for someone as intelligent as you." I could tell my words were starting to have an effect. He started to sweat and his lip quivered. The waitress came up and asked us for our drink orders. Don ordered a Coors Light, I asked for a glass of Cabernet Sauvignon. Don's eyebrows went up and he looked at me with a bit of astonishment. "I didn't realize you were a connoisseur, Mr. Biggs." I smiled and said, "Well, in the detective business you need to know your wine, your women, and your guns." I meant it as a joke, but I'm not sure he took it that way. When the drinks arrived he said, "I order the Coors Light because it slightly reminds me of a Spanish beer, a Mahou Classic. I don't suppose you've heard of that brand?" I shook my head as he took a sip.

He was relaxing, the familiarity of the restaurant and the beer had given Don a chance to catch his breath and regain his poise, but only for a second. Two sips of his beer and he began acting like a regular on an Oprah Winfrey tell all.

"I am a lost soul," he began, "I'm in love with two women and I don't see any way out. I don't want to be in this situation, it just happened, but I don't know anything about where Patsy is or what happened to her."

"Ok, Don, let's just say for the sake of argument I believe you, which I don't, but fill me in on what did happen between you two. Think of it as a practice for when the police interview you." I said it sarcastically but he didn't take it that way, he approached it as if engineering a solution for his textile mill.

"I saw her on Thursday, two weeks ago, at the Grill for lunch. She seemed in a good mood, but I said I had something to say. I told her I couldn't go on like this anymore. My betrayal of Candi and the children were weighing heavily on my soul and I had to end our, um, friendship." It had sounded like a confession to a priest until the last part.

"And how did Patsy take it?" I asked.

"Surprisingly well, I thought. She said she understood, but said to give her a day to make sense of it. There were no tears. Indeed, if truth be told, I may have cried more than her. The next day, she called, and said she had a solution, but she needed to make some arrangements first. I told her there was no solution but she said she'd see me Sunday night and we would both be happy. That's the last time I talked to her."

"Why didn't you tell me that in our conversation earlier? It could have kept me from chasing after some very false trails."

"I was worried about, about . . ." "Patsy??" I challenged. "No," he said, "not Patsy." "Candi?" I asked incredulously. "No," he laughed, "not Candi."

"Who, then?"

"Mr. Cline."

"Mr. Cline! He's in his eighties, for God's sake."

Don shook his head, "Not Mr. Cline personally, but that assistant of his, Indian Bert."

"Tell me about him, Don. All I know is that he is a hulk and a possible sociopath. What do you know about him?"

"I know too much, I know what he did during the attempt to unionize the mill and I am worried that knowledge might make Mr. Cline do something."

Now it was my turn to shake my head, "That's not enough, Don, explain yourself."

"When the union began its efforts, there was a real possibility that the mills might become unionized. Four of their organizers came from out of state and were having a real effect. Bert caught these guys outside a bar in Burlington and beat them."

"Why didn't Big Bert get arrested?"

"Two reasons. He beat them in a way it didn't show and Mr. Cline ran interference for him. The Union officials went back home and the organization attempt ended in failure shortly afterwards. Oh, by the way, don't ever call him Big Bert. I once saw him pummel a guy for calling him that."

"Pummel?"

"Yes, pummel, you know beat them senseless."

I thought, *why didn't you just say so*? It wasn't just his accent the Hispanics had trouble with, it was his erudite vocabulary.

"Okay I guess I got the pummel thing, now go back to that part where he beat them in a way that it didn't show."

The hand holding his beer was shaking slightly and I detected a slight quiver in his voice when he began, "Mr. Biggs, Bert had learned techniques in his short stay in the special forces to beat people with things that didn't show bruises. It was as much psychological as actual physical brutality."

"Short stay in the Special Forces, how short?"

"You know what you said about sociopath? Well, the Army agreed with you."

"Who told you this?"

"Mr. Cline told me one evening when he invited me up to dinner at his house. We had beef noodles." Damn, I thought I was special; obviously it must be the meal he fixes for all his visitors.

"Okay, assuming all this is true, how is it connected to Patsy?"

"Don't you see," he said almost pleadingly, "I had told Patsy, and she probably picked up some things from Frank, and she went to blackmail Arch. When I figured that out I decided to get out of town and I didn't tell my wife because I wanted her to be able to say nothing if anyone called. She always tells the truth if she knows it."

I sank back into the booth and wondered if any of this could be true. The waitress came to get our orders. I was so spooked she had to ask me three times what I wanted. Finally, she suggested an order of lasagna and I nodded my head. I was on some very shaky ground here; it didn't make a lot of sense. It seemed too much like a plot out of some 1930s movie. But I had to admit Big Bert was an imposing figure, and Arch Cline had survived in a business that was dying all over the South, perhaps with some illegal techniques. Was it too much of a reach to think that he could order others to commit violence to keep his life style afloat? But could Patsy have had the gumption to blackmail Arch Cline on his own turf? Well, yeah, that part I could believe. She was just crazy enough to try such a scheme, especially if she thought she could win the heart of the man she loved, but was she self-delusional?

"Don, supposing she had pulled off such a stunt and returned with more money than you could dream of, would you have run away with her?"

Now he sank back in the booth, and there seemed to be at least two minutes of dead silence. Finally, he spoke, "I'd like to think I wouldn't have, but I can't honestly be sure."

Good answer. He's covered both bases and didn't try to wriggle out of it with some sort of self-serving statement of innocence and protestations of love for his wife. About that time two Raleigh police officers walked in. I could see them at the front, Don was turned away from them, and I considered the possibility of going up to them, turning in Don and washing my hands of this increasingly confaluted tale. But the officers went to sit on the other side of the restaurant and my lasagna showed up. My stomach demanded I put off these pressing decisions until I could stuff myself with some very good ricotta cheese.

We settled down for a delicious dinner and the conversation turned to lighter topics. Don talked about his engineering courses at N.C. State, his first meeting with Candi and his experiences at the Cline Mill.

"You'll never guess where I first met Candi," he started, "I met her at the Baptist Student Union. I went there for the doughnuts and the coffee, and there she was. I can still remember her standing there in a polka dot sundress, as beautiful a girl as I had ever seen." He sighed and took a sip of his beer. He made a face and said, "Well, sometimes the Coors tastes like Mahou Classic." He continued, "It's just not the same, but you Americans do doughnuts better. I love those Krispy Kreme's. You know I once dreamed of getting a franchise for Madrid or Barcelona," he chuckled.

I asked him about his work at the mill. He confirmed the story that Etta Mae had related. "They really did hire me as a translator as much as for my engineering skills. I'm convinced the workers could understand me, but I had enough of a dialect and they had their own slang that they could pretend otherwise and slow down the line. I fixed them. I brought in new time-study techniques that weren't that modern but they were for the Barrington Mill. Soon production was going up and overtime was going down." He seemed proud of his accomplishments and nothing seemed to indicate either a kidnapper or a murderer.

I found both the conversation and the meal interesting. I commented on the memorabilia that covered every nook and cranny in the restaurant. Don claimed he wasn't much of a sports fan but he had information on more than a few of the athletes or championship news articles on the wall. "State," he said, "has a better winning tradition that a lot of people realize. It's just that with Duke and Carolina around, we always seem to be the third wheel."

"Yeah," I said, "that coach at Duke seems to have all the luck."

"Or else pays off the referees," interjected Don. We both laughed, but I had a thought that might give me an opening to other topics. "You know," I started, "my dad always believed that N.C. State used up all its luck on that basketball championship run back in the 80s and they just haven't been able to catch a break since."

"Oh, I don't know," said Don, "this football coach we have now has been doing pretty well and I think the new basketball coach might just . . ."

"No, no," I interrupted, "you're missing my point, Don. I'm talking about luck and its consequences now. What I'm trying to say or what my dad meant was that everybody has a bit of luck with them and when it runs out you've got to realize it and face the consequences. You've had a good run of luck for a long time now, Don, but it's over and you need to see that. It's time to pull back before someone gets hurt, perhaps someone you love."

It had an effect on him. He slumped back in the booth and stared at me for a minute or two. Finally, he spoke, "Perhaps, you're right, C.W. Maybe it's time for me to stop running. Maybe I do need to go home and explain myself to my wife, Mr. Cline, Frank, everyone. Are you going to arrest me, Mr. Biggs?"

Interrupting my fork moving a bit of lasagna to my face, I replied, "I wasn't given that authority, Don. In fact, I'm not sure I could plausibly arrest or detain you for anything right now, but I do think you need to clear up a lot of things. Although, if you're right about Mr. Cline, and I don't think you are, but if you are, you might want to go to the SBI. I think the Sheriff might be in Arch's pocket."

He smiled, "I wouldn't be surprised, I wouldn't be surprised at all." The waitress approached with our bill. Don looked at me with his most charismatic smile and said, "Do you think we have time for dessert?" I said why not. He looked at the menu and said to the waitress, "I think I'll have the chocolate cheesecake. Would you like some, C.W.? It's my treat, and coffee, too." I said sure and wondered if it would be the last thing he'd ever treat anyone to.

Within a few minutes the waitress returned with the cheesecake. Don looked at the cheesecake and the young lady, smiled and said, "Ah, a beautiful dessert brought to me by a beautiful young lady. Who could ask for anything more?" Now if I had said such a corny line, I would have gotten slapped or laughed at, but the waitress blushed and gave him a wink that spoke volumes on Don's amazing charisma. As the young lady and her smile left, Don took a bite, "Umm, this is delicious. You know I almost always got a piece to take home to Candi, but I never tasted it myself."

"I know," I blurted as I forked a nice chunk of chocolate cheesecake into my mouth.

Don gave me a quizzical look, "How do you know?"

"Candi told me," and the look on Don's face made me realize I might have made a tactical error, but there was no turning back so I plunged ahead. "She said she could tell when you had been with Patsy because you would always bring back a piece of cheesecake to her after your date. Didn't you ever wonder why she went into the kitchen to eat the cheesecake?"

"I thought she didn't want me to see her devour the slice. You know she has gained quite a few pounds in the last few years."

Exasperated, I raised my voice, "No, you Hispanic Casanova, she didn't want you to see her crying her heart out."

Don dropped his fork on the plate, pushed the plate back and whispered, "I didn't know. I thought she was embarrassed to eat in front of me." I just stared and he got emotional. How could a guy who had such great people skills be so far off base with understanding the woman who loved him? The only answer that crossed my mind was he truly believed the world revolved around him. Damn, this cheesecake was good.

There were several moments of silence, the kind where you can hear all the conversations around you but nothing at your table. Three times Don tried to say something but nothing came out. Finally, I said, "Mr. Rivera, I think you have some 'splaining' to do. I suggest the first person you see or call is your wife."

"Yes, I know, but what do I say?"

"The truth would be a good start. I think Candi has known and, amazingly, forgiven you for what has happened, though I wouldn't talk about Patsy too much. She deeply loves you and deserves more than a piece of cheesecake. Although, I must admit, this is a very good substitute."

"I love her, too. I just got off track. Patsy was so alluring and sympathetic at the same time. I just couldn't resist."

I had a feeling he didn't resist too much, but I kept my mouth shut. Like I said sometimes I'm too soft hearted for this job. "Okay," I began, "this is what we're going to do. You go back to the motel and start . . ."

"And start what, Mr. Biggs? A letter, a phone call, packing?"

"Shush," I whispered as loud as I dared, because a tall figure with long hair nicknamed Big Bert had just walked into the restaurant and was beginning to talk to the cashier. "Indian Bert just walked in, DON'T look," as Don began to turn around in the booth. Now the only thing that crossed my mind was that I had been set up as a patsy again. I knew there was a reason I didn't like that name. Arch Cline must have had Bert following me or tracking me down ever since our dinner, but for what purpose? Was it just to keep Arch informed or something much more dangerous for me and Don? Whatever the case, Indian Bert showing up at this restaurant was too much of a coincidence and trying to get out of here without encountering the big Indian looked like an impossible task. If Bert stayed at the cashier's station he could watch anyone who left. Admittedly the restaurant had lots of little nooks, but if he didn't move we were trapped like canaries in a cage.

I had to think fast and looking around at the memorabilia on the wall gave me an outlandish idea. "Don," I said quietly, "Are you good enough friends with the kitchen crew to sneak out the way you came in?"

"Yes, I think so."

When I tell you to move, you head for the kitchen and don't look back. Go straight to the motel and get your stuff."

"But I'm paid up through Sunday!"

"Tough shit, Don. If Bert is half the character you and others have described and he's here to find you, losing your damn payment is the least of your worries. Toss some money on the table and get ready."

It had occurred to me that here in the midst of NC State's Valhalla that I might be able to create just enough misdirection to get Don, and maybe me out of there. Bert was tall enough to look like an ex-basketballer. If I called out that a famous State player was at the cashier's station, it was possible that two or three autograph seekers might approach Bert and keep him occupied. I mean, it was pretty dark in the restaurant. Ok, it wasn't a great plan, but it was all I had. The problem was trying to think of a name of a State basketball player who looked like a 6'6" Native American. Tommy Burleson? Too old. Archie Miller? Too short. Todd Fuller? Too light. Brandon Costner? Too dark. I needed someone exotic. I took another look at a photo autographed just to the right of the booth and I had my name.

"Look everybody, it's Engin Atsur!" I shouted and told Don to go as he looked at me like I was a fool. And he was right, but it was the best I could do. I mean, Atsur was from Turkey which was kind of near India, and Columbus thought Native Americans were Indians. Stupid, stupid, stupid, but in the dim light of the restaurant, it worked. In fact, it worked better that I could have ever imagined.

Indian Bert had spotted me just as I shouted my infamous alert and began to move towards me, but three small fry, the oldest was no more than ten, had sprung up with ink pens and napkins in hand and headed for the tall dark Turk, er, Indian. Bert was accosted by the little ones all begging for his autograph. Bert handled kids as badly as he handled union sympathizers. Moving towards me, he pushed one kid down and another back in a booth which of course set off mothers and fathers standing up to the ungrateful celebrity. Quickly he was surrounded by a small crowd of angry fans. I saw Don had made it back to the kitchen, so I decided to head for the door. For once, the Biggs luck held. The two cops who had entered earlier were moving towards the cashier. They confronted Bert about the fracas and asked for identification and an explanation.

Bert was now temporarily occupied. All I needed was something to push him over the top and into a real frenzy. I could make my escape and probably nobody would remember me. I neared the confrontation, looked at him and grinned, "Hi, Big Bert!" It worked, "Arrgh" he growled like a pirate and lunged at me as I moved as far over in the narrow aisle as I could without falling into a pretty blonde's lap. One of Raleigh's finest moved between us just as Bert's big paw took a swipe at me and connected instead with side of the cop's head and all hell broke loose. Bert's other hand grabbed the back of my jacket but the cop's partner had brought out his baton and swatted it. Bert let go of me and I beat it for the door.

As I got outside I heard something like a table turn over and angry shouts. Praying Bert was not on my tail, I walked as quickly as possible. And praise be, my prayers were answered. Walking up the sidewalk were two more officers. I immediately hollered, "Hey, you guys, some of your buddies are inside and they're trying to control a real troublemaker. Big guy, you might need more cops." The shorter cop rushed in and the taller one said thanks as he got on his shoulder phone and called for backup. About that time a plate or a tray went through the glass door entrance. I turned one more time to see Big Bert wrestling with cops, employees and patrons. It looked like he might just win so I headed for my car and didn't look back. Forty-five minutes later I was back at the Sleep-Easy Inn, but Don was gone and there was no note for me. All the half–awake clerk could remember was that he had paid in cash. I drove around the parking lot and up and down the road looking for his car but to no avail. I was back to square one. I turned back down the interstate and headed for home hoping Don had done the same.

.

Sunday, Sun Drop and Sunsets

By the time I got home it was getting close to midnight. I went by my mother's house and the lights were on, so I stopped. She met me at the door and said she was tired of running down to the basement to answer my phone.

"The Sheriff's called twice. An older gentleman named Arch Cline called and asked how you were doing. He sounded very nice. And a girl named Rita has called four times. Each time she sounded more frantic. You aren't in any trouble, are you C.W.?"

"No, I'm not in any trouble," I said without an awful lot of conviction. I should have known better to sound so dejected. Immediately Mom jumped to conclusions.

"Oh, no, you haven't got that girl pregnant, have you? She sounded so young."

"No, mother, you haven't got anything to worry about and Rita is a tough girl who can take care of herself."

"So, she's not your girlfriend?" My mother suffered the same malady many mothers do when their son gets into his mid-thirties and isn't married. It would have been worse but my other two brothers had given her several grandchildren so her biological countdown for me wasn't quite as intense. "No, Mother, she's not my girlfriend. I hardly know her."

"Well, she seemed nice. Are you going to stay the night?" Now the answer in my head was no way, I've got to get out of here to avoid a two hour grilling, but what I said was "No, I need to get back to the apartment to check my mail and write a report for the Sheriff." I gave her a kiss good night and headed back to the car. On the drive back I decided I wasn't calling anyone tonight. Once I got to the apartment, I took the phone off the hook, took a long shower and tried to get a good night's sleep.

The next morning I put the phone on the hook and it immediately started ringing. I wasn't interest in answering; I didn't have any answers anyway. I decided to get out of town and find some place where maybe I could figure out something before Monday came and my future as a detective would very likely be over. It was getting close to 11 when I left the house. I deliberately decided to call the Sheriff and give him a message about what had occurred. I knew he wouldn't be able to pick up. He would be campaigning, er, attending church services. I left a message that summed up the major events on Saturday, emphasizing that I had asked Don to come home and contact him. With that, I headed to where I could be alone and think.

Now, some people who need to think go out into the country, some go see a movie, some take a walk and some get a bottle of whiskey at a bar and find a nice quiet corner to reflect. But Southern country boys are a little different. You see most of us didn't get a chance to drink alcohol, unless it was moonshine, because we grew up in dry counties. We had to find another drink to clear our thoughts and see our way to the truth. In Central North Carolina that beverage was probably going to be a soft drink. You get to become quite a connoisseur of soda pop. Some will turn to root beer, others get a Nehi, and still others yearn for a Cheerwine or Yoo-Hoo. But in my family, if you wanted to clear your head and get a handle on the future you turned to Sun Drop, the golden elixir

I had been introduced to the cola when I spent a summer with my uncle who lived on the west side of Charlotte and worked in Gastonia where the drink of the gods was bottled. I almost became an addict, but there was a problem. The drink is not nearly as popular in Eastern North Carolina and it's almost impossible to find it at a restaurant. You had to go clear over to Asheboro to find a grill that sold the wonder drink from the tap. But that was okay. A nice long trip to Asheboro might keep me invisible from a sheriff and a nosy reporter.

It was a beautiful Sunday as I headed west for Sharkey's Grill, the aforementioned restaurant that carried Sun Drop as a fountain drink. Sharkey's was on the far side of town and it was late afternoon before I arrived. I ordered a cheeseburger and fries to go with the Sun Drop and settled down at a table that faced the main entrance. After Indian Bert, I was obsessed with always finding a seat that could watch the front door.

As I sipped on my dream of a soft drink, I tried to make some sense of this perplexing case. First off, had Patsy really gone to the proverbial mansion in the sky or had her craziness led her beyond Edenton and to another state? The Sheriff had said nothing had happened with her checking account so she had to be running out of money. I didn't see Patsy living out of her car if she had any money at all, and where was the car? Nope, I had to admit it. Patsy had probably shuffled off this mortal coil.

And if that was the case, who was the prime suspect who had squeezed the life out of sexy Patsy? Frank? I couldn't see it. I could see him misplacing her and forgetting where he had taken her, but Frank was just too out of it to do harm to anyone. Don? I had to admit Don seemed the most likely candidate but there was something about his lost soul conversation that convinced me he was innocent, a very mixed up dude, but not a killer. Indian Bert and Arch were my personal picks, but if they had gotten Patsy out of the way, why were they following me? Tying up loose ends? I suddenly had a shudder go up and down my spine, but it could have been the Sun Drop. Then there was Mama Eu, she had been almost too nice the last time, but killing your own daughter? It seemed too diabolical even for Old Lady Worsham. There was the possibility of a total stranger, but I was inclined to agree with Dr. Morganstern that Patsy could take care of herself. First, she wouldn't pick up a hitchhiker and secondly, Patsy would find some way to get out of that kind of trouble, if you know what I mean.

This investigation was driving me, well, crazy. My condition wasn't helped any by the weird music playing in the background at the restaurant. It was a strange mix of oldies, reggae, pop and soul. I know within a half hour I had heard Gwen Stefani, followed by The Carpenters, Barry White and Madonna. Now they had on Bob Marley singing "I Shot the Sheriff." Hmm, I wonder? No, I'd never get away with it. I couldn't concentrate despite the wonderful effect of my second refill of the golden elixir. I was just about to give it up and head home when it happened.

I looked toward the door and four attractive women walked in. One in particular caught my attention. She was wearing a white skirt and jacket and the setting sun caught her perfectly showing off a gorgeous figure and beautiful legs. The piped in music was playing an old song that I usually detested, the Pina Colada song, but the refrain about "making love at midnight" seemed to match every move she made.

Of all the soda pop joints in all the world, she had to walk into mine. Yep, Mabel had come back into my life in the most unlikely of places. The group began to move to the counter and I sat there in amazement. So, I did the only thing a man could possibly do when seeing the girl of his dreams for the first time in five years. I drooled.

I don't think Mabel saw it as I grabbed for a napkin as swiftly as I could. I thought she was going to pass by me without speaking, but all of a sudden she cocked her head took a good look at me, and said the most wonderful words I could imagine.

"Don't I know you? You look familiar."

"Yes," I said and stood up at the same time, "we met in Edenton a few years back."

"Oh, yes," she replied, "your Bria . . ." "C.W.," I interrupted. "Yes, Yes, C.W. Post."

"Biggs, ma'am, C.W. Biggs."

Suddenly, she smiled, and a sense of recognition dawned on that pretty face, "The detective, I remember now. What brings you to Asheboro?"

"I could ask you the same," as I tried to regain some equilibrium from the dizziness I felt when I stood up and it wasn't from the Sun Drop. "I heard you had left Edenton and gotten married, but I didn't know you had come to the western part of the state."

"Well, I did leave Edenton, but the marriage part didn't exactly work out," she said with a rather sad look. My heart skipped a beat and asked if she'd like to sit down.

She looked over at her friends and told them to go ahead. Two of them gave her a meaningful look, winked and whispered something to the third member that caused her to snicker. Mabel sat down across from me, and said "What you drinking, C.W?"

I told her and she laughed heartily, "I don't know if I can handle that hard a drink. I think I'll stick with something a little lighter," and hollered to her girlfriends to get her a Michelob.

I began, "How in the world did you end up in this hole in the wall in Asheboro?"

"Well, I'm from Ramseur originally. Do you know it?" I nodded yes; I had passed through it on the way to the restaurant. If I had known Mabel was there I would have camped out there. "Anyway," she continued, "the marriage only lasted a few months. It was a sham. He seemed wonderful. He was from one of the leading families in Edenton."

"Hewes???," I interrupted.

"No," she giggled, "but perhaps just as arrogant. It seems he was gay. You aren't, are you, C.W?" I shook my head vigorously, perhaps a little too vigorously. "Well, that's good to know," she said with a little smile and patted my hand, a gesture that warmed me all over.

"The family was more than gracious with a settlement, as long as I kept my mouth shut, which is why I can't tell you his name. I came back to Ramseur where my parents had left me a very large house. I have four sisters, they opted for the money from the will. I was satisfied with the house. I turned it in to a bed and breakfast and it's been a surprising success which has made all my sisters jealous. I run it with the help of the three girls I came in with." She gestured over to the other table and pointed, "That's Cheryl, the pretty blonde is Monique and the one looking enviously at you is Christie." They all looked at me and waved. They were all pretty but none held a candle to Mabel.

"Now tell me how you got here, C.W."

"Well, strangely enough it's connected to the Patsy Cline case that led me to meeting you in Edenton. By the way I never got a chance to thank you for your help. Patsy was right where you predicted," and I held out my hand to shake. She took my hand graciously and I held it as long as I dared. She didn't draw back. "Now Patsy has gone missing again and I have hit a dead end in trying to find her."

She sat back in her chair, "I'm intrigued, let me get another beer and you can tell me about it. But first I need to see my friends."

"Go ahead," I said, "I'll get the beer, maybe you'll see something I have missed just like last time."

"We'll see, C.W.," she said as she moved towards her friends' table.

I floated over to the counter got her beer and my third refill of Sun Drop, something not recommended by doctors but it was a special occasion. She had returned by the time I got back and I began to summarize the main elements of what had happened to me over the past week. I thought she'd be bored but Mabel listened intently, just like she did five years before and interjected comments and asked questions that showed she was fascinated by my predicament. She agreed with me that Frank was probably unable to brew a pot of coffee, much less plan a murder, and she wasn't totally convinced that Patsy wasn't out on a lark. Don intrigued her, but she wasn't as sure that he was as unlikely a candidate as I was. She said it sounded like a lot of men she knew. I immediately let her know I wasn't like that and she smiled again. It was a whimsical kind of smile that left her right upper lip slightly higher than the other. I thought it was adorable. Still, Mabel finally agreed that his actions didn't sound like a murderer; going to Raleigh to run away seemed more like a desperate and lame attempt to keep the cops away from Candi and the children.

When I got to Arch Cline, it became obvious that she didn't have quite the high opinion of him that I did. "I know a few people who worked over in the Barrington Mill or in one of the others when they were open," she commented. "He's a skinflint who rarely paid more than minimum wage for his line workers. I hear he has property on the Outer Banks, financed, so I'm told by pension funds that were misdirected into his account. C.W., I don't know if he could have done it but I can see him serving as a puppet master. Watch out for him."

I told her about my conversation with Dr. Morganstern. It surprised her how I had gotten so much information from a trained psychologist. She smiled and said it must be because of my charming disposition and my willingness to listen. I then turned to my narrow escape at Armadi's. She laughed heartily at Indian Bert's comeuppance. Suddenly she turned serious. "Wait a minute," she said, "go back to the conversation you had with Dr. Morganstern about Patsy's sister." I went over the part about Patsy losing her sister at an early age and its effect on Mrs. Worsham.

She pondered on that a bit and said, "I got a theory, C.W., now hear me out. Did you have any sisters?" I told her all I had were brothers. "Sometimes sisters don't get along, believe me, and if Patsy showed any jealousy towards Barbara Jean while she was sick, well, it could lead to real problems. You said that Mrs. Worsham seemed to favor Barbara Jean over Patsy. If she perceived that Patsy seemed unresponsive to her sister's illness, it's plausible she might have taken it out on her after Barbara Jean died."

"I don't know, Mabel, that seems a little farfetched and, besides, Mrs. Worsham was genuinely concerned about Patsy when I interviewed her."

"That's just it, C.W. Here's a woman who spoke contemptuously of her daughter and her son-in-law, suddenly she changes. Doesn't that seem suspicious?"

Well, I must admit, Eurydice did seem like an entirely different creature this time around, but murder?

Mabel continued, "I know it sounds weird and I may be way off base, but I think you've got to go back and interview that old lady. She knows something; a tiger can't change its stripes that quick."

"But I only have till tomorrow morning," I lamented.

"Trust me, C.W., I've got a bad feeling about that woman," as she grabbed my hands and held them. Well, that did it. I wasn't going to reject the advice of my beautiful Greek Oracle.

"Alright," I said, "I'll head back for Barrington tonight, although I'm not sure I'll make it back in time to do much."

"Don't be negative, something will shake loose, I promise; and I'm so convinced I want you to come to Ramseur after this is over and tell me all about it."

I almost licked my lips. I looked into those beautiful black eyes and said I promised. "You've been wonderful, again, I don't know how you do it," then foolishly, I asked "Can I kiss you?"

She looked at me kind of funny, giggled and said, "Well, I don't suppose a quick peck on the cheek would hurt me." I got up and moved to kiss her on the cheek but at the last minute she turned and her lips met mine. It was the most wonderful kiss I'd had since Samantha Shields had snuck up on me in the third grade, caught me by surprise and said I was her boyfriend. She moved the very next year. I held Mabel's kiss for as long as I dared. It seemed like minutes, but it probably wasn't more than five seconds. As she pulled away, she pulled me down and whispered in my ear, "I think you're sweet and you've got pretty blue eyes." They're actually hazel but I wasn't about to spoil the moment. Her girlfriends hooted. She looked at them and told them to shut up, "Let's go, before I get another proposal." They all laughed. I didn't know if she meant the incident in Edenton or this was a common occurrence for Mabel.

She started walking towards the door with her friends, but as she got to the entrance, she turned and came back to me.

"C.W.," she began, "do you know anything about Greek mythology?"

"You mean like Hercules and Xena? Sure, I know some." *After all*, I thought, *I do watch cartoons and shows about scantily clad women.*

She gave me that funny smile again and began "Well, Eurydice was the name of the wife of Orpheus who went to the underworld to find her." She pulled me close and said "Don't let Mrs. Worsham pull you down to hell, I would miss you". She gave me a heartfelt and wonderful hug, quickly turned and left.

I had told her I would pay for her and her friends' drinks, a courtesy that almost took the last dollar out of my billfold, but it didn't matter, I nearly danced out of the little bar and grill and headed for Barrington.

Walking, After Midnight

I was floating on air, which is difficult to do in an Aspen, after my meeting with Mabel. I was feeling so good I decided I could even handle talking to the Sheriff. About halfway back to Barrington I gave him a call and asked for an update on Don. "Not a word," said the Sheriff, "I had the Wake County boys drive by his house every hour to see if his car was there. As of 5 PM, he hadn't shown." I was a little disappointed, but the Sheriff was very frustrated.

"Listen, C.W., I hope you got some good news for me. I really could use some and what's going on with the Rita Worthington? That snoopy reporter has called me ten times since yesterday afternoon. She is mad as a wet hen. What in the world were you thinking sending her to Edenton?"

Hell hath no fury as a woman newspaper reporter scorned. I tried to explain my actions to the Sheriff to keep Rita off my back. He wasn't impressed. The glow of my romantic encounter with Mabel was beginning to fade. I began to speak rapidly about the other events, especially my narrow escape from Indian Bert. He said the Wake County officers had said something about it but they didn't have many details. He wouldn't let go of his determination to get some good news for the news conference he had called for Monday morning. I decided I would tell him I had a lead, but needed some more time.

"Sheriff, I've got some new evidence that might break this case wide open."

He leaped in, saying "What? This better be good."

I couldn't tell him that my theory and Mabel's intuition had led me back to Mrs. Worsham's doorstep, so I lied. "I found some evidence about Eurydice Worsham that I need to go check out. It's possible she's being blackmailed over Patsy's disappearance. I'm going to go by the house and check it out."

"Blackmail? Maybe I should send over my boys to interview her."

Now I knew that "my boys" meant the one detective on the Branch County payroll who was inundated with unsolved stolen lawn mowers and farm equipment cases, but I couldn't say that without getting the Sheriff mad. I replied, "No, no, Sheriff. I don't want to put your guys on the spot if this turns out to be a false lead. In fact, can you keep your boys away tonight? I don't want anything to spook her."

"Hmm, that's mighty nice of you, C.W. I must admit I wouldn't want my boys serving papers on a little old lady's telephone records if it turns out to be a dead end. It'd look bad in the papers."

"Yeah," I assured him, "you wouldn't want that, and can you keep Rita off my back until about noon tomorrow?"

"How do you expect me to do that? That woman is a bulldog."

"Umm, tell her that I took sick and got admitted to the Cape Fear Hospital." Now I knew it was another lie, but I really didn't want to see Rita unless I had to, and there was a Biggs in the Cape Fear Hospital. It was my cousin Curtis, who was either the world's biggest hypochondriac or really at death's door depending on who you talked to. Nobody in the family could get a clear answer because nobody wanted to visit Curtis. He was the family's biggest gossip, and once he got started he wouldn't shut up. Come to think about it, he and Rita might just hit it off.

"Now, how's that going to help me, I mean you, C.W.?"

I had to admit that was a good question on both parts. Thinking fast, I said, "Tell her I'm on medication and talking crazy stuff about Patsy. She's just the type of reporter to think that she can get the real story while I'm in my delirious state, and if she goes to Fayetteville, she probably wouldn't be back to Barrington by mid-afternoon."

"You know," perused the Sheriff, "that just might work and I could hold off on my press conference until she got back." *Even better*, I thought, and added, "And Sheriff, can you get the city cops to cut their patrols by the Worsham house to a minimum?"

"Now, I'm not so sure about that. Though, it's on a short road that ends on a cul-de-sac."

"Tell them I'm bird watching and don't want to be disturbed."

"Bird watching, that's pretty sharp, C.W. The old lady is an odd bird."

"Really, Sheriff?" I thought he actually was complimenting my acumen.

"No, C.W., can't you spot sarcasm when you hear it? This better lead somewhere or you're going to be one dead bird, figuratively and literally."

Thanks for the support, I thought, but all I said was, "I promise I'll have something for you by noon tomorrow. Goodbye." I clicked off before he could make another biting remark. All the euphoria of my heady ride back had evaporated by the time I reached the Barrington city limits.

I vaguely remembered that the house across the street from the Worshams had a For Sale sign and could make a nice stakeout location. I really didn't know what I was going to do when I got to the old lady's house. All I really had was Mabel's cockamamie theory that seemed lamer every time I tried to wrap my mind around it. I thought the stakeout was the best way to start. I didn't think confronting Mrs. Worsham right away would work. I got to her road and drove down the street. My memory was correct about the house across the street and the road was just five blocks long. I figured the Barrington cops would only make one pass on a Sunday night, if I could wait and let them do their tour of duty, I could . . . I could what. Well, maybe I would think of something.

I turned into the driveway at the vacant house. It was almost as large as Eurydice's and it had a hedge that was just as broken and dying as the one across the street. I pulled across the yard between a large elm and a much smaller oak. It gave me a pretty good look at the Worsham's front door and if I slid over to the passenger seat to avoid a small dying cedar, I could also see the garage and most of the right side of the house. The lights were all off except for a basement light. Interesting, it would make more sense to have the front porch light on, but Mrs. Worsham might have turned off one and turned on the other by accident. I turned off the car lights and began to wait. Parking between the two trees didn't give me much maneuver room but in the dark it was hard to see the car unless the light beams hit it head on.

About an hour later, Eurydice drove up. As she entered the driveway and got close to the house, security lights popped on. That's why she didn't need the front porch light, but the basement light was still visible. She turned slightly to pull into the garage and the doors began to go up. For just a second, I thought I got a glimpse of a dark colored second car. Why would she need a second car? Pride, I guess, but considering the fall in the family fortunes it seemed a foolish pride. Nevertheless, I thought I'd start my casing of the property there, if I could figure out how to avoid the security lights. Mrs. Worsham hit the remote and ended my review of the garage. She was carrying at least two bags of groceries as she teeter tottered towards the front door.

I settled down in the passenger seat and checked out my binoculars, a standard piece of equipment for private eyes who couldn't afford video equipment. They weren't much good in the dark except when cars went by, which didn't happen often on the cul-de-sac. About 11 PM a Barrington police car drove by. Now I waited for the old lady to go to bed. The lights were still burning bright downstairs and she still hadn't noticed the light in the basement was on. If I was lucky, she'd leave it on, and I'd have some light to guide me when I went skulking around. I tried to think of all the events of the past few days to see if I could think of anything I had missed in my investigation that might help solve the case, but my mind soon drifted to Mabel and that beautiful outfit as she entered Sharkey's. It was certainly a beautiful vision for a cool, but not frigid, late fall night. I kept a small blanket in the car, leaned the passenger seat back, and . . . promptly went to sleep.

Okay, that was not standard detective procedure, but, in my defense, it had been a couple of fast paced days without a great deal of sleep. I did have some very nice dreams but you don't need to hear about that. I was awakened at about 4:30 by a chattering noise coming from the hood of my car. It was a squirrel and he was obviously quite upset. I tried to shoo him away by turning the windshield wipers on but all that did was make him madder. I got my mini-flash light and shone it in his eyes. The only effect was to make him look demonic. Now I had a gun in the dash pocket that could have blasted the little varmint to kingdom come with one shot, well, maybe two or three with my ability, but that seemed a little much for a furry rodent. So I quietly opened the passenger door and got out to confront my new nemesis.

I was worried about making any major sound. I whispered, "Get away" several times, with no effect. Finally I decided to just try to sweep him away with my arm, and the lousy critter tried to bite me. What in the world had I done to make him so mad? I took another swipe at him with my arm and this time did push him off, but in less than a minute he was back at me, chattering away with his little teeth and the equivalent, I guess, of a Bronx cheer. This was getting ridiculous! I thought if I just turned around and ignored him, he'd get tired and go away. But as soon as I turned away, the little bastard bit me in the heel. I danced away, shaking him off my leg as I went. Were squirrels rabid? I didn't think so, but I could be wrong.

By now, I had become convinced that there was some malevolent spirit operating in this squirrel. It had to be the reincarnated spirit of Reggie McElhenny. Reggie was a real know-it-all pain-in-the-ass that I had picked on from elementary school to graduation. I wasn't the only one, but I was the only one with a conscience. When Reggie was killed in an accident about twenty years ago, I became convinced that any bad occurrence I had with animals had to do with the bad karma I had created with him. Whether it was a cockroach in the bathroom scaring me at midnight or a black cat running in front of my car on a dark and snowy night, I was sure it was the new spirit of Reggie. With as loud a voice as I dared, I tried to placate the critter, I said "Reggie, Reggie, listen, I didn't mean it. I was just a young kid, can't you forgive me?"

It didn't work, the fanatical rodent charged again. He leapt. I put up my arm, and he gave me another nip.

"Oww!" I yelled loud enough to wake up the entire neighborhood, "Come on, Reggie give me a break!" I waited for lights to start coming on up and down the street. No lights came on while I tried to take off my jacket and shake this tree beast of Kali. I needed something to stop the rascal. The next few minutes was a comical back and forth of me charging, dodging behind my car, and kicking away a whirling furry demon that had all the intelligence of Chip and Dale and a mean streak from the Tasmanian Devil. I would have laughed if I hadn't been too busy running. I briefly reconsidered the gun, but decided to see if I had something in the trunk. I popped it open and saw a golf club and a tennis racket.

I chose the racket, it gave me more coverage. I turned around and stuck it up just as the animal jumped from somewhere right at my face. He collided with the strings and bounced back several feet. He came again, I didn't remember Reggie being this determined. I swung down and knocked him to the ground. He seemed to limp off, but as I went back to the car, he attacked from out of the darkness. I had sensed his movements this time. Turning back around, I was prepared enough to display the best backhand I had used in all my years of playing tennis. SWACK, went the tennis racket, catching him head on. The squirrel did a 180° and went flying into the bushes. His bushy tail was the last thing I saw. I jumped around three or four times waiting for the next attack, but it never came.

I limped back to the trunk to put the racket up and see if I had a first aid kit, but just as I got to the rear, I heard a car coming up the road. I ducked down and watched as a white Mercedes slowed down to turn in to the Worsham driveway. It was Frank.

I moved to the hedges to see if I could get a view, but by the time I reached the line of thinning bushes, Frank was out of his car. I stood watching and listening in the cool morning air as the dawn sky began to lighten the darkness. Suddenly, there was the retort of what sounded like a pistol. But it was so faint, the only thing I could think of that would make such a small sound was a small firecracker or a derring . . . "Oh, God, Frank, what have you done?" And I began to run.

Crazy, Maybe, Psycho, Definitely

I crossed the road and headed up the driveway huffing and puffing as I went. Lights were appearing at the houses near Mrs. Worsham. The sun was peaking over the horizon, and I hoped folks were just getting up for the workday. Right now I didn't need any snoopy neighbors. Or maybe I did. It dawned on me as I reached the open front door that, in my race to help Frank, all I had with me was an old tennis racket and a mini-flash light. Neither gave me a lot of confidence. I briefly thought about going back to the car to get my gun, but a quiet audible moan ended that idea. I crossed the threshold to who knows what.

The foyer was just as I remembered it except that Frank was lying at the bottom of the steps groaning. I ran over and tried to revive him with a push and a pull. I looked for his gun, but couldn't find it. I quickly searched for a gunshot wound thinking maybe Mrs. Worsham had surprised him with her own gun. There was no gunshot wound. The mark on Frank's head looked more like he had been hit with a frying pan not creased with a bullet.

"Frank, Frank," I said, "are you ok? What happened?"

Frank groaned again, muttered "She's got . . . gun."

"Who's got your gun, Frank? Patsy? Eurydice?"

"Patsy," he groaned again, and threw his arm over towards the far side of the steps, "Go. . . ."

I looked that way and for the first time noticed a door under the stairs with a light shining under the sill. This must be where my mysterious light was coming from. "Are you going to be okay?" I think he said "Uh-huh." "Okay, I'll go see about Patsy." What was I saying? She probably had a gun, and I had a tennis racket! I went to the door and carefully turned the knob.

The door was smaller than a normal one and led to a tiny landing leading to steps. Those turned back towards the front of the house. As I stepped on, it became obvious that this door was added later, perhaps when the house's heating system converted from coal. There were eight to ten narrow steps to the basement; it was hard to tell despite the light that had been left on. It was a good thing I still had my mini flashlight. It allowed me to see a rickety handrail on the left side of the steps. I took two or three steps and still saw nothing. I found out why when the furnace started up and startled me. There was a heat vent right next to the steps that went almost to the floor and obscured my view.

The basement was small. The furnace seemed to take up much of the left portion. I now could see the transom window that allowed light to be seen from the outside. I squatted down as I reached the final steps and was shocked at what I saw. Sitting in what looked like an oversized high chair was Mrs. Patsy Cline! She was bound with masking tape on her wrists and legs and another piece covered her mouth. Her clothes were filthy and she was wearing what looked like a big diaper. I covered the short distance to her, dropped the tennis racquet, and began to pull the tape off her hands.

"Patsy, what in the world is going on?"

She gave me a sarcastic look while I realized it was going to be difficult for her talk with masking tape over her mouth. I knew I was going to get lambasted for stupidity as soon as I removed it, but instead she gasped, "C.W., look out!"

I turned back toward the steps thinking I would see Frank, but those were a woman's shoes. An elderly hand held tightly to the handrail and in the other hand was a small Derringer. Mabel's intuition had been right, Eurydice Worsham had gone psycho. Psycho! That was it, she reminded me of Anthony Perkins, and this?? This was the set of the movie.

The old lady took another step and spotted me. I grabbed the tennis racket and jumped towards her. The sight of me moving towards the steps seemed to surprise her and she switched the gun to her left hand. As she moved to fire, I swung with my second best back hand of all time. I hit her hand and simultaneously the gun went off. The bullet buried in a plywood wall only inches away from the furnace. Eurydice lost her footing when she stopped and tumbled down the last couple of steps hitting her arm and head on the concrete floor. I didn't have to do much to subdue her: Mrs. Worsham's frailties had caught up with her. I did take the Derringer for what it was worth.

Patsy had finished getting the duct tape off her. Shaking, she got up, but fell back into the high chair. I went back over to steady her and asked, "Okay, Patsy, now tell me, what in God's name is going on?" But I never got an answer.

Someone else was coming down the steps. It was Frank moving slowly but steadily. "Honey," he said, "Are you all right?"

Patsy got up and stumbled towards him as he reached the final step. "Frank, I've been such a fool. Can you ever forgive me?"

"Of course, Patsy, I love you," he said quietly. And they collapsed into each other's arms. I gagged.

There were new sounds coming from upstairs. Others had arrived. Rather than breaking up the loving reunion, I went upstairs. I ran into two deputies almost as soon as I emerged from the Harry Potter room under the steps. Funny, I thought, that deputies would be here instead of the Barrington city police. I looked through the window and saw an unmarked car. Intrigued, I asked, "What are you doing here?"

One of the deputies said "The Sheriff wanted us to check on Mrs. Worsham. We were supposed to let her know there would be a press conference at 11 AM at the courthouse about Patsy and to drive her there if she wished." He looked back at the basement entrance and saw Frank helping Patsy up the stairs. "It looks like it's going to be a very different conference than the Sheriff originally thought," and grinned. "So, what happened here?" he asked.

All three of us began to talk at once. "Hold it, hold it," I said. "Let's just let one person speak." I began to give as brief a description of the events as necessary. About halfway through my narrative, another car pulled up in the driveway. It was the Sheriff. He walked in, took a look at the situation and said, "I think we need to come up with a good story before we head to the press conference."

About an hour later a story emerged that had Patsy going west, suffering a severe illness that had led to a hospital stay and an inability to get in touch with her family until yesterday. I got physically sick listening to this crazy story but the truth might seem even stranger. The Sheriff told me to go home. I left. I needed a shower and a good day's rest, plus I wasn't about to be around for that press conference.

Epilogue

It's been about three months since the "press conference". I'm not frothing at the mouth so I guess I don't have rabies. The doctor says rabies in squirrels is very rare. That leaves me with the Reggie explanation. Anyway, the "press conference" was a preplanned farce. The fact that it was rehearsed was no surprise. The fact that all the reporters accepted the story was, except for Rita. Rita asked about thirty questions. The rest of the assembled group, two to be exact, asked about four. The story went that Patsy had gone to Tennessee to view the fall foliage, had become desperately ill and unable to communicate her predicament to her family. They became worried about her and started an investigation. The only reason they pulled it off was the claim that Patsy recuperated at a little hospital in Maryville. All sorts of records were provided except for the fact that it was begun and still funded by the Cline family fortunes.

This was the story in the Barrington Stars and Bars. *Mrs. Patsy Cline has returned from a vacation in the Great Smoky Mountains that was cut short by a severe illness. She would like to thank the staff of the Maryville General Hospital and appreciates all of you who have sent get well cards. She is recuperating at home.* It ran in the society section of the paper that only comes out once a month. I bet Rita was fit to be tied. I've been trying to put together the pieces of what happened on my own, helped considerably by Etta Mae and, reluctantly, by Rita. I've finally got enough to give you the rest of the story, plus things are really slow during the winter months for investigating. I've had plenty of time to write and reflect.

Patsy had indeed gone to see her mother on that particular Sunday, but it was to demand help to run off with Don, who may or may not have known how far Patsy was obsessed with him. Eurydice had reacted in horror and told Patsy she wouldn't or couldn't help. Patsy threatened to tell everyone the truth about the Hewes. It seems Patsy had done some investigating too and discovered Eurydice's proud genealogy was a house of cards. Ironically, I was right about the blackmail. Patsy's threat snapped something inside the old woman and she started a wild, wicked, spontaneous and ultimately disastrous plan.

She began with a cup of tea, loaded with enough sleeping pills to put Patsy out for several hours. I have no idea why or how Patsy fell for it. Patsy awoke down in the basement tied down in the high chair with Eurydice hovering over her feeding her and calling her Barbara Jean. For almost two weeks Patsy never left that chair. Eurydice treated her like a three year old, and if Patsy wasn't crazy before, she probably is now. The Clines, the Sheriff and even Don cooperated enough to keep what happened hidden, thanks, in part, to Eurydice Worsham's sudden desire to 'retire' to Edenton. I understand Mrs. Worsham is now at Mrs. Beasley's Home for Wayward Women. She has a whole wing and, once again, the Cline's money is keeping the place afloat.

Patsy and Frank seem happy together again. I have doubts on how long that will last. They've begun to sell off much of Eurydice's prized possessions and have put the house up for sale. It's old enough to be an historic landmark, especially since the whispers of the strange occurrences at the house have made it seem exotic by Barrington's standards. I understand the offers are pouring in despite the poor economic climate.

Don and Candi are also back together. From what I can gather, Don did everything but scrape the driveway with his tongue to get Candi's forgiveness. I think she might just make it work. I hope she holds out until the freezer is filled with chocolate cheese cake.

I have it on good authority that Indian Bert will be in jail for several years. It seems that after I left Armadi's, Bert briefly cleared the restaurant of police before they sent in reinforcements to subdue him. Final Score: Bert—Four cops and two civilians treated at the hospital, Raleigh Police—One Big Bert incarcerated. He was charged with six counts of felonious assault, damage to public property, damage to private property and two counts of breaking the young hearts of North Carolina State University fans, plus the civil suits. He could be in jail for a long time. Raleigh cops don't like being shown up. Even Arch Cline can't save him this time.

But Indian Bert continues to hold up his end of that strange relationship. He hasn't said a word about Arch's role in this affair and it looks like the old man will never have to reveal any details about what Arch intended. I can only speculate that he was attempting to guide events in the same way he had guided the fortunes of the mills. I think he sensed that Eurydice was at the bottom of the affair but had no way to prove it. He had sent Indian Bert to keep checking on me to see if I might stumble on the truth. He might have succeeded if Bert hadn't gone berserk at Armadi's the night before my epiphany from Mabel.

Speaking of Arch, I hear that he has given up any active role in the mills, reportedly because of ill health. He let another fifty employees go and handed over the directorship to Don, Frank and four others. That was enough to get past the bad publicity of the downsizing and shortly afterwards Don worked out a deal to sell yarn to several mills in France and Spain. It made big headlines in the business section of the Raleigh News & Observer. The company is back on sound footing. About Christmastime, Arch's oldest son, Mike, came to visit me with a check for $2,500.00. I thought I had died and gone to heaven. It also included a promise of another 5k if I didn't say anything about Arch's role in this affair, or if he died. So, if I ever get this published, you'll know that Arch Cline has died or I have had to change the names to protect my investment.

Well, I guess that ties things up. What? You want to know about Mabel? Oh, how cruel the affairs of the heart! A few weeks after this adventure ended, I went to see the best little boarding house in Ramseur. It was just where she said it would be, but she wasn't there. A lady by the name of Michelle said she had gone on a six week cruise in the Bahamas. I can just imagine her sitting in a chaise lounge in a string bikini surrounded by suitors. Her tanned skin covered in sun lotion being rubbed on by some guy named Raoul. Ok, enough of that. I'm getting hot and bothered. Needless to say, I was crushed and may never recover, although the money helps a bit. I think I can promise I'll never fall in love again, unless Mabel comes back or someone of roughly the same stature and looks shows up. That is so unlikely to happen I've desperately considered calling Etta Mae.

Now that should about cover everything. So, what do you think about a murder mystery without a murder? Although if I were Don and especially Frank, I'd watch my back. Well, it isn't quite true there weren't any murders. There might be a squirrel named Reggie. But if the park rangers ever charge me for that one, I'll swear it was self-defense.

123

The Correlation Between Alien Abduction And An Increased Divorce Rate:
A Case Study

In Partial Completion for an Associate of Arts Degree in Sociology
By
C.W. Biggs - North Central Carolina Community College

Directed by Dr. Marjorie Dellbridge

The correlation between alien abductions and a high divorce rate has been well documented in both the popular literature (*Playboy, Vogue, People, and Cosmopolitan*) and the scientific literature (*Alien Abduction Quarterly, Journal of Close Encounters of the Third Kind, Annual Review of Extraterrestrial Contacts, and Popular Mechanics.*) Notable cluster events have been seen in Las Vegas in the aftermath of the death of Elvis Presley (*Playboy,* June 1978 and *People,* Dec. 12, 1977) and in Roswell, N.M. (*AAQ,* Spring 1996, *ARofEC,* 1988.) However, there is much less reporting on events in rural America. This paper will attempt to close that gap with a scientific sociological review based upon qualitative interviews and quantitative surveys in central North Carolina on events in the late fall and early winter of 2008.

It is, perhaps, not surprising that the national press took little interest in the events occurring in rural North Carolina in 2008. Most of the nation was focused on a financial crisis and an intriguing national election. Still, it is hard to understand why scholars have not followed up on well documented reports from that area in the following years, particularly since there were significant newspaper stories over several weeks in the <u>Barrington Stars and Bars.</u> However, it has allowed this reporter the ability to till unsullied soil with the sociological interview skills taught by Dr. Marjorie Dellbridge in her Sociology 201 course in writing this required paper of not less than one thousand words, nor more than three thousand, and at least eight sources.

A review of the literature shows strong evidence for the hypothesis that alien abduction has a strong effect on divorce rates. The Roswell incident was not well documented at the time of the initial event in 1947. Since that time ufologists have mined this area with historical studies and sociology reports. In 1991*The Journal of Close Encounters of the Third Kind* reports that divorce rates rose by 17% in the six months after the "landing" (p. 13). The authors also state that the rate may have been higher than reported because of the cheap and easy access to Mexican divorces at the time (p. 15). In interviews with the divorcees thirty years after the fact, there was a near unanimity among men that this was the fourth most important reason for their marital troubles. Women, however, placed it only at number twenty five (ibid). Five years later, the spring edition of *Alien Abduction Quarterly* interviewed ten widows of men reported to have had sex with alien seductresses. Each woman stated that their deceased husbands saw a green haired woman with glowing eyes before their sexual encounter (p.6). Remarkably, every woman said that the men all had first seen the woman in the back of the Roswell Atomic Cantina (ibid). Unfortunately, this cantina was closed down because of moral charges in 1972. (Roswell Daily Record, July 11, 1972, p. 5). It is also interesting to note that all these men died before their thirty–fifth birthday, each under mysterious circumstances (*AAQ*, Spring, 1996, p. 7).

The Las Vegas incident is more recent and was recounted in more popular literature. There was a three page review in *Playboy*, June 1980. The Playmate of the Month reported that she saw Elvis in Las Vegas just after his reported death and just before her subsequent divorce (p. 79). Several attorneys reported a rise in divorce petitions in the three months after the King's death. Each incident cited irreconcilable differences revolving around eleven women and one man, all of whom reported a sexual encounter with a greenish looking Elvis (ibid).

Later empirical evidence was sought by the 1988 *Annual Review of ET Contacts*. Unfortunately the investigators were met with a wall of silence. They reported that, over and over again, they were told by various officials, "What happens in Vegas, stays in Vegas" (p. 23). Interestingly, this may be the first use of that memorable phrase.

Popular Mechanics tabulated the number of coincidental peaks in divorce rates and alien abduction reports as of July of 2005 at thirty one, over a thirty year period, in the Western Hemisphere alone (p. 86). However, twenty-nine of the thirty-one were in urban areas. The reports in rural areas have far less documentation. The two that were reported were near isolated military posts. Therefore, the incident in Branch County, North Carolina in the fall of 2008 offers a unique opportunity for research.

As stated before, the election and financial events of that year pushed the UFO sightings out of the mainstream press, but a review of literature found nothing in the regional press either. The local newspaper did have three articles over a ten week period. The first was simply a report that strange craft had been sighted in the sky near Barrington (Oct. 5, 2008 Barrington Stars and Bars p 5). A follow up article came out the next week stating that several observers reported an oval craft landing northwest of Barrington near an area referred to locally as the Devil's Tramping Ground, a local legend that is associated with many unexplained events. Many wondered if the old stories were being mixed with new myths (Oct. 12, p. 7).

Nothing appeared for the next few weeks but, in December, a new report mentioned several names all revolving around one female and an encounter with several males in connection with the aliens. The police declined to investigate further because of the reputation of some of those involved. "Our main report," stated the police chief "came from a young woman known for her gossip and fabrication of reports. We have decided not to pursue it." (Dec. 17, p. 11). That seemed to end the October UFO occurrence of 2008 until this intrepid reporter decided to pick up the trail in the spring of

2011 while taking a course requiring a sociological paper using survey and questioning techniques.

The reporter will use both quantitative and qualitative approaches as described in our excellent textbook *Sociology: A Common Guide to the Daily Use of Sociological Research,* 4th Edition. The quantitative approach will be used primarily with the ten male subjects who elected to participate in the survey and the qualitative approach with the one female subject who participated. The female subject was the only one who insisted that she be referred to by letters instead of numbers (hereinafter she will be referred to as EMW). All the males will be referred to by number.

The basic story reported by the interviewees followed this repeated pattern. All of the events happened at night over a three week period in October of 2008. The participants were less certain about how the incidents began. Most, however, said they remembered going out to a bar and drinking (male participants 1-6, 8 and 10 and the female participant). Four of the males vaguely remembered meeting the female participant at a bar (participant 1, 6-7 and 10). The female participant remembered meeting all the males in quite vivid detail, including discussion of their anatomy. (After conversations held with the directing professor, it was decided not to include this information because of lack of corroborating evidence – Conversation held 3-11-2011.) Eight of the ten vaguely recall meeting a tall, dark haired alien woman (only participant 3 and 9 couldn't remember any details). Therefore, much of the details of the encounter had to be supplied by the female participant.

EMW stated that, in October of 2008, she saw four sightings of an alien craft, oval in shape with flashing lights. She believed it to be the same craft. Three nights after the first sighting, she said two tall, blue haired, possibly male, aliens accosted her at her house. She quoted them as telling her to not be afraid and that they were interested in human courtship practices. They told her that they would bring several males and wished to watch her seduce them. They would provide medications to help her control the men and asked her to wear several disguises. They would be in her closet and observe the action. She said she was forced to comply by a golden cord tied around her waist that only she could see and feel. It would burn any time she tried to end the experiment (Conversation with EMW on Feb. 11, 2011 and a telephone conversation to confirm material on Feb. 12th).

In the survey material with the males, questions were asked about the events leading up to the meeting with EMW, remembering that night and what they remembered after the events. Nine of the ten males remembered a telephone call with EMW and an offer of fun, games and sweet tea. Six of the ten were sure they drank from the sweet tea. Only two could recall anything of value after they had drunk the liquid. (Questionnaire Survey results returned and tabulated 2/10-2/18, 2011).

Participant number six remembered that EMW was wearing a certain perfume his wife often wears, and that the female participant had a large mole on her left thigh (Survey #6). He refused to answer any follow up questions about any other physical characteristics of the other participant, nor could he confirm any sexual activity that occurred. He did volunteer that his wife had left him within one week after his overnight stay at EMW's residence (ibid).

Participant number nine vaguely confirmed some of EMW's story by stating, "I remember she said something about aliens, but I thought she was talking about migrant workers. After that, I sort of blanked out until the next morning when I found my pants neatly folded over a chair next to the couch." (Survey #9).

The other eight participants declined to provide any corroborating evidence other than to confirm they had had some contact with EMW (Surveys 1-5, 7-8 and 10). Four of the ten male participants stated they were involved in divorce proceedings. Two stated that their divorces had been final, and the other four said they were no longer a part of their 2008 relationships (ibid).

EMW reported that all the men seemed to enjoy themselves and the aliens were quite pleased with her "techniques". "They said they had never seen a sexier female in their research of courtship practices on seventeen worlds." (2/11 interview). The following is a summation of the more relevant parts of the interview using questioning techniques described in our textbook.

"Did any of the aliens ask to have carnal relations with you?" (Researcher follow-up question).

EMW: "Not at first," she replied, "they were perfect gentlemen. Although they did decline to drink my famous sweet tea. However, they changed their mind after I did my famous tango dance"

Researcher, continuing: "And then what happened?" (Much of this part of the interview was redacted after conversations with the supervising teacher. We pick up our talk after some discussions of alien anatomy) (Conversation on 2-11).

Researcher: "I'm sorry, did you say three?"

EMW: "Yes, three."

Researcher: "Was that for separate individuals or together?"

EMW: "Separate, of course."

Researcher: "Did the aliens state why they came to Barrington?"

EMW: "Well, not in so many words, but they did imply that they felt my romantic vibrations as soon as they passed the orbit of Venus."

Researcher: "Did they say where they came from?"

EMW: "Planet D, about three light years from Earth."

Researcher: "I was under the impression that the nearest star was four and a half light years away from here."

EMW: "It is, but they were using their distance measurements. I'm afraid I can't remember much else and my mother is calling, we'll have to continue this conversation at a later date." (Conversation 2/11).

Unfortunately, the researcher was unable, or unwilling, to have another conversation with EMW before the end of this project. In conclusion, this review presents compelling arguments that aliens visit rural areas, also. In addition, the divorce or separation rate for males is quite similar, and perhaps a little higher, than in urban areas. Although, admittedly this was a very small sample, I can conclusively state that there is a direct correlation between alien abduction and divorce rates and suggest that further studies be done in rural areas.

The researcher would like to suggest that the female subject might be a valuable asset for further sociological studies. In truth, she suggested it and even gave the researcher some possible topics. They include, *"Lonely Southern Women and the Men Who Adore Them;" "Romancing the Bag, Stories of Sweet Tea and Seduction;" "The Dreams and Desires of Tall, Thin* (rail thin, researcher's words,) *Women;"* and, *"Dangerous Liaisons, the Women of Branch County."* There were many other suggestions, but in the interests of brevity and the fact that I'm almost at the end of eight pages, I will forego those. However, the female subject was more than willing to provide her address and phone number. You may contact the researcher or the supervising teacher for the information.

BIBLIOGRAPHY

"Famed Cantina Closes," <u>Roswell Daily Record.</u> 11 July, 1972 Section A,   p. 5.

Ciccone, M. "The Fashionable Alien" *Vogue,* October, 1991, p. 122-125.

Durkheim, Emile. <u>Sociology: A Common Guide to the Daily Use of Sociological Research, 4th</u> Harper-Row, 2010, New York.

Fixit, Canhe. "Strange Symmetry: Aliens and Divorce." *Popular Mechanics,* July, 2005.P.85-87.

O'Hara, Martin and Tim O'Hara. "Green Eyed Ladies" *Annual Review of Extra-Terrestrial Contacts.* 1988, p. 19-24.

Reston, Jim. "Interview with Honey Melon: The Last Time I Saw Elvis. (with Pictorial)" *Playboy* June, 1980 p. 74-80.

Reynolds, B. "The Aftermath of the Death of Elvis," *People,* 12 Dec. 1977. P. 66-67.

Scott, R. "The Continuing High Rate of Death and Divorce in Roswell: The Legacy." *Alien Abduction Quarterly.* Spring 1996, p. 4-11.

Spillsbourg, S. "The Hidden Cost of the Roswell Cover-up: The Destruction of the Institution of Marriage." *The Journal Of Close Encounters of the Third Kind.* Sept. 1991, p. 12-19.

Wells-Brown, H.G. "What Really Happened to Elvis." *Cosmopolitan* Aug. 2002, p. 41-47.

"Strange Lights over Barrington." <u>Barrington Stars and Bars.</u> 5 October 2008. P. 1

"UFO'S in Barrington?" <u>Barrington Stars and Bars.</u> 12 October 2008. P. 2

"UFO'S are Humbug, says Police Chief." <u>Barrington Stars and Bars.</u> 17 December, 2008. P 8.

Bright Lights, Biggs' City

Well, I'm back. Don't act too surprised. There were a few folks who liked my first story and asked if I had any others. I did have at least one more, so this is dedicated to you three readers. Plus, I got finished with my Associate's Degree in Sociology. Now I've got more time to write. I guess I first need to let you know I'm out of my mother's basement–but it didn't happen the way you might think. I was actually quite happy to stay there and use the money from the Cline's for other important things like an Xbox. But my mother went and got a boyfriend and it was more than I could take. You see, my mother is a pretty good looking woman to be in her mid-sixties, if I do say so myself. I would say a cougar but calling your mother a cougar just doesn't sound right somehow.

Mother has taken up with a younger man, younger being relative. He's in his late fifties and they like each other a lot, as in an intimate lot. I could have probably survived that if it hadn't been for that song. Which song? There was a popular little ditty playing when I was a young boy called *Afternoon Delight.* You might remember it. I do, and it led to one of the more embarrassing moments of my early life. Mother and Dad loved it and sang it all the time. Now I must have been a pretty sharp little kid back then because I had learned the words by age three. I wish I knew what happened to my cognitive skills. If you remember the song you know it has some pretty risqué lyrics. That wouldn't have mattered if Mother hadn't gotten religion and decided to take me down to the Evangelical Episcopal Baptist Church in Green Top. Dad didn't care much for church, but Mother was determined to give me a spiritual background, so when the Reverend said they were looking for kids to sing for the Christmas program, I got volunteered.

It was early December and the Choir Director decided to see what kind of children's choir she had. She auditioned us one Saturday afternoon. Dressed in my Sunday best, Mother paraded me down there in front of the preacher and several of the prominent granddames of the congregation. The Choir Director asked several of us kids to sing. Most sang things like "Jesus loves me." I thought about it but I didn't know that one as well as I should have. Still, I might have tried it until the curly haired little girl with three missing teeth sang just in front of me. She began, *"Yeth, Jesuth wuves me, Yeth Jesuth wuve me"*. The words didn't sound right and I just felt uncomfortable following with the same song. When the choir director asked me to sing I launched in the only song I felt confident with. You remember, *"Gonna find my baby, gonna hold her tight, gonna grab some afternoon delight, rubbing sticks and stones together...."* That's as far as I got. The director gasped. The preacher grabbed me by my collar and escorted me to the door letting me know exactly how he felt about that song. It really hurts the psyche of a four and a half year old kid to be called the Spawn of Satan. Needless to say, we never went back to that church again, and I never got another chance to be in a Christmas pageant.

So that song brings back very bad memories for me. You can imagine how I reacted, sitting at my little desk, when I could hear the song through the vents as my Mother and her new beau sang it upstairs. That was bad enough, but you remember that part about skyrockets and how the band would make that woo sound? Mother and Clyde, her new beau, would make that sound when, well, I don't like to think about it. Let's just say it happened often enough in the middle of the afternoon to drive me out of the house. Oh, I keep a cot over there in the basement but my office facility just couldn't handle the noise.

I have now moved to the old bus station. It was owned by a friend of mine, Bud Ragsdale. Bud's not the sharpest tool in the shed. When I got me an office at the station I had a friend of mine print C.W. BIGGS, P.I. on the door. Bud was always asking about what kind of pies I sold. I'm not sure he was kidding because every time I made a little extra he'd expect a pie with the rent check.

Bud dropped out of school in the 11th grade but he was a good mechanic and had made enough to buy the station when Green Top went off Greyhound's stop list. It was barely on there anyway. By the 80s there was only one bus stopping per day, so Bud picked up the place for pretty cheap. He used the main part for the garage. The area that served as a waiting room is now Arlene's Beauty Salon and the old luggage area (closet might be a better description) is mine. It's just big enough for a desk, a file cabinet and two small chairs, one for me and one for my client. If there was more than one they sat on unopened boxes of books I should have read to get my private investigator license. The only window is up about nine feet and almost impossible to open, and the fan is one of those old timey ones that turns about once a minute. As you might imagine, it can get quite hot in there. Bud did cut a hole over the door and stick in a tiny 3500 BTU air conditioner that I have to get in a chair to turn on.

Still, the rent is cheap and it does have one advantage. I punched a small hole in the wall next to Arlene's that they haven't seen or don't care to notice. I get to listen to all the gossip in town and it's led to a couple of decent jobs-not the one's I like, but beggars can't be choosers.

Business has been okay but the Cline bonus from the Patsy Cline investigation only went so far. Eventually I had to look for new streams of revenue. One of my specialties is bounty hunting. Now don't get any notion about courageous C.W., I'm not Dog the Bounty Hunter. I'm more C.W. the Bottom Feeder. It works like this. I do have a computer and I can scan most of the state's major newspapers in the morning while I'm waiting for my phone to ring. I've come up with a scheme that has kept me in business, barely. It has a lot to do with big cities and small counties. Small counties have a tendency to set higher bails for lesser crimes than the big cities. I guess it has something to do with crowding and the need for more money in the small towns. Anyway, when somebody from my home county skips bail, I check the big towns in the hope they've been picked up by local authorities for some other crime. It's amazing how they'll leave court here and get in trouble somewhere else.

Here's the tricky part. The bail has to be less than it is here to convince Chico and Riley, the two big bondsmen for Green Top, to go along with my scheme. Say they got a $500 bail in Greensboro but a $2500 bail here, Chico and Riley will give me the money to bail them out of Greensboro to bring them back for trial here. It can't be too much or the bailsmen will go to get the miscreant themselves, or too little, and I can't make any money on the trip. It's surprising how often I get jobs. You have to remember our class of criminal isn't bright or rich enough, to get too far away. It also helps that both my mother and father had big families. I got cousins and uncles and aunts scattered from Atlanta to Richmond where I can stay while I pick up my meal tickets. The ones I pick up are pretty docile. In fact, we've had some interesting philosophical discussions on the way back. We've discussed things like the constitutional basis for the American legal system and why the sun comes up in the morning-important stuff like that. Almost without exception, they're ready to go back and get a home cooked meal, so there's no violence, no confrontation. Pretty tame compared to what you see on TV. I won't get rich, but most of my relatives will feed me when I visit.

My reputation for being quick and discreet had led me to finally get a bond collection that was worth big bucks. It was a surprise when I got a call from Leonard Whitmore, Boger's biggest celebrity. Now, bear with me while I explain how this most recent venture had the potential for a big payday. First, I have to tell you about the political situation in my home county, Boger County. Let's get the name out of the way first. My county is named for Hugh Boger, the youngest colonel in the Confederate Army. He was only sixteen when he went to war and by 1865; the South was getting desperate for officers, so Hugh got his chance with the 182nd Regiment that held off a much larger force of damn Yankees at Averasboro for a good four hours. North Carolina was not blessed with many famous military officers in the War of Northern Aggression, so when my county was formed in the late 1800 choosing Hugh Boger to be the namesake was the logical, and perhaps, only choice. It helped that he was a big wig in the Democratic Party and he had just passed away when our county was created. There was only one problem, one that I ran into at about any jail I visited. Hugh's name should be pronounced "Beau-ger," but the sheriffs, deputies, and even the magistrates loved to pronounce it Booger. I used to get mad but it didn't do much good, so now I just grin and bear it.

Now Booger County politics, sorry I got carried away, Boger County politics were a mess, which may explain why the economic expansion of the state had jumped right past us. The county was small and had three towns: Hughville, the county seat, Green Top, the largest town and Sterling, closest to the Interstate. All three had a population of about five thousand which meant that all three had about the same political influence. None of the three were willing to give up their political sway for fear they would be left in the dust of their "rivals". It led to things like three tiny high schools and fighting over every possible improvement to highways or infrastructure. For years these rivalries let nearby counties get the bigger share of everything. We couldn't even get a representative elected to the General Assembly even though we were part of a district that was primarily based on Boger County. That is, until Leonard Whitmore showed up.

Leonard, or Len to his friends, was a handsome charismatic forty-three year old, who got elected to the General Assembly when he was 27. Len was smart; he kept his law practice in Hughville, his mailing address in Green Top but sent his kids to Sterling schools. He had triangulated the county rivalries and in the process become a master politician. Indeed, there was serious talk that Leonard was going to run for Lieutenant Governor in the next election. There was only one problem.

It was his ne'er-do-well older brother, Bradley, nicknamed Beetle. There was an old comic strip called Beetle Bailey. I think it's still around, all I remember about it is a dog named Otto, but Bradley must have loved it. He had his parents read it to him every day and somewhere he picked up the nickname Beetle.

Beetle's problem was that he drank like a fish, a big fish, a really big fish. Worse, he often drank and drove, or tried to drive. He wasn't a good driver anyway-add the drinking and he was horrible. He was so bad that the county Mounties would look for him whenever they did a DUI checkpoint. Beetle racked up about twenty-six DUI's in about thirty years, but a very smart lawyer had managed to keep him out of jail until about three years ago. Bradley finally had an accident that Len couldn't get him out of. He hit a car loaded with kids going to the prom, too many as a matter fact, but that was beside the point. Luckily no one was killed but three were seriously hurt with lengthy stays in the hospital. Beetle got the book thrown at him by a judge from out of the county. Len knew it was a helpless cause as soon as he saw the 'hanging' judge but he did get the sentence reduced to six months in minimum security (which ended up being the county jail because of overcrowding) and a large restitution.

A remorseful Beetle came back after two years in self-imposed exile and seemed to be making progress until about a month ago when he plowed his car into a telephone pole and ran away. The Green Top police tracked him down, brought him in, and the magistrate slapped a $10,000 dollar bail on the county drunk. Somehow, Beetle got the bail money, perhaps with help from Len. That gets us to last week when Bradley didn't show up for a preliminary hearing. The bail went up fifteen thousand, a warrant was issued for his arrest and I got a call from Len.

"C.W., this is Len," he began.

"Len who?" I countered. I wasn't trying to be smart, but I had only met Len three times in my life and every time, until this one, he had messed up some part of my name – C.P., P.C.,W.C. and he kept mixing me up with my brother who worked in Sterling. So I wasn't familiar enough with him to know him from Adam's house cat.

"Len Whitmore," he said with an exasperated tone.

Ok, now I knew who he was.   "Oh, how are you, Mr. Whitmore?"

"Not so good, C.W., do you know my brother, Beetle?"

"The town dru . . . , er, yeah, I know Beetle."

"Well, Beetle had gotten in trouble." *So what else is new,* I thought. "He skipped his hearing today for drunk driving and his bail is $25,000." My ears perked up. "C.W., I hear you can get things done without an awful lot of noise. I'd like to hire you to find my brother. I'll pay the expenses and make sure you get your fair share of any bounty money, IF you can find and return him discretely."

I said I thought I could handle that, then asked, "We've only met a few times and I don't think I mentioned at any of those occasions what I did for a living. How did you get my name?"

"I heard you were the best detective in Boger County." I was the only detective in Boger County. "And I've done some legal work with Arch Cline. He recommended you highly." God bless Mr. Cline. "He said you could get things done and keep your mouth shut. I need that right now, C.W. I hate to put pressure on you but I need to find Beetle as quickly as possible. I have some other business coming up in the next few months and I need to get this handled soon." In other words he was going to announce for Lieutenant Governor and he needed this behind him as fast as possible.

"I think I can be discreet, but my fees have gone up to $50 a day plus expenses." I had suddenly decided it was time for a new fee schedule. The man sounded a bit desperate and he could certainly afford it.

He made a growling sound, but agreed. "I'll go along with that, but in exchange I want results within ten days."

"Ten days? I don't even know where to start to look."

"Ah, well there I might be able to help you. The last three times something like this has happened, Bradley has gone to Charlotte to visit a friend named, uh, Frenchy. She lives off of Central Avenue. Are you familiar with Charlotte, C.W.?"

"I know how to get around the town, if that's what you're asking." My favorite uncle lived on the west side of town and I had spent many a summer there, especially after my parents separated.

"Well, some people from around here don't like driving in the big city and avoid it like the plague." *Some people from around here think Charlotte is in South Carolina*, I thought, but all I said was, "Oh, I'm not one of those, I feel pretty comfortable. You just got to know some main streets and you can get around. I may need some money up front in case he's been picked up," I ended hopefully.

"I think I can handle that, would two thousand be enough to start?"

I hoped he didn't hear me gulp, and I was pretty sure he couldn't hear me lick my lips, as I said, "I think that will be fine for now. I'll come by your office leaving town."

Hush, Hush Sweet Charlotte

I began to ruminate on Mr. Whitmore's call and got a funny feeling I had been through this before. I sensed that I was being used like in the Cline affair. That one worked out okay but it didn't mean it was a trend. I decided to ask some more questions when I went to see him and pick up money at his office, the biggest office building in the county.

"Mr. Whitmore, do you think Beetle will come back with me amicably?"

He leaned back in his leather padded chair, "Do you know him, C.W.?" I did. Everybody who hung around the county jail knew Beetle. He had his own cell and his own pillow for the cot. They usually gave him the run of the place because Beetle normally wouldn't run away. One, he was more out of shape than I was, and two; he had every reason to believe his brother would get him out every time. Well, almost every time. Either the fear of getting another out-of-county judge or the possibility that his brother had enough and might abandon him had led Beetle to skedaddle.

Len interrupted my ruminations saying, "You know he's a pretty friendly guy when he's sober and usually he's a happy drunk. Oh, I know my brother can't hold his liquor, but I don't think there's a mean bone in his body. He was truly remorseful for what he did three years ago but he seems unable to change his ways. I think if you approach him and tell him I will stick with him, he will come along. I just don't want him getting into any more trouble in a big city than he doesn't know and that doesn't know him." It was a nice little speech delivered with a respectful style but there was something about the smile on his face that worried me. I sensed that the real answer was 'you bring him back, and this time I'll make sure no one will hear about my brother again".

That didn't bother me as much as what would happen if I didn't bring him back. "Am I in competition with anybody?"

"What do you mean, Mr. Biggs?"

"Am I the only one looking for Beetle? I don't care to do the leg work and have someone snatch him up at the last minute."

"I assure you no one else is looking for him at this time. In fact, I've asked the Sheriff to hold off on any APBs for a time."

I wasn't surprised at that. Most of the locals believed our sheriff would become Len's head of security if he moved up to a high political position.

"Okay, but I want you to know that if I sense someone's on my tail, I'm pulling out." With that, and two thousand bucks in my pocket, I headed for Charlotte. It was a nice two and a half hour drive, an hour and a half to get to the city limits then forty five minutes to wind my way through Charlotte traffic to get to Elizabeth Avenue near the local community college. When I arrived at the address on Elizabeth, I found an abandoned house. I wandered around, knocked on a couple of doors but no one knew of a Frenchy. I was about to call it a day when I stopped at a ritzy looking gas station near Presbyterian Hospital. After I filled up, I asked the powerfully built clerk if he'd ever heard of a woman named Frenchy.

"Woman?" he snickered, "Yeah, I've heard of Frenchy. Most everyone recognizes Frenchy. If you want to see 'her,' stick around. You see that bus stop over there," pointing toward a sheltered stop over near the hospital. "Hang around there until about dark and you're liable to see Frenchy."

I thanked him and pulled the car over to the side. I got a cup of coffee and watched. A little after seven I saw a woman moving up the sidewalk—at least I thought it was a woman. She was wearing a silky black top, a white skirt and red high heels. She was the hairiest woman I have ever seen. In fact, she had more of a moustache than I had. I walked up to her with a little trepidation.

"Ma'am, sorry to bother you, but are you Frenchy?"

"Who wants to know," she answered in a gruff, husky voice.

Now I'm no Sherlock Holmes, but I was having a strong suspicion that Frenchy wasn't a woman. Still, I plowed ahead. "My name is C.W. Biggs and I'm looking for a fellow by the name of Bradley Whitmore, most people call him Beetle."

"Bradley, huh, I didn't know that. I always called him Beetle."

"Oh, so you do know him."

She, er he, put her hands on his hips (I was getting very confused) "I didn't say yes, and I didn't say no. What do you want him for?"

"His brother sent me to bring him home."

"What for?"

"I'm not at liberty to say, ma'am."

"He's in trouble isn't he? He's always in trouble when he comes up here to see me." Suddenly, her voice changed and she purred, "What's in it for me?"

I had to think how much of my money I was willing to risk on this source. I decided to try enough to maybe hook her (I later learned that was a bad phrasing choice). "I'll give you fifty dollars if you have some worthwhile information and I'll come back tomorrow and give you another fifty if it turns out to be accurate."

She looked me up and down and said, "I might be able to do something for you for a little more."

This was getting me nowhere; I said "Look, I'm tired. I've been hanging around this street corner all day. If you want the fifty, fine. If not, I'm leaving." I turned around to head for my Dodge.

"Okay, okay, just hold on, you don't have to get upset. A girl's got to make a living. I just thought you might be the kind of guy who wants a little action on your first visit to the city."

"It's not my first trip, I've got relatives on the west side and I'm through messing. Either put up or shut up." It was another poor choice of words, but a car had driven up and the driver had whistled at Frenchy. At least I hoped it was at Frenchy. It seemed to motivate her to end our conversation. "All right give me the fifty. The last time I saw the bastard was yesterday afternoon. He said he was going to the north side of town somewhere near Statesville Road, probably that tattoo parlor he frequents. If you see him, tell him he owes me and he better not come back to me with a new name shining on his backside."

She turned and headed over to the car that had whistled at her. "What kind of car was he driving?" I hollered. She turned back and said, "An old Toyota, I think."

That fit the description of the car Len had told me he might be driving, so maybe she wasn't feeding me a line. I got back to my car. It was 8:00. I decided I'd look for Beetle tomorrow. I just wanted to get over to my uncle's house, have a nice shower and get a good night's sleep before I went looking.

My uncle lived off Oakdale Road near Sunset about halfway between Highway 16 and I-77. It was an older ranch style house located in a decent neighborhood although new developments were crowding around his quiet enclave. He and his wife had three kids. Two were grown and out of the house: his youngest, Sandy, was a junior at UNCC. I hadn't seen her since she was thirteen, so when a pretty blonde waved at me as I drove up, I didn't recognize her.

"Sandy, is that you?"

"Yeah C.W., it's been a long time. Good to see you." She gave me a hug. "I'm going out with some friends, wanna come along?"

I must admit I was tempted, but I remembered our age difference and the fact I was related, "Uh, no, I need to talk to your dad. Thanks, anyway."

"Ok, we'll talk tomorrow." She got into a car that made my old Dodge look like an antique and headed off.

Uncle Barry met me at the door and welcomed me in. He was a bit shorter than my father and somewhat rounder. He had a good sense of humor and always treated me well when I had spent summers up there. He could also read my emotions and saw that I wasn't in much of a mood to talk. "Long day, huh? Marian's gone to church but there's some leftovers from dinner. Eat something. Relax before we talk."

About an hour later after I settled in to the guest bedroom, I came back to the living room where Marian and Barry were watching a local newscast. I gave Marian a big hug and thanked her for the food. We exchanged information about the families while we watched the news. I had called Barry while I waited for Frenchy and kind of filled him in on the case I was working on. I was just telling Marian about Mother's new boyfriend when Barry suddenly turned my attention to the TV.

"Look at this, C.W. I bet you don't have to deal with this much in Boger County. It's another drunken driving accident. I swear it seems like every night somebody's getting killed on the roads around here."

My head turned towards the TV. The reporter was describing an accident on Harris Boulevard near the university. The pictures looked pretty horrific. T he car was burned beyond recognition and the reporter was saying there had been a fatality but the victim wasn't identified. I was about to restart my conversation with Marian when my head snapped back around. The anchor was saying the car was a white Toyota and liquor was suspected to have been a contributing factor the accident.

I had one of those sinking feelings, turned to Uncle Barry and asked, "How far is that from Statesville Avenue?"

"Not far at all, why do you ask?"

"My source said the guy I was looking for was up that way."

He stared at me. "Oh, come on, C.W., it would be a thousand to one chance that would be your man."

"Yeah, but you know the Biggs luck, Uncle Barry. It wouldn't surprise me given this guy's past history."

The conversation turned somber afterwards and Marian and Barry went to bed when the newscast finished. I couldn't sleep. Charlotte TV has a lot of newscasts. I watched three more before I went to bed. Each one gave a little more detail, and each time it seemed more like my trip to Charlotte might me a short one. It sure sounded like Beetle. I decided to start my investigation tomorrow with a visit to the Police Department, and maybe the morgue.

I Get To Meet a Celebrity

I headed out about 8:30 the next morning. It didn't take long to get downtown to the police station, by then the traffic had thinned out. I had been to the central station and the jail before, so I knew the layout, but I had never been to the morgue. I didn't get much money bringing a dead bail skipper, especially at the rates I was charging. The fact I had never been to the morgue turned out to be a problem.

The officer on duty was amiable as I explained who I was and what I was doing there. He verified that no one matching Beetle's description was in lock up and checked the County Jail sheet to make sure. That left me with yesterday's accident.

"Oh, from what I heard that was a bad one. The car burst into flames and the body was burned beyond recognition. It's at the morgue," he said.

My uncle said that was on North College Street, but I decided to check just in case. The officer gave me a look, "You're not from around here, are you?" I answered negatively. "Where are you from?" I always hated this question. Because Boger County is so small and unknown, I have to launch into a dissertation of thirty minutes to explain where to find it. It was no different this time. Two more cops walked up as I began. "It's in the eastern part of the state."

"Oh, towards the beach," one of them interjected. "Which beach?" said the other.

"No," I began again, "it's sort of east central, nearer Raleigh."

"Right near Raleigh, oh I know where you're talking about," said Ferguson, the cop at the desk.

"Well, no it's not that near Raleigh. It's still about an hour and fifteen minutes to get there. It's more south central."

"Fayetteville?" said Turner one of the officers who had

150

walked up. "I was stationed at Bragg in the 82nd. Do you know the Cross Creek Mall area? There was a little Thai restaurant down near there that was really good. You ever been down there?"

"No, and no, it's not right at Fayetteville, either."

Ferguson began again, "If you flew there from here, would you fly to Fayetteville or Raleigh?"

This was getting frustrating, plus I didn't know the answer. "Fayetteville, maybe. Actually, I think the closest airport is Greensboro."

"So, you're close to Asheboro."

"No, not exactly."

MacManus, the other cop, chipped in, "You don't know exactly where you live, do you?"

"NO, it's just you can't get there from here easily. In fact, it's hard to get anywhere easily from Green Top," I shouted.

The three looked at each other, smiled and seem to commiserate with me. "We get a lot of folks coming in here that say that," said Ferguson. "I better give you some detailed directions to the morgue," he continued. "It's not on North College anymore. It's moved to Reno near Rozelle's Ferry."

"Rozelle's Ferry!" I exclaimed, "I know where that is! I passed it coming in from my Uncle's house. I probably saw it without even realizing it."

"I wouldn't go that far," finished Ferguson, "it doesn't stick out like some neon sign, but if you can get to Rozelle's Ferry, you'll probably find it. It's one of the newer looking buildings over there."

I had probably wasted forty-five minutes, but these guys seemed friendly, so I didn't consider it a total loss as I headed for the new morgue location. I approached the location with a feeling of trepidation. I really expected to find Beetle burned to a crisp. I thought about what I knew about him. I already said he wasn't overly intelligent and he also wasn't overly handsome either. Life isn't fair. He was a couple of years ahead of me in school, but not at Green Top. He went to Hughville where he was the star player on his baseball team. That wasn't a great honor-remember what I said about our weird county. All three of our high schools were tiny, so being the star of the team wasn't necessarily a great accomplishment, for example, I was the star for Green Top. That was a bit of an exception. My team was fairly good, we made the state playoffs all four years I was there, but Hughville won like two or three games each year.

That's how I knew him. I was mainly an infielder, a pretty good one, too. But when we played a team like Hughville, Coach Rimmer would run me out as the pitcher, figuring we could survive my lousy pitching against a lousy team. I did get by, but I couldn't get Beetle out. It wasn't necessarily his talent. Beetle had a really bad case of acne when he was in school and I swear every time I faced him, he would have this oozing pimple in the middle of his forehead. No matter what I tried, all I could do was stare at that pimple and it spoiled my concentration. I walked him three times and hit him twice. The only time I ever got him out was when I threw right at the pimple. He jumped back but kept his bat over the plate and hit a dribbler back to me. I still remember hearing old Coach Rimmer from the dugout hollering, "It's about damn time!" I had seen him at the jail several times since. The pimple was no longer on his forehead, it had mysteriously moved to his chin.

There was one other thing that hurt Bradley's appearance, though it was less visible. It also came up during a baseball game. I said I hit him twice. One time I plunked him pretty hard in the ribs and he jumped right up and headed to first base without even wincing. After I got back to the dugout I commented on that. Another player said it was because he was wearing a protective vest. Obviously I had to ask why. He told me Bradley had curvature of the spine and he wore a truss to help keep his backbone in line. It wasn't noticeable unless you knew, but now that I knew whenever I saw him, he looked slumped over. That may have been the liquor, but it led to another memorable Biggs faux pas.

I arrived at the county morgue at about 10:30. It took a while to get through security. Just being an out of county detective wasn't cutting it, but when I mentioned Len Whitmore, things began to move. It seems Len has a very good reputation with law enforcement agencies. Suddenly, I was heading down the hall to meet or rather view my suspect. The Medical Examiner who escorted me was named Gene. After we exchanged pleasantries he gave me a word of warning.

"I thought I'd let you know who's in the lab today. It's 'she who must be paid homage to.'"

"I'm not following you."

"You know, the famous one. The one that they've written books and made TV shows about."

"You mean the one they've nicknamed Boney?"

He chuckled at my error. "I think you mean Bones. Yep, that's the one."

"But I thought she was just a fictional character. I had no idea she was real."

"Well, she's sort of fictional. Nobody could have that many murder cases to solve in the short period of time they show her on TV. But the woman she's based on is in there," pointing to a door on the right we were approaching. "And she's every bit as beautiful as the actress who plays her on TV," he continued, "and with just as many quirks."

Wow, I thought, this was my chance to meet a big time celebrity, a pretty big time celebrity, one who wasn't much older than me. Not that it mattered. I could be some cougar's plaything and be remarkably happy. All I had to do was impress her with my medical knowledge and my sparkling personality and we'd be going for our first date on Len's retainer. I summoned up my three semesters of biology study and knocked on the door. Okay, it was actually two, but I did sign up for an anatomy course that third semester. I just never went to class. I waited for a moment, and heard a soft but strong "Come in, but don't bother me." I crossed the threshold and thought, "Time to hit a home run!"

She was just as pretty and just as imposing as Gene said. She was a little taller than I expected and had just a touch of gray in her hair. But for this woman, that just added to her allure. "What do you want," she challenged as I walked across the room. I explained who I was and what I needed. Here was my opportunity for my big move.

"You know, I'm kind of the medical examiner for my home county. Could I help you?"

She looked up at me for the first time, squinted her nose and said "I suppose. You'll need to come closer and put on some gloves and a mask. They're over there on the lab table." Her voice was commanding, but somehow sexy. I was already fantasizing about my upcoming date. As I reached the autopsy table, I saw an incredibly burned victim who looked as if the bones would fall apart if I touched anything.

"Pick up the tibia and take it over to the microscope," she commanded, "I want to see if there was any damage to the bone before the accident. I suspect our victim may have already been hurt before the accident. If that's the case, this might lead to a murder investigation."

Ok, now I was in trouble. My anatomical studies were limited to "the ankle bone was connected to the shin bone". I looked over the body and decided to make a guess. I picked up a bone and turned to the table with the microscope. She looked up, gave me a quizzical look and said "Hold on, that's the femur. Here's the tibia."

"Oh, I guess it's hard to tell since the body is so burned." It was a lame attempt to cover up my mistake and I could tell by the look on her face it didn't work. *STRIKE ONE,* I thought. I needed to recover quickly if I was to have a chance. Then I remembered Beetle's spine curvature, if I could just remember the official name, ah, that was it.

"The person I was looking for had curvature of the spine, you know, he had halitosis." I said with confidence.

She looked at me and laughed, "Do you mean scoliosis?" *STRIKE TWO.* But suddenly she stopped giggling, "He, he" she continued, "Did you say he?"

"Yes, his name was Bradley Whitmore."

"Mr. Biggs, look at the pelvic area." *Pelvic,* I thought, *that was near the hips as best as I could remember.* I looked that way. She said, "Do you notice anything?" I had no idea what she wanted me to notice so I all I could say was 'uh huh'. "Well," she continued, "what do you see?" Again, there was no reply from me. "Mr. Biggs, this is a skeleton of a young woman, between 23 and 25 who has never had a child. Where did you study anatomy?" *STRIKE THREE AND YOU'RE OUT OF HERE.* I could either tell her my two courses came at North Central Carolina Community College or I could beat a hasty retreat. I decided the latter was the better choice. The chances of me ever having a date with this beautiful medical examiner diva were now about nil. I pretended my cell phone vibrated and went through the process of answering it with a made up conversation. I don't think she bought a minute of it, but I carried through and said how much I enjoyed meeting her, but I had been called back to Green Top and had to leave immediately. I basically ran out before she could say anything more, knowing I could never show my face at the Mecklenburg Medical Examiner's office ever again.

Always Check Your Trash

I had hoped for a speedy departure from the site of my humiliation, but it wasn't to be. The old Dodge wouldn't start and I had to get a jump. It must have been about lunchtime because just as I was clamping the jumper cables, the Queen of Forensics walked out. She looked over my way, our eyes met and she just shook her head. She gave me a look that seemed to say 'What a loser.' Could this day get any worse? Unfortunately, I knew the answer to that. I just wanted to confirm my miserable existence.

I headed back downtown, or uptown, (Charlotteans have an on-going argument on what to call their center city) and the law enforcement offices. I really didn't want to talk to anyone, but I needed to locate Beetle and get out of town as fast as I could. Yet, everywhere I went, the answer was the same. No Beetle Whitmore. The desk cop commiserated with me. He turned to speak to an angular, grizzled black man. But the black man grabbed my shoulder and said, "Say, bro, did you say you were looking for Beetle Whitmore?"

"Yeah, do you know him?"

"Hell, yes. I was drinking with him just yesterday."

"Can you give me an idea where to look for him?"

He pointed his finger at me and said, "I can do better than that. If you can give me a ride home, I'll take you to him."

This sounded too good to be true, but I was in a desperate position. I looked over at the desk cop hoping for some confirmation. He looked up at me and then over at the Good Samaritan and said, "Well, if anybody can help you find somebody on the west side of town, it's probably Leo." He motioned me closer and finished, "Just don't buy him a drink."

"I heard that, Officer Robb. There ain't no call for those kind of remarks," said Leo.

Officer Robb answered, "You be nice to this fella. He's from out of town and has a tendency to get lost." That really wasn't true, but I wasn't going to break this last straw of hope. I introduced myself to Leo. He told me his name was Leo Jenkins. That name sounded familiar but I couldn't quite place it. He said he needed to go to Beatties Ford Road. This sounded promising. Beatties Ford was near that tattoo place Frenchy had mentioned. Maybe I was gonna catch a break.

We exchanged pleasantries and I told him where I was from. He surprised me when he said he knew where Green Top was. He said he was from Winterville, near Greenville, where his daddy worked at the university. "Oh," I said, "did he teach there? I was a student there once."

He stared at me, "Are you stupid? Do I look like my old man taught at East Carolina? Hell, no, my dad was a janitor. He worked in the administrative office and Old Man Jenkins was always kidding my father when he saw him about which Jenkins was in charge. My old man liked Dr. Leo and he named me after him 'cause he liked him so."

I realized that was the connection, Leo Jenkins. I went by the medical building named after him several times during my four month stay at that college that should have included a class in anatomy. I told him that was a good story and congratulated him on being Dr. Leo's namesake.

"How many black dudes do you know named Leo?"

I had to admit I didn't know many. "I've hated that name all my life, just call me L.J. and don't ask me any more questions."

Great, I thought, another brilliant introduction. I was just full of them today. We hardly spoke for the rest of the drive, which was mercifully short. His directions were terse but I knew enough about the area to make sense of them. Somewhere off of Beatties Ford, he told me to stop and started to open the door.

"Wait a minute," I yelled, "you were going to take me to Beetle. Is he around here?"

He looked at me with an exasperated face. "Damn, you're dumb. I just needed a ride up home and you were the perfect sucker to bring me here. Now, if I were you, white boy, I wouldn't hang around here too long. The home boys ain't likely to strip this piece of shit you're driving, but they might just want to use it for target practice."

The look of disappointment and shock on my face must have led to some sense of compassion by L.J. He sighed and said, "Jesus, I'm getting too nice. Listen, go up Statesville Road and take a left on the first road past Sunset. Look for a big neon sign that says MINDY'S TATTOO. I think that's the place you might find your meal ticket back home and if I were you I'd head that way as fast as you can." As he turned his head slightly to the right, I saw two men moving towards the car. Neither looked friendly. I took Leo's advice and gunned it out of there, which meant I peeled off at 30 miles an hour.

Under cloudy, threatening skies, I got to Mindy's about dusk and was helped immensely by the neon sign L.J. had said to look for. The sign also said you could get a massage there, too. It sounded like a really friendly place. I walked in and an older lady welcomed me, "Are you here for a tattoo or a massage? We can do both at the same time if you got the money."

"Are you Mindy," I asked.

"Yeah," she replied, "who wants to know?"

"I'm looking for someone."

"Honey, you've come to the right place. We're a full service establishment." She pulled back a curtain so I could see an old man. "That's Jim, best damned tattoo artist in the Carolinas."

It looked to me like he was dead. "No, I'm not interested in a tattoo."

Mindy broke in, "Of course not, I could see that you were a man looking for a little fun as soon as you walked in," as she pulled open another curtain. I was looking at two scantily clad young ladies who immediately began to move in exotic ways as soon as they saw me. I was fascinated, but it didn't help my investigation.

Now looking back at it what happened next might not make any sense to the casual observer. In fact, it looks pretty dumb but I was so fixated on finding Beetle and getting the hell out of town, I may have missed a few obvious clues. Okay, maybe a few dozen obvious clues. It's my story and I'm sticking to it. Besides, my mother may read this someday. I digress, back to the action.

"No, I'm here on another matter. I'm looking for a guy by the name of Beetle Whitmore. I got a picture of him. Frenchy told me I might find him here."

Mindy's voice suddenly changed to a shrill shout, "FRENCHY! What did that ugly trannie tell you? We run a legal establishment here. You're not with the Vice Squad are you?"

"No ma'am, I'm a private eye hired to find Beetle."

"Let me see that photo," and she snatched the picture out of my hand. "I think I do recognize him. I think he saw Brenda the last time he was here. Brenda, come out here."

A leggy, slightly overweight redhead stepped out from the glass partitioned room. She took a look at the photo and her eyes got as big as saucers. She whispered something to Mindy and Mindy sent her back, telling her to move quickly. Mindy looked over at me and said, "I think we might can help you, Mister. Just sit down there. What did you say your name was?"

"I didn't say. It's C.W. Biggs."

Mindy gave what amounted to a grin and asked, "Why do you want Beetle?"

"I'm here to take him back for an important legal matter. I'd appreciate any help I can get."

Mindy looked worried by my statement. About that time Brenda came back out and whispered in Mindy's ear. Mindy looked over at me. "I believe we can help you find this fella. Just give me about thirty minutes and I believe we can solve all your problems. Would you care to see one of the ladies while you wait? I'm willing to give you a discount, fifty dollars for the half hour."

I'd never had a massage in my life, but what the hell, you only live once, so I agreed. Mindy signaled for the other girl and she led me to a back room of the establishment. This girl was a young brunette who said her name was Trina. We got to the back and she asked if I wanted to take a shower first. I thought that was a little funny, but said no, I'd wait. She started to take off her top. "Wait a minute," I said, "I thought you were giving the massage, not me. I'm not paying fifty dollars to give someone a massage!"

Trina stared at me with the same kind of look that the famous doctor had given me. "Are you stupid? This is a massage parlor. It's fifty dollars for me to be topless, more if you want me completely nude."

I must have looked like a big guppy fish as my jaw dropped three feet. I was in a MASSAGE PARLOR. "No," I sputtered, "I'm here to find a guy by the name of Beetle Whitmore. I didn't, I mean, I wouldn't, I mean, not to say you're not a pretty girl. I..I..I."

Trina started to laugh, "What was it my mama used to say, 'did you just fall off the potato truck?' What did you think this was?"

I didn't know how to respond. I decided to play the naiveté card. It was about all I had available except for the expense account of a lawyer who would pay dearly to avoid bad publicity. So I began telling her as much of Beetle's story and my day in Charlotte as fast as I could. Fortunately, she listened intently. She got up, opened the door, looked up and down the corridor, shut it and came over to me. "Listen," she began, "I shouldn't be doing this but it's obvious you're in over your head. The guy you're looking for was here earlier today begging for help from Brenda. He said he'd seen something he shouldn't have and Big Ed was after him."

"Who's Big Ed?"

She looked at me with wide-eyed astonishment, "Christ, where do you come from? Big Ed is guy who runs the largest drug ring between here and Atlanta, AND, he owns this place. So when Beetle unloaded his life story to Brenda, she told Mindy, and she called up Big Ed's place to come and get him, only Beetle overheard the conversation and hightailed it out of here. Big Ed's people are mad as hell Mindy had lost him but now Mindy's got someone she can trade and hope Ed forgives her."

"Who?"

"Who!! You, you fucking idiot! She's holding you here until Big Ed's boys get here and wring out any information they can get out of you as they beat the shit out of you."

Jesus, what have I got myself into?! Luckily, Trina was smitten with my puppy dog eyes or maybe the five hundred bucks of Len Whitmore's I offered for an escape route. She said she'd help me get out through the back door, but then I was on my own. She went out of the room again, came back in a few minutes, held her finger up to her lips and we snuck out. The back door was only a few feet away. Trina unlocked the door, wished me good luck, and pushed me outside into the darkness of an alley. I got back to my car and climbed in just as two black SUV's came roaring up. It didn't take a genius to figure out these guys were not here for either a tattoo or a massage.

The SUVs pulled to the front which gave me a chance for a get-away. I tried to start up the old Dodge, but it wouldn't turn over. Now I was in big trouble. I grabbed my pistol out of the dash pocket and slid back into the alley trying to get into the shadows and out of that big, glowing neon light. I could hear Ed's henchmen talking to Mindy and they didn't sound happy. It gave me a chance to consider my possibilities. I knew a shootout was not good for me. All I had was an old .38 Policeman's Special - and I mean old. My great-grandfather was given the gun when he was on the police force in Gastonia in the 1930s. He begat it to my grandfather, who begat it to my father, who begat it to me. It worked fine; it just was a little obsolete to go up against the gansta's guns I imagined I would be facing. Couple that with the fact that I wasn't the best of shots. Private investigators have to pass gun efficiency and safety course every so often and I had passed it every time, just barely every time. If the score to pass was 72, I'd make a 73, if it was 77, I made 78. The evaluators had a standing bet on whether I would ever make five points higher than proficiency. Part of the problem was the old gun seemed to shoot high and to the right every time. So when I went to the target range I often looked like I was shooting at the target on my left and at its toes.

I decided the best strategy for me was to try and hide. There was a big trash bin in the alley, I ducked down behind it and prayed. It didn't work. Three hoods came to the front of the alley, one of them hollered, "Come out of there, you son of a bitch or we'll start shooting!" But something about the way he said it made me think he was not certain who he was up against. Now I had to make a big decision. Do I try to stay as silent as a mouse or do I see if I could scare them off with a couple of well-placed shots? Stupidly, I chose the latter. From my point of view beside the trash bin, I could see their feet at the front of the alleyway. I shot towards the left corner and sure enough it drifted up and right, catching one of the bad guys in the lower leg. Now I had them.

"Shit!" shouted the 'victim', "Kill the bastard." A hail of bullets followed his command. I was absolutely sure that back home my lucky shot would have ended the confrontation, but not here. I slid down beside the bin as bullets pinged off the wall and the container. After about 20 seconds that felt like fifteen minutes, there was a lull. I decide to take another shot. I rose up and started to shoot, when suddenly, the big lid on the bin flew open and a man stood up. I turned toward the sound and shot at the same time, wilder than usual even for me. It went real high and real right.

KABOOM went the shot, followed by sparks going everywhere and glass shattering in a series of lesser pops. I had hit Mindy's neon sign. The explosion nearly made me drop my gun, as I looked over at the individual in the trash bin.

"Beetle Whitmore! What the hell are you doing in there???" I screamed

"C.W. Biggs! What the hell are you doing in Charlotte???" he shouted back.

I began to laugh and laugh hard. I could do that because the sound of that explosion and my lucky shot seemed to have sent our opponents scrambling for safety. As sirens sounded in the distance, we heard their cars pull away.

Now Beetle began to laugh a little, too, but I was laughing so much I was having a hard time catching my breath. "What are you cackling about?" he asked.

"Either, either…" I gasped, "You've got the strangest earring in history or you've got a condom hanging on your left ear!"

He reached up and pulled it off, shouting, "That's not funny, C.W."

"I hope it's yours. Ouch!" grabbing my side from laughing so hard. The sirens were upon us, but it was a fire truck and it sped right by followed by the sound of more sirens, I was sure the police would be coming at any time. Finally catching my breath, I looked at Beetle and asked "What the hell is going on?"

"C.W., help me get out of here. I'm in a shit load of trouble and I don't want to talk to the police."

I held the trash bin lid while he crawled out. Once he got on the pavement I asked, "What are you talking about, Beetle? Len sent me up here to bail you out. You haven't got anything to worry about. Len will cover for you, and you haven't committed any crimes, have you? Jesus, Beetle, can't you stay sober for a few days?"

"I've been sober the whole time I've been in Charlotte, but I wish I hadn't been. C.W., two nights ago, I saw Big Ed and a couple of his boys shoot somebody over on Beatties Ford Road. At least I think it was Beatties Ford Road." The sirens were fast approaching. The police would be there any minute. "Listen, I don't want to talk to the police right now. Get me out of here, and I'll explain what's happening. I'm afraid if I tell the cops what I know AND who I saw, I'm going to be a dead man real soon."

Ordinarily I wouldn't have agreed with him, but having survived my encounter with Big Ed's thugs, I saw his point. I came up with a dumb strategy but it was the only idea I could come up with at the time. I stuck Beetle in the trunk of my car and waited for the Charlotte police who pulled up within a few seconds after I hid him.

It began to rain. Blue lights pulsed in the darkness. With the neon light gone, the headlights provided the only illumination in the alley. I put the revolver on the ground, got my P.I. license out of my wallet, and held it up high. The cops approached with their guns out, but my visits to the Charlotte Police Department in the past two days paid off. One of the officers was Robb who had warned me about L.J.

"I know you," he said with his flashlight pointing right in my face. "You were looking for someone up this way. Did you find him?"

Well, here was my moment. I could tell the truth, open the trunk, and wash my hands of the whole thing. That would be the wise thing to do. But one thing about the Biggs, we weren't very wise. "No," I said, "I think someone named Big Ed may have got to him first, or at least was looking for him, too."

"Big Ed?" Officer Robb boomed with rain droplets now running off his cap. "Damn, you're lucky to be alive if Big Ed was involved in this." The other three officers looked at me warily. "We better call in the detectives on this one. Simpson, why don't you get Mr. . . . what did you say your name was?"

"Biggs, C.W. Biggs, and can we get out of this rain, I'm getting soaked." I spent the next two hours telling my story four times to different officers and detectives. I've found that in situations like this, it's best to tell as much of the truth as possible. I told the story exactly like I've told you, except for the part about Beetle. They seemed to buy it, partly because of my visits to ask about Beetle, and partly because I was the only witness. The ladies at the establishment had all left as soon as gun shots began, and Jim, the tattoo artist, swore he didn't hear a thing, which seemed plausible given his age and physical condition. The cops counted thirty two cartridge casings in the alleyway. Thirty were not mine.

As we walked back to the cars I finally got up the gumption to ask, "Who is this Big Ed, anyway?"

The officers stopped as if hit by a thunderbolt. There was a moment of silence before Officer Robb spoke up, "What planet did you say you came from? You've never heard of Ed Malekola, the biggest, baddest, meanest gang leader this county has ever seen?" I continued to look stupid; I wanted to find out more about my nemesis. Robb shook his head, "Look, it's raining. I'll ride down with you and give you the lowdown on Ed, but you ain't gonna like it. If the guy you're looking for is mixed up with Big Ed, you might want to contact the funeral homes in town and make an appointment for the disposition of the body." I hoped Beetle didn't hear that.

I got into the old Dodge and it still wouldn't crank. I think that corroborated my story as much as anything I had said. The police officers decided that no one in his right mind would have come to this place and faced off with Big Ed's boys with a car that wouldn't start. So I was either telling the truth or I wasn't in my right mind. I kept quiet as they jumped me off and Officer Robb and I headed downtown.

Robb looked over at me. "You're not shittin' me, are you? You really never heard of Ed Malekola? I shook my head. Robb stared at the top of the car, whistling through his teeth, "Jesus, alright, P.I., here's the main facts on Big Ed. He's 1/4th Samoan, 1/4th Cuban, 1/4th Irish and 1/4th Japanese.

"He sounds like a regular walking United Nations."

"A UN of crime. Every one of his grandparents is connected to a major mob from those groups. It's like he's been picked as the crown prince. He's 6'3" and weighs at least 450 pounds. He could dominate most of the drug traffic of the East Coast."

I stared at him, "Why don't you guys go in and get him? It sure sounds like you got enough to charge him with something."

"Three things" Robb said. "First, he's smart. Second, he does almost all his main activities outside of Mecklenburg. And third, I said he was smart, but he's also lazy or either so smart he does just enough to stay under the radar of the Feds. He is also very territorial. One of the reasons we've got an uneasy truce with him is that whenever a rival gang moves in, he'll make sure they behave, or he'll hand them to us."

"Sounds like a real pussycat," I said.

"Wait a minute," Robb interrupted, "I didn't finish. He'll hand them to us, in pieces. One time the Bloods and the Crips tried to take him on. He turned them into the Blips!" Robb laughed long and hard at his lame joke. I gave a forced chuckle. I sure hope Beetle wasn't getting any of this.

"Your friend isn't a drug dealer, is he?"

"No," I said, "He's basically the town drunk. I came up here to pick him up for an outstanding warrant. I can't imagine why Big Ed would be interested in him at all."

"You're going to a lot of effort for part of the bail money." Robb looked at me quizzically. I realized I might have made a strategic mistake. I didn't want to bring up that he was Len Whitmore's brother. I told him, "Look at the piece of crap I'm driving. I need every bit of bail money I can get. Plus, I got relatives up here. I'm just trying to make ends meet. I'm probably going to head home right after I get a good night's sleep. This mess is way over my head."

The answer seemed to satisfy Officer Robb. The rest of the ride was about how bad the Bobcats were playing this year. Before too long we arrived at the main station.

Three hours later, the new set of investigators I talked to were satisfied with the story I had given and didn't press me too hard on Beetle's whereabouts. I think they were just relieved that they weren't investigating a murder. Several officers continued to compliment me on my "miracle near the Catawba". By the time I headed back to my uncle's house, I was feeling pretty lucky, until I remembered my "hostage" in the trunk. Beetle started beating in the back seat almost as soon as I pulled out of the parking lot, but I didn't stop until I reached a gas station on Belhaven.

I let him out and he immediately apologized. "It's okay, Beetle, I would have tried to kick in the back seat if I was in there for four hours, too."

"No, C.W., it's not that. I just couldn't hold it any longer." I looked in the trunk and it was very wet, nothing the Dodge hadn't seen before, but that's another story. I told him it was fine, but he was still apologizing all the way home. We pulled into the driveway but before we went in, I asked Beetle to fill me in on how he had gotten mixed up with Big Ed.

"I came up here to see a friend of mine named Frenchy," he began, "and hide out for a few days while I got straight. Trouble is, I forgot Frenchy and I had a disagreement the last time we met. She wasn't overly interested in talking to me."

"She, She?" I interrupted. Obviously, all that drinking had affected his eyesight.

He gave me his dumb puppy stare, "Yeah, she. What's the matter with you, C.W.? You act as if you've met her."

"Some people have told me about him, uh, her."

He gave me a funny look, "Anyway, I left in a bit of a hurry and got confused and lost. I stopped somewhere uptown and asked for directions. No one seemed willing to help me until this black fellow said he'd help me if I'd give him a ride to Beatties Ford Road."

"Wait a minute," I said, "this guy wouldn't happen to call himself L.J.?"

He looked at me in amazement, "How did you know that?"

"Let's just say I've got a nodding acquaintance."

"Wow, small world, huh?" *Yeah, and full of strange coincidences*, I thought and I keep having them. "Well, anyway," Beetle began again, "we got up to the road and I let him out but he double crossed me. He said take a right and I could get out of the city. I took a right and came right back into the city! It was about 11 PM and thunderin' and lightnin', so I stopped at what looked like a municipal building to check to see if I had a map in the dash pocket. Suddenly, I saw flashes of light. I didn't hear anything but I was pretty sure the flashes weren't lightning 'cause I didn't hear any thunder. I got out of the car and walked over to the fence when another round of flashes went off. I saw something fall, a body, I guess and I let out a gasp."

Beetle took a gulp of air. He hadn't talked this long since his last bail hearing. After another moment he continued, "I didn't mean to, C.W., but I couldn't help myself. I heard someone say, 'Don't anybody screw with Big Ed's boys!' I scrambled back to my car, but they heard me. This time shots hit near the back of the car. I don't know how much they saw, but I was parked under a street light, so I'm sure they saw the color."

I suddenly spoke up, "Wait, so you really didn't see much of anything? How did you know who Big Ed was?"

He looked at me like I was a fool. "Do you ever talk to Len?"

"Not as much as you, obviously," I answered crisply.

"Len talks about Big Ed all the time. Well, not all the time, but enough for me to know that he's a criminal mastermind and you don't want to be messing with him or his people."

"Yeah, but you said you just heard the name and you aren't even sure you saw anything. Why would he even suspect you?"

"Uhm, you didn't let me finish my story. I drove around for a while, pulled off at a gas station and kind of went to sleep."

"BEETLE!!"

"I was really tired, C.W. The next morning I felt like I needed to relax, so I went to a really nice place called 'Mindy's'."

"BEETLE!!"

"They were real nice, I spent the whole morning and part of the afternoon there, but I think I might have mentioned to Brenda what I had seen."

"BEETLE!!"

"I needed someone to talk to and Brenda was so comforting, if you know what I mean. Somewhere around 1:30, she said she needed to make a phone call. A few minutes later, one of the girls came in and said I was in lots of trouble and Big Ed's boys were coming to get me."

"I don't suppose her name was Trina?"

"Yeah, I think so, how do you know all these people?"

"Well, that's what I get paid the big bucks for," I said with a commanding voice, but deep down inside, I was hurt that Trina was willing to help any guy with puppy dog eyes or five hundred dollars.

"She said she'd help me get out for a little money, I gave her what I had in my pocket and hightailed it out of there just as Big Ed's crew was arriving."

"Okay, so why did you come back and how did you end up in a trash bin?"

Beetle sighed, "I had lost my wallet. I thought maybe I had left it there when I gave the money to Trina. Though, now that I think about it, I got my money out my pocket. I came back a few hours later after parking my car a few blocks down the road, just in case there were people looking for my old Toyota. I guess I got there a little after you had arrived. Trina intercepted me and sent me back outside. I went out into the alleyway and there was Big Ed's boys coming in the front door. I dived in the trash bin, you started shooting and here we are."

Like I said, Beetle had a way of finding trouble again and again. I told Beetle to keep quiet as we walked to the bedroom I was using.

"Don't wake anybody," I whispered, "It's past two." Beetle never heard me. He fell across the bed and was asleep before I could tell him where the bathroom was. I kind of trundled him up and went to sleep on the couch in the den.

The next morning, I gave my uncle and aunt a quick overview of what was happening leaving out the gunfight at the massage parlor. Everybody was gone by the time Beetle woke up in the early afternoon which spared me any uncomfortable introductions. I decided we needed to get his car back, so we drove up to Statesville Road. We found the abandoned gas station where

Beetle thought he had parked his car, but it wasn't there. It did have a big sign about towing abandoned vehicles under the name of Townley's Towing. I called the phone number given, and sure enough they had a white Toyota which we could claim for $250. I was beginning to sense I might lose money on this "milk run". I gave a quick call to Len and let Beetle explain what was happening. That didn't go well, so I took back the phone and gave a brief description of the events that made sure to include the expenses I was racking up. It didn't seem to faze the noted attorney. His only comment was "Get back here immediately." I said we'd start back as soon as we got the car.

On the way to Townley's I decided to go by this municipal building where Beetle had seen the purported murder. It was called Vest Water Works and it was a historical landmark. It had been Charlotte's first real water pumping station from the Catawba. It was a low profile building that had been built in the 1930s. It also looked like a mini Fort Knox. It was surrounded by barbed wire fences and black steel bars. It definitely did not look like a place for a gangland murder. In fact, it looked sturdier than the county jail. I questioned Beetle "Are you sure this is the place?"

"Yeah, yeah, I remember these black bars. This is the place."

I scanned the vicinity and immediately noticed that just to the north was a Charlotte police sub-station. "Hold it a minute, Beetle. Look there, do you see that police station?"

"Oh yeah, I hadn't noticed that before."

"NOTICE! Beetle, how could you miss it? Are you telling me that you witnessed a murder in as secure a place as I can imagine, and right next to a police station?"

He shrugged. "Well, yeah."

All of the sudden I was beginning to get very nervous. Either Beetle was crazy, or Big Ed was as vicious and daring as any crime lord I ever read about. There was one other possibility. "Bradley Harold Whitmore," I began, "were you drunk that night?"

He gave me a sorrowful, whipped puppy look, "Nobody's called me that since my mama passed away. I swear to you, C.W., on her grave, that I was stone sober that night. I wish I had been drunk. I wish I had never come anywhere near here. But I know what I saw."

I sat there in silence for a minute and pondered the implications of everything I had heard. It was just weird enough to be true, especially given Beetle's predilection towards bad luck, drunk or sober. No, I think I believed him. And that meant we needed to get out of town as fast as possible. We reached the towing service a few minutes later. I introduced myself and Beetle and started to collect the car, but the owner said he needed to see some kind of identification. I looked over at Beetle. He gave me something between a grin and a mope and said. "I never found my wallet."

Oh, Christ, I thought. *Could it get any better than this?* The next fifteen minutes both of us tried to convince Mr. Townley that Beetle really was the owner. We made a little headway by getting him to get the registration card out of the dash pocket, but having only called Bradley by his nickname since we arrived, I couldn't convince him of Beetle's identity.

Empty-handed we headed back to the northwest side of town. I asked Beetle where he thought it could be. "Well, I know it's not in the trash bin. I'm pretty sure I searched the bottom of that place thoroughly while you were engaged in my defense."

"How did you pay Mindy? Surely you had to get your wallet out there."

"Now that you mentioned it, I don't remember taking it out there and I don't think she asked for any money."

"Didn't that set off alarms in that brain of yours?"

"I, uh, thought it might be a reward for my past business and my, um, special relationship with Mindy."

I realized Beetle and I were fish out of water and needed to get back to our little pond as soon as possible. "Do you think you could have lost it anywhere else?"

"I might have lost it at the water plant. I remember I pulled it out to see if I had a pre-paid telephone card. I felt like I needed to talk to Len, but then the shooting started"

"I wished you'd had that feeling about fifteen minutes earlier."

"Me, too, C.W., me too."

The rest of the trip was done in silence, well, almost silence. Beetle kept trying to hum a Taylor Swift song and he did it so badly, I turned on my radio.

"Put it on a Country station, C.W. I like country music. He said it as if he didn't have a care in the world. I hoped he was right.

Lost and Found

I took Beetle back to my uncle's house. I felt he would be safer there and I would see if I could find out what happened to the wallet. It was probably just lost, but if he had lost it at Mindy's it was possible Ed's boys knew who he was, and worse, would be looking for him in Green Top. It was easier to hide in Charlotte than Green Top and I was nervous about what kind of trouble a couple of henchmen could cause in a little town like mine. I called up Len again asking him to fax the garage some sort of picture I.D. I also reminded him my expenses were piling up. I decided not to mention any more about Big Ed. I didn't think it would do anything for Len's confidence in me.

I wasn't going to try to look for the wallet at Mindy's. I decided to see if I could have any luck at the water plant. It took me several phone calls to negotiate through the labyrinth of Charlotte Mecklenburg government to find the right person to talk to, but when I did, things went surprisingly smooth. I got up with Rick, the public information officer for the utilities department, and he was willing to help. Again, I gave out as much of the truth as I dared. I told him I was a private investigator and had been called to Charlotte to help a friend who had a tendency to get a little drunk and may have spent an evening of reverie in the Vest plant parking lot.

"I'm not sure I'd have picked that spot for starting my night life in Charlotte," began Rick, "though you do have a nice view of the Charlotte skyline."

"No," I laughed, "but my client never had a real sense of the romantic life. Do you have any kind of lost and found at the plant? That wallet had some important information."

"We do keep a lost and found at the plant for a few days but only what we find on the inside when we have tours, but that doesn't happen very often. I don't think we keep anything that's on the outside of the gates. Nobody has said anything about a wallet though they might keep something from the parking lot I don't know about. I'll let the chief operator, Taylor, know you are coming. Just go up to the gate and speak into the intercom. What kind of car do you drive? He'll have you on camera. It's a pretty secure facility."

"I drive an Aspen. Yeah, I noticed that when I went by there and I'm not holding much hope that we'll find anything but I told him I'd try." I drove to the facility on Beatties Ford without a lot of faith. I stopped in the parking lot for a few minutes just to look. I still couldn't visualize what Beetle had seen. The strong iron bars and the barbed wire were impressive, but the elevation of the lot sloped down from the north to the south. It made me think that Beetle might have seen something through the fence outside the facility. That made it more unlikely I was going to find anything. The building itself was an impressive example of old architecture with big glass windows and a front that vaguely reminded me of the Alamo for some reason.

I walked to the intercom and said who I was. Within a few minutes, the gate began to pull open. I got back into my car and drove in as the gate closed behind me. Taylor popped out of a door and loudly called me. He was about my size, perhaps a little shorter, and seemed a friendly fellow. I said "seemed" because as soon as he opened the door, I was almost deafened by the noise from the pumps inside. I could see how somebody might not hear a commotion outside the gates.

"We don't get many adult visitors," he started, "lots of kid's groups and their advisors, but not many older folks are interested in a water plant, even a historic one."

I really didn't want to disillusion him, so I sounded intrigued as he began the story of the plant and its place in providing water to Charlotte, especially downtown Charlotte, and looking south you could clearly see it was downtown. I let him go on for a while but I finally interrupted and mentioned the lost and found.

"Oh yeah, Rick said you were interested in that. We have found a few things in the last week and they were on the inside of the gates, though how they got there is a bit of a puzzle." I told him I had noticed the security. He kind of chuckled, "Well, it is unless you're determined to get in."

"Oh, does it happen often?"

Taylor slipped his security card through another locked door as he said over this shoulder, "Rarely, but every now and then someone will slip in when a truck comes through the gate. We even had one of these cards stolen once," holding up his. "But as far as anyone knows it was never used. Besides, once you got in, you'd be lost pretty fast."

"Really," I asked, and Taylor responded, "Yeah, let me show you." Thus began my tour of the Vest Water Plant.

He was right. The three tiered building was a maze of closed doors to the upstairs that ended in other locked doors, all stating access by cards. The hum of the pumps deafened me. Taylor had to take me outside before I really could hear anything he said. "These are our reservoir pools. The water for Charlotte comes in from Mountain Island Lake and begins the process of cleansing for use." I was looking across dozens of pools crisscrossed by concrete beams that were strong, but relatively narrow. I started towards them, but Taylor grabbed me saying "Let's walk around the edge. There's more of a sidewalk and if you fall in and one of the suction pumps is on, you might lose a shoe-plus you would have contaminated the water and we'd have to start the cleaning process again."

"Really?" I asked in wide eyed innocence.

"Well, probably not," he laughed, "unless you can't swim.

"How deep are those pools?"

"About ten feet. Some on the upper end are deeper than that. It allows us to use gravity for some of our settling process."

"Speaking of the upper end, that's where my friend was in the parking lot up there. That's a lot of parking for a facility that doesn't seem to have that many employees."

"Yeah, we are pretty automated now, but in the past we had a lot more employees," stated Taylor. "The parking lot up there is used for some local community events and there's a social club across the street that sometimes uses it for overflow. Matter of fact, they used it the other night when I found the lost items. I just figured one of them might have dropped something. Only, like I said, I couldn't figure how they got inside the gate."

"What did you find?"

"We found a baseball cap, a shoe and a wallet?"

"I thought Rick said you didn't find a wallet?"

"Well, it really isn't a wallet, it's one of those little card carrier deals. It's torn and there's nothing in it."

Uh-oh, I thought, that didn't sound very good. "Where did you find these things?"

"Here, I'll take you up there," and we walked up toward the north end of the facility, the one close to the police sub-station. He took me to a large basin that was at least twenty feet across and very deep. It had only a small amount of water, but there was a very obvious watermark two-thirds of the way up a circular wall that I guessed was just as tall as the well was wide.

"This is our recycling well. We use the water here to clean out the sludge that collects at the bottom of the pool.

"Is it always this shallow? It looks like there's not much more than two or three feet of water there."

He motioned toward the line I had noticed earlier, "Oh, no. It takes a lot of water to carry the recycling process. Occasionally the water will be twelve or fifteen feet deep. After that, it will slowly be pumped out leaving the sludge at the bottom."

Again, I noticed how the department used the effect of gravity. The basin didn't sit too far above ground but it was enough elevation that I suddenly saw that some of the plant was at least twenty five feet lower than the upper parking lot. Someone could be down there and not be seen by the police or almost anyone else.

We walked back in to the little fortress that protected Charlotte's water supply. I stopped short when I noticed a small electric substation. "You've got your own power supply, too?" I asked, somewhat in amazement.

"Yeah," said Taylor, "a relic of when this was the principal water supply station. It looks imposing but it's kind of old. We've had some problems in recent years. It leads to a few outages."

"Don't you have a backup generator?"

"We do, but, it provides just enough to keep the lights on. We're high on Duke Power's emergency list but usually when something happens like that, we switch over to Franklin, the main plant on Highway 16 and Franklin controls all the water until the power is back up. Now, they've got some big emergency generators."

"Have you lost power recently?"

Taylor gave me a quizzical look, "Yeah, as a matter of fact it happened the night your friend said he was up here."

That gave me something to think on. I thanked Taylor and took the lost items from him. I told him I wasn't sure about the baseball cap but I'd take it anyway. I knew the shoe wasn't his but, what the heck. I could toss it away when I got down the road. I got back on Highway 16. Maybe Beetle wasn't quite as crazy as I thought, though I still wasn't sure about his new found sobriety. I hate being so prophetic.

And Lost Again

I called my uncle's house and Sandy picked up the phone. "Hi, C.W.," she said with a teenager's lilt in her voice.

"Hey Sandy, how are things going?"

"Oh, pretty good. The garage called and said Beetle's brother had sent them the information and paid the bill with a credit card. So, I took him over there and we got his old car in no time at all."

"Fantastic! We can head back home now. Put him on the phone, will ya'?"

"Well, uhm, he can't come to the phone now."

Suddenly, my voice tensed up and I stepped on the accelerator. "What do you mean he can't come to the phone right now?"

With a forced chuckle Sandy said, "He's not here."

My voice went up another octave and the car sped up another five miles an hour. "What do you mean, he's not here?"

"Well, he said he felt so good, he wanted to celebrate."

"Sandy!" I shouted in a soprano's voice and almost rammed into the back of a truck. Fortunately, I hit a railroad track at the same time. It slowed me down, but I lost a hub cap, the last one on the old Dodge. I pulled to the side of the road and ironically found myself at the Franklin Water Plant, Vest's larger counterpart. "Sandy, what is going on? Didn't your father tell you Beetle had a drinking problem?"

"Well, he might have. He did ask me if I wanted to go, but I didn't want to be seen in public with such an old man." He was about my age, but I decided to let that go. "Did he say where he was going?"

"I think he said Wilkinson Boulevard or maybe it was South Boulevard, I remember he said he was going to some Country and

Western hangout. That was another reason I decided not to go. I'm more of a Rihanna/Jay Z kind of girl."

I had only a vague notion what she was talking about, so I tried to find out which direction he had gone.

"I don't know," said Sandy. "The weirdest thing happened. As I started to pull out of the garage, this black SUV pulled out of nowhere and cut me off. Beetle took off and so did the SUV. I couldn't tell which way they went."

I bit my hand so I didn't curse in front of Sandy, but she probably heard the horn when I slammed my head. "What's the matter, C.W.?"

"Nothing, sweetie," I said through clenched teeth. "Just tell your dad I might be a little late."

"OK, I'll see you later," she said cheerily and hung up. Ah, the innocence of youth. I dropped the phone and picked up the first thing I could grab–the baseball cap–and began to try to tear it. It was made of very good material so I didn't get very far, but all of the sudden a small card fell out from under the sweat band of the old cap. I picked it up, written down was something like 'rat' followed by the name Ubaldo Echevarria. It didn't take a genius to figure out that I was holding either the name of the person Beetle may or may not have seen, or a contact person for the "victim". I was now convinced Beetle had truly seen something and I might be holding some very important clues. All that didn't seem to help me at all with Beetle's disappearance, but by now I was grasping for straws. As if things couldn't get worse, the phone rang. The ID screen said it was Len Whitmore. Damn, I might as well face the music and lie through my teeth.

The Search Begins

I answered the phone and tried to regain my composure at the same time. It didn't work. "Hi, Len, it's so good to hear from you." There was a pause at the other end of the line.

"C.W., why are you so cheery and why is your voice so tense?"

Damn lawyers, I thought. This is probably how they get people so upset during cross-examinations. I took a deep breath, "Oh, nothing, I had the window down and was hollering at some guy who had cut me off on the road, but I'm sitting in parking lot now."

There was another pause, but Len must have decided to get on with the conversation. "I sent the information to the garage. They should have gotten it by now."

"Oh, yeah, they got it."

"Okay, let me talk to Beetle."

"Uh, he's not here right now." God, I was sounding like Sandy.

"Where is he?"

"He had to drive his car back."

"Why aren't you with him?"

Man, these attorneys don't let up, do they? "Well, I had to drive my car back."

"But you were supposed to stay right with him."

"I did, but I got cut off, like I said. I'm sure he's back to my uncle's house by now."

"C.W., are you sure everything is all right? You still sound agitated."

"Things are fine. Me and Beetle will start home tomorrow morning after we get something to eat and a good night's sleep."

"Anything more come up about Ed Malekola?"

"Uh, no. Why do you ask?"

"That guy had a bad reputation. You and Beetle need to steer clear of him at all cost. I don't need any kind of . . . . well, never mind. I'm just glad you haven't heard anything more."

What he meant was he was just glad that there was nothing that might appear in a major city newspaper before he began his campaign. Man, if he only knew. But at least for right now, what he didn't know was more important to me. I said "Yeah, I'm glad too."

"Tell Beetle to give me a call as soon as he can." He hung up and I began to breathe again. I obviously needed to find Beetle as soon as possible, but the question was where to look in a city of nearly three quarters of a million. Sandy had said something about South Boulevard or Wilkinson. I wondered how many bars there were on those two streets, considering one stretched to the South Carolina line and the other all the way through Gastonia. Wait a minute, I thought. What did Beetle say when he was humming that Taylor Swift song? And Sandy said something about he liked Country and Western. Maybe, just maybe, I could cut my search down by starting at Country and Western Bars. I stopped at a convenience store and borrowed a forlorn telephone book. There were more than I expected. It could be a long search.

I headed for South Boulevard, visiting anything that could classify as a restaurant, bar or pub. Some of the stops I just took a look at and could tell it was not Beetle's kind of place. The rest went something like this. *"I'm a private investigator and I'm looking for a guy named Beetle Whitmore." "What's this guy to you?" "Just a client." "What does he look like? Well, he's kind of my height, and he's got the same color hair." "So, he's your brother/cousin/nephew/son?"* That last one hurt the most. *"NO! He doesn't look exactly like me. He weighs more than me." "How much more?" "I don't know fifteen or twenty pounds." "So, he looks a lot like you." "NO, he's got acne and scoliosis." "Scoli what?"* In other words, it was futile.

I got to Wilkinson Boulevard hungry and thirsty. This time I thought I'd try a different approach, and actually spend some of Len's money. I ordered a drink and an eight dollar hamburger that you could get for $3.95 at a local fast food restaurant. I asked the questions again and got the same answers. I was ready to give up, when a beautiful, black eyed, black-haired woman walked in. Of all the honky-tonk bars in all of Charlotte, she had to walk into mine. Yep, Mabel was back into my life.

"Mabel! Is it you?" I asked hesitantly, even though I knew exactly who it was. There was only one Mabel—a smart, tough talking perceptive woman who had a soft spot for lost puppies and forlorn private eyes.

"C.W.?" She remembered my name. "What brings you to Charlotte? Not another case . . . it is, isn't it?" She turned around to three friends I vaguely remembered from the last time I saw her. She tossed her head my way and introduced Cheryl, Monique and Christie. "You remember me talking about C.W. and his missing woman. What happened in that case, C.W?"

"You were right. It was the mother, she had gone over the deep end and was holding Patsy hostage in her basement. A scene straight out of a horror movie. I guess I owe you another kiss." I said hopefully.

"Oh, I've got to hear the rest of this. Girls, I think I've found my date for the night. That is, if you don't mind." She said I was her date, ahh, all I could do was nod. She scanned the small crowd, "I don't think you girls are going to do any better than me." Cheryl winked and they moved on towards the small stage in the center of the bar. I pulled out a chair for Mabel, gave her a quick hug and kiss, and sat down. She looked at my drink, "Giving up Sun Drop, C.W.?"

"Drowning my sorrows," I replied.

She sat back in her chair and looked hurt. "What about my sorrows? Why didn't you come see me in Ramseur?"

"But I did. Didn't the girl tell you? I can't remember her name, but she said you'd gone on a month cruise of the Bahamas. I thought, well, as pretty as you are with all those rich men on board that you'd found somebody, so I never came back." I didn't include the part about being brokenhearted. I didn't want to sound any more desperate than I already was.

"It was only a week. And no, she never told me. You've just got some bad timing, honey. There were some good looking men on the trip, but no, I haven't found Mr. Right yet. At least, I don't think so," and then she seemed to blush.

I was bowled over. I was sure she was sending me a signal. I took a big swig of my beer and immediately blew it by coming up with some lame line about how beautiful she looked in the dimly lit club.

That seemed to snap her back from the brink of a romantic moment, "Explain yourself. No, wait a minute. First tell me about Patsy."

I filled her in on what had happened after I saw her in Asheboro. She smiled often, even at my desperate fight with the squirrel, and gasped in horror at the description of my encounter with Eurydice Worsham's little basement of horrors. "No wonder Patsy was crazy. Why didn't I read about any of this in the paper? It sounds too good to be true."

"Maybe it was," I said. "In any case, between Mr. Cline's money and the sheriff wanting to keep the whole incident quiet, it just got swept under the rug and Mrs. Worsham has a whole wing out at Mrs. Beasley's little resort."

"That place is still open?"

"Barely. If it weren't for the Cline money, Eurydice would have been out on the street or maybe in a cell at Butner."

She took a swig of her Michelob Light that had just arrived. "OK, what brings you to Charlotte?" I could ask her the same but began to tell her the saga of Beetle Whitmore, the poor, out of luck dope who may or may not have seen a murder committed by Charlotte's biggest crime syndicate. She gave me that wonderful laugh when I described what happened at Mindy's, and rolled her eyes when I swore I didn't know what kind of place I was in when I asked for a massage. My muse turned anxious when I talked about Big Ed and even briefly held my hand. It was wonderful, and time seemed to stand still. When I started to berate Sandy for letting Beetle get away from her, Mabel spoke up and said, "No, I think she made a wise decision not to try and follow. You don't know what she might have had to deal with if they had followed her instead. In fact, it might be a stroke of real luck that they didn't come after her."

"Yeah," I said, "I guess you're right. I just don't want to tell Len Whitmore that I had his brother and then let him disappear again."

"Screw Len Whitmore and all politicians. You've got to stop worrying about impressing them and take care of Beetle and the ones you love," she said emphatically.

"But I don't know where to look, Mabel. I'm a duck out of water in this city and it's too big to cover effectively without blowing who Beetle is related to."

Mabel slapped the table, "Maybe that's it, C.W. Maybe you need to let them know who they've got. Didn't you say this Big Ed was smart and avoided doing things that might bring the law down on him too hard?"

"Well, that's what the Charlotte police said, and it seems to be confirmed from what little I can find about him."

"Ok, play that angle. This guy doesn't want the kind of publicity that might come from kidnapping the brother of a prominent politician. It might bring down a lot of scrutiny on his operation that he can't afford."

"So, you really believe they got him."

Mabel looked at me with eyes that left my heart racing, "Yeah, I do C.W. He's even more of a fish-out-of-water than you."

"Duck"

"What?"

"I said duck, not fish."

"Duck, fish, it doesn't matter." Holding up her hands as if to say I was going off course, "My point is that Beetle would have gone back to one of the few places he's familiar with and feels safe at. No, I think they've got him and you've got to make them think it would be a huge mistake if he was killed. That means you need to let them know the possible consequences for them if Beetle ends up as a dead duck."

"Fish"

"Whatever. Have you got anything else you can use for leverage?"

"I have a cap, a shoe and part of a billfold. The cap had a name under the bill, Ubaldo Echevarria, who I think may have been the victim."

"Great, so you've got something. Now, you just have to figure out how to use it. I think I need another beer. You want something, C.W.?"

"Yeah, a coffee, black. I think I need to clear my mind. If I'm following what you're thinking, I'm going on a suicide mission."

"C.W.! I have faith in you. You're one of the bravest men I have ever met." She reached out, cupped her hands and held my face. "I think you're a lot smarter than these guys. You just have to realize how smart and wonderful you are." Suddenly I felt a foot taller. My shoulders felt a foot wider. In fact, nearly every part of me seemed to be growing.

I looked into those wonderful, big, black eyes and dreamed of sitting here with her forever and sighed, "Do you really think so?"

"I know so." She leaned over to give me a wonderful passionate kiss that went on and on until suddenly a wolf-whistle came from one of her friends at a nearby table. She snapped back, smirked, and shot them the bird. "Get a room," hollered Christie.

"Listen, C.W., when all this is taken care of, I want you to call me and maybe we can have a real date." She took out a pen, pulled a napkin out of a dispenser and wrote down her phone number. I put it in my shirt pocket and dreamed. Suddenly, a vision of Big Ed crossed my mind and I shuddered.

"Mabel, I'm scared. These guys don't mess around. And what if it's too late, what if Beetle is already dead?"

"Well, it might be more important for you to bluff your way out of this, particularly if they made some sort of connection with Sandy. In fact, you need to really start moving on this issue. If something has happened to Beetle, you're going to have to convince them that you've got information you can use to put them away. You make coming after any of your relatives a losing proposition for them. You can do this. You have to do this, C.W., plus if you told this story to the police, I'm not sure they'd believe you."

"You're right about that," I chuckled. "They think I'm either the luckiest or dumbest detective they've ever met."

"Well, they're wrong, and you're going to show them. Come on, C.W., you can do this. Win one for old Booger County."

"Boger!"

"I know," She laughed and said I needed to go and figure out what to do next. She stood up and walked to my side of the table. I didn't move, I didn't want her to leave. She leaned over put her knee in my lap and nuzzled my cheek and whispered, "I want to see you again, so don't do anything too foolish." She turned back towards her friends and waved, gave me a quick kiss on the cheek and headed back to her friend's table.

I didn't want to get up, for a couple of reasons, but if I was going to live up to her expectations I needed to start taking some action. I needed to arrange a meeting with Big Ed and tell him what a valuable person he was holding and try to work out a trade. If I could convince them that Beetle and I would leave town without any word on the possible murder; and if I could trade the few bits of supporting evidence I had that something has occurred and if I could somehow get Beetle out in the trade still in one piece, I could go see Mabel with lots of money in my pocket. That was a lot of ifs, I know she had confidence in me, but I needed a miracle to take care of all those ifs.

First off, how does one go about arranging a meeting with Ed Malekola, or at least a meeting that I could survive? Mabel was right. What little evidence I possessed was not going to convince the police to bring an awful lot of resources to bear for an out of town hick detective who had shown no expertise other than luck. Who did I know in Charlotte that might have a connection, any connection, with Big Ed? The only persons I knew who weren't relatives included a female impersonator (or a very ugly woman), some employees at a massage parlor, an engineer at the Vest Water Plant, and a friendly con man, in both senses of the word.

Wait a minute. Leo Jenkins just might be the answer. Leo seemed to know a lot of less than reputable people and he had taken me to the northwest side of town where most of the "action" had taken place. Maybe, just maybe, Leo might have some connection that I could use. Of course, he could also deliver me into the hands of Big Ed Malekola and that could be the end of the best detective Boger County had ever produced. Now, what was the best way to find Leo? Well, it was a Friday night, so I thought it made sense to stop by the Mecklenburg County Jail. In a city of 700,000, it might be my only hope to find him.

Cat's-paw

I was familiar enough now with the Mecklenburg County Jail that I knew where to go. One of the bailiffs quickly checked the computer and gave me the news I half expected. "Nope, Leo's not on the list today, hmm, that's unusual for him. Wait a minute. Let me check something." He went to another station and checked the radio log with one of the dispatchers. A few minutes later he returned and said, "Yeah, they just picked up L.J. on West Trade trying to sneak out with some gum at a convenience store. L.J. never does anything big. He's just real bad at getting caught or real good, depending on your point of view. Who is this guy to you?"

Here was my moment again. I could tell them my tale of the adventures of Beetle in Charlotte or I could stretch the truth once again. Guess which one I chose. I know. I'm the brightest detective in Boger County because I'm the only one. "Ah," I began, "he's important to an investigation I'm conducting about a missing person."

"Maybe, I could help you. You want me to check the computer again?"

"NO!" I said a little too forcefully. "The family wants to keep this under the radar for now. That's why they got me to investigate."

"Hmm, you know this kind of thing usually turns out bad, don't you?"

"Uhm, maybe not. I think L.J. can help me, he has before. What do you think the bail will be?"

"It depends on who the magistrate is tonight, but, honestly, it wouldn't surprise me if he got released on his own recognizance."

"Oh, that would be great."

The bailiff chuckled. "You don't know L.J. that well, do you? He'll protest and beg to be kept for the weekend. At the very least, he wants a free meal and a checkup by the nurse before he leaves.

If he doesn't get it, it wouldn't surprise me if he doesn't do something by midnight to get back up here."

I didn't need that. I needed to intercept L.J. as he came in, or hope the magistrate put him in jail with not too big of a bond. Len's money was starting to run low and I surely didn't have any. About a half hour later I saw a police car roll in. I hollered and tried to get L.J's attention. I think he saw me and gave me a quizzical look. "I've got a business deal for you," I yelled. He kind of nodded, but that's all I got to say. A couple of beefy deputies came jogging over and asked what the hell I was doing. I tried to explain, but they made it clear that no civilian was supposed to be down in the parking lot when a prisoner was being brought in and told me in no uncertain terms where I needed to go. I took their advice.

Over an hour later, the bailiff who had befriended me came by and said Leo was probably in until the next morning. I asked if I could see him. "I don't think that's likely, but he's entitled to a phone call. If you want I can give him your number. If he wants to call you rather than his bookie or a bondsman, I guess he can." I told him thanks and said, "Tell L.J. he can make some money if he gives me a call."

I spent the next half hour trying to figure out what I could say to Leo to convince him to help me meet my doom. I half hoped he wouldn't call, but I knew that wouldn't do Beetle any good. Then the phone rang.

"Hello. L.J., I think I can help you get out of jail and make some money off the deal to boot."

"Who the hell is this?" Leo fired back.

"L.J., it's me, C.W., the guy who gave you a ride up to Beatties Ford Road the other day. You know, in the old Dodge. Remember you sent me to Statesville Road to Mindy's."

"Oh yeah, the dumb white dude. Did you ever find that fellow?"

"Yeah, and you "helped" him, too. L.J., he's in big trouble and I need your help."

"What's in it for me?"

"I'll take care of your bail."

"Maybe I want to stay in here for a while. What do you want, anyway?"

"I want you to arrange a meeting between me and Big Ed Malekola."

"What!! Are you fucking crazy? I knew you were dumb, but I didn't think you were that dumb. Why don't you just shoot yourself? It'll save Big Ed the trouble."

"No, listen, we haven't got a lot of time. I need to find out if Big Ed has that fellow I was looking for. It might be he doesn't even know anything in which case I'll pay you for your time arranging the meeting, and you're out of there."

"It ain't enough, it ain't nearly enough. You may have a death wish, white boy, but I don't wanna be no corpse."

"Just get me a contact, L.J. I'll take care of the rest, but I got to move fast. Help me, Leo, you're my only hope." Jesus, I couldn't believe I was using a Star Wars cliché with this guy. I had to be desperate.

"Okay. I'll consider it for my bond and five hundred bucks up front."

"L.J., I ain't falling for that stuff again. You get me a contact, just a phone number, and I'll pay the bail and a hundred."

There was a moment of silence. "Well, I might know one of Big Ed's boys, but I ain't getting nowhere near that man. Give me two hundred and that Dodge of yours and I'll do it as soon as I make bail."

"Are you crazy, L.J.! How would I get home? Besides you called my car a piece of shit."

"Yeah," philosophized Leo, "but a piece of shit is better than no shit at all."

I had to think about that for a minute, but somehow, in the surreal situation I was in, it kind of made sense. Desperately I said, "If you get me a contact and I get a talk with Big Ed, I'll put two hundred in the dash pocket and leave it for you somewhere on Beatties Ford, but only AFTER I talk with Big Ed." I figured, what the hell, I might be dead anyway. Nobody else would want that car. "So, who do you know that can help me?"

"His name is Alphonzo Latour. He's not really a part of Big Ed's gang, but he does some odds and ends for them."

"He doesn't sound like a native."

"Oh, no, he's from Chalotte, No' Kalina."

I had to chuckle. My uncle had told me long ago that you could tell a true native of the Queen City from the way he said the name of his hometown. The old timers always dropped the r's and always made it clear, sort of, what state they were from. It was the newcomers that put in the R's to make it sound so much more cultured. "Okay, L.J., you convinced me. You do know Chalotte. I'll talk to the magistrate and begin arranging your release. When you get hold of him, tell him I got some things Big Ed might be missing-enough to tie him to my friend, should he show up in less than one piece."

Now L.J. chuckled. "You know that might work, if you're not bluffing. Big Ed likes to cover all his bases. What kind of things you got?"

"You don't need to know that right now. Just tell him I got some incriminating evidence." Jesus, I was going out on a limb. But that started as soon as I came to the big city.

"OK, Ok, they want me off the phone. Listen, don't hang around, I'll give you a call. I don't need you screwing up my contacts."

"Now why should I believe you?"

"Well, A) what choice do you have and B) all you got to lose is a few dollars and a crappy car." True, but not comforting.

I laughed again. "All right, L.J., you're probably right on both counts. But if I don't hear from you first thing tomorrow morning, I'm coming looking for you and you won't get either money or my crappy car."

The rest of the night was spent tossing and turning wondering if I had put all my eggs in a ratty basket. I was sure Leo had contacts all through the criminal underworld of the city. I was less sure he would risk any foul up for what little I offered him. Of course, another way of looking at it was L.J. wasn't risking nearly as much as I was, particularly if he made his connection in a roundabout way that couldn't be traced back to him. I was the one who could be walking into a trap, but if I was, I'd be damned if he got either my car or my money.

I decided I needed some sort of insurance that didn't risk my uncle and his family. I didn't have a lot of cards to play without going to the city police. Actually, the only cards I had were a baseball cap, a shoe, and part of a billfold. I needed somebody else to see them and make pictures. Maybe, just maybe, I could see a friendly face at the Medical Examiner's office that had enough curiosity to try and solve a mystery that at the moment had no body, no crime, and no leads. I spent the rest of the night trying to think of a convincing enough story to get into the facility and get them to look for something from the little bit of evidence I had.

Saturday Morning - The Plan

My first task was to convince Uncle Barry that there was nothing out of the ordinary and I wasn't mad at Sandy. That part was easy. Sandy was oblivious to how upset I had seemed yesterday and talking about going to the library at the University to study with some friends. Still, I worried about whether Ed's henchmen had noticed her car. I told Uncle Barry that the folks at Townley's said her car sounded a little ragged when it left the garage. Barry played the concerned father perfectly and said maybe she should use the family car. He'd take her car for a checkup at a local repair shop. Great, that would get Barry out of the way and have Sandy in a car they wouldn't recognize, just in case they tailed her on Friday.

That was the easy part. Now I had to convince someone at the Examiner's office to check my flimsy evidence without giving too much away. Jesus, what had I gotten myself into! So, I did the only logical thing I could think of. I went to breakfast-a two hour breakfast-trying to think of a convincing story. I drank about two pots of coffee at the local pancake house going through various scenarios that might be realistic to a gullible Medical Examiner, if there was such a person. I couldn't tell them it was part of a murder investigation because they would immediately call the Charlotte police. I could try the missing person's angle again, but that had already blown up in my face. If it was a new guy, I could pretend to be a big wig from a federal agency, but that depended too much on not seeing anyone from the first visit. Nope, it was beginning to look like I was s.o.l.

Curiosity! Maybe that was the answer. Those M.E.'s were always so curious on television. Perhaps I could convince them that I had a mystery only they could solve. A mystery that could help find a missing man. I know, you're thinking that this could only work in a novel or a movie, but hey, it could happen. On that slender thread I headed for the Mecklenburg County Medical Examiner's Office one more time.

I would lie that Beetle was still missing but I had found this "evidence" at the last place anyone had seen him. Plus, I could only loan them the stuff for a few hours because the Charlotte Police were now interested (another lie), and I needed them to take pictures and I.D. the information before I took it away. That, of course, was not a lie. It might be the only way anyone would know I was no longer a member of the P.I. fraternity should this quixotic attempt at rescue go awry. *"Should go awry"*. That was a joke, when it went awry. I wasn't going to get by the front gate, was I?

I arrived at the barred facility off Rozelle's Ferry and saw cars in the parking lot. I guess that was a good sign. I went up to the gate and called in. "What do you want?" said a rather agitated voice. I identified myself and gave enough of the story to hope for entry. I heard my disembodied greeter talking to someone in the background.

"It's that rube from Hicksville," he said to the other person. Rube! I hadn't heard that word in twenty years. Matter of fact, I'm not sure I had ever heard that word, but I knew it was not a compliment. Nobody from around here would use the term. He couldn't be a native of Chalotte. I heard a feminine voice laugh and say, "Let him in, I need a good laugh on a day I wasn't expecting to work." It was her, the one they called Bones, the one who had so enjoyed my last calamitous visit to this facility.

The gate opened. I went in carrying the precious cap, shoe, and billfold insert. "She who must be paid homage to" came out into the visitor's area and said, "Ok, what you got, W.C."

"It's C.W., Ma'am. I'm still looking for my missing man, but now I've got convincing evidence he was in Charlotte. I was wondering if any of you could take a look at it and see if there is anything that might help me in my search."

"Where did you find this?"

"At the Water Plant up on Beatties Ford Road."

She took them out of my hands, "Have they been in these plastic bags the whole time?"

"Oh, absolutely," I asserted. The items had been in those bags since this morning when I had borrowed three sealable bags from Aunt Marian's kitchen cabinet.

"A ball cap with WC on it, a shoe, and billfold insert with no cards or any ID's. Not much to go on C.J."

"C.W., Ma'am. A name did fall out from under the bill of the cap. It said 'Ubaldo Echevarria'. I'm guessing he was the owner of the WC cap."

She looked at the material carefully "Hmm, not necessarily. WC on the cap could stand for West Charlotte High School and I'm pretty sure Beatties Ford Road is in their attendance area. It could be just a random coincidence but that hat could have been there for weeks. Or it could be a softball cap for a church. W could stand for any number of churches and the C is obvious."

"Oh? How?"

"Church, C.W."

"Oh, uh, yeah of course."

She gave me an exasperated look. "Look, C.W., I'm supposed to be doing some examinations for the state, but you are obviously in over your head. Let me take a look at this and I'll give you a call."

I was both happy that she'd help and disappointed that my reason for getting help showed such desperation. I tried to recover "Uh, but I need these items back right away."

"Jesus, pushy little country bumpkin, aren't you?" She saw I looked hurt, actually it was a frown, but she apologized which made me feel better, for a moment. "I'm sorry," she said, "I'm just teasing you, R.C."

"C.R., Ma'am, I mean, C.W." Now I wasn't even sure who I was. But at least she was willing to help. I tried to change the subject. "What about this Ubaldo fellow?"

"Well, he could be the owner of this cap, but he also could have been the person someone was looking for. Tell me more about this fellow you're looking for."

Uh, oh, now I was in a bind. How much could I tell her without giving it all away? "Well, like I said last time, he has some characteristics that make him easy to spot if you know what to look for."

"Scoliosis is not easy to spot, C.W., any more than this shoe tells me the wearer was probably about 5'8" and tended to drag his heel, wait a minute! Did you look inside this shoe?" I shook my head, "Did your friend bleed easily?"

"No, not that I am aware of."

"Look inside the shoe, what does that look like to you?"

It looked like ketchup to me, but I wasn't going to admit that, so I said, "Yes, I see what you mean."

"That's pooled blood and enough to get a DNA sample. It will take a couple of days, but I think I can get you a good guess as to who this is."

"A couple of days! I can't spare a couple of days. I need this stuff to make a, er, I mean get it down to the city police to prove I'm not making up anything."

"Ah, now we come to the crux." She laughed, and when she did I finally saw something that showed me how men might easily fall under her spell despite her hard shell façade. "OK, C.W., this intrigues me more than the stuff I'm doing for the state. Let me do a scraping from the shoe and I'll see if I can pick some hairs out of the cap. I might be able to get enough to confirm if they belong to the same person. What about the little billfold inserts? Surely I can keep that."

"Yeah, I guess so. But I really need the other parts."

She took everything back inside to her lab and I sat for what seemed an eternity but was probably less than forty-five minutes.

"Ok, I got some blood that pooled in the shoe, I got several hairs from the cap and I took a quick look at the billfold. It looks like there some impressions on them. I'll put it under an electron microscope and see if I can see something. Satisfied?"

"Completely," I said. "I owe you a cup of coffee."

"You owe me more than that, C.W." she said in a stern voice as she handed me the shoe and the cap. "You owe me the real story rather than that cockamamie nonsense you've said so far, but I'll wait. I must admit I'm intrigued now, but don't expect that to last. I have a very short attention span for private investigators who think they can pull anything on me."

I thanked her and headed out the door. At least I had someone who might remember me if I disappeared, and maybe some evidence that could be linked to Big Ed, too. I felt better for about two seconds. Then L.J. called. He didn't even say my name, he just jumped in. "C.W., 'Lonzo wants something for proof."

"I don't follow, L.J., proof of what?"

"Proof that this is important enough to take up with Big Ed. He don't like anybody taking up his time."

"Hmm," now the question was how much I tell him. It dawned on me that everything I had heard about Big Ed said he had a good deal of political savvy. Like Mabel suggested it was just possible that Beetle's connections might be worth something. "Okay, tell them the guy I'm looking for is the brother of a very important politician who could bring down some heavyweights on him if something happened."

L.J. thought for a moment, "That might be the first real sign I've seen that you've got some intelligence. Only, you'd better not be bluffing, if you are, his boys will come looking for you, and me, too."

Ok. I was in this deep, I might as well jump in feet first. "Oh, I'm not bluffing. Tell them I've got some things that might link Big Ed to a murder." There was a long pause. I realized I had miscalculated. L.J. began, "I'll tell them C.W., but I'm not sure if you want to get involved in a high stakes game with Ed. He makes sure he wins. I'll pass it along but you better have something good to back this up." I felt miserable. I was sure I had played my best cards too soon and couldn't think of what else I had to use. The next few hours were agony waiting for a call that might determine Beetle's fate.

Finally, L.J. called again and surprised me. "C.W. they want to know what you're holding." Ok, I've got a nibble. How far do I yank? "Tell them I got a cap with a name in it, a very important name." Maybe he'd jump to conclusions and think it was Big Ed. Instead he fired back, "But not a wallet."

"A wallet?" Now why would they want to know about Beetle's wallet? They already had that with his identification and everything. They could put two and two together just like me, unless…. I had a hunch. Maybe somebody else's wallet was missing. "Yeah," I finished, "I got a wallet." Ok, that was an exaggeration. I had a wallet insert with nothing in it but it just might work.

L.J. spoke to somebody in the background "Ok, where do you want to meet? They want you to bring everything, plus some money." More money? Where the hell was I going to get more money? Too late, I pushed ahead. Now the question was where I would feel comfortable meeting for this little party. I didn't have an awful lot of choices. I didn't want them near my uncle's house. I wasn't about to go back to Mindy's. It occurred to me that if this went down wrong, I would find a sympathetic audience at the morgue if they brought my bullet ridden body to a place where people knew I had been. It was a bit morbid but I wanted some sort of vengeance if I was dead.

"How 'bout the Vest Water Plant on Beatties Ford?" That just might worry them. I heard L.J discussing again. "Sure, that'll be fine. Alonzo says about midnight and no surprises."

That was too easy. What part of the puzzle was I missing? About an hour later another phone call gave me one piece. It was the voice of "she who must command". "C.W.," she began, I've got some news for you. First off, this Ubaldo Echevarria character isn't on our radar. I can't find any mention of him on any state or local data banks. You sure you got the spelling right?"

"Yeah, well, I guess it was. I mean that's exactly the way it was spelled on the piece of paper that fell out of the cap."

"Okay, I'll check with a friend of mine at the FBI and see what they turn up. We got some hair from the cap but don't expect any DNA results for a week or two. The hair doesn't look like it came from a Caucasian, so it's probably not your friend."

"Hmm, well I guess that's good news. Anything else?"

"Well, I put that billfold insert underneath a high powered microscope and there were some indentions like somebody signed their name on a check and used it for a surface. As best I can tell it has an Al, and a z, a capital L and maybe another a, and then it gets fuzzy. Mean anything to you?"

Yeah, a lot, but I didn't want to share it. It would seem that my hunch was correct and somebody other than Ubaldo had left part of a wallet at the party scene at Vest. Alphonzo Latour was suddenly becoming a key member of my little circle of friends. But if he suspected I had something that important, why was he willing to meet me right back at the scene of the crime? My stomach was turning cartwheels. I was walking blind, smelling a trap and seeing nothing but disaster for myself and Beetle at every corner. I needed a drink.

Three Blind Mice, A Beetle and A Whale

It was a dark and stormy night. Okay, okay, just stop. I can hear the collective groan all the way to Green Top. It really was a bad night. Storms began moving into the region around eight and just kept coming. I didn't know whether it was a good or a bad omen. My plan was to grab Beetle, toss the bad guys against the metal fence just as lightning hit, and fry them. After that, me and Beetle would scurry home. Not exactly a top notch plan for saving the day, but desperate circumstances call for desperate, hmm, desperation. My real plan wasn't a whole lot better. I was going to go up to the well I had seen before, put my "evidence" on one side of the upper basin, and have the bad guys send Beetle around the other side. We both get what we want and amble out of the Water Plant parking lot. Good, huh? Okay, back to the lightning.

Actually, I felt pretty good about having a plan at all. I mean who would believe that a would-be girlfriend would send me in the right direction to find a lost Beetle in a city of 700,000 AND that I would find someone who could arrange a meeting with the bad guys who I had never met until I went to the county jail AND I happen to have some leverage to use against the bad guys totally by accident. It's like something out of a …… maybe we better move on.

I said my goodbyes to Uncle Barry and Aunt Marian. I had told enough of the story to Barry that he understood I was doing this to keep any trouble out of his house. Marian thought I was going out on a late date and Sandy was clueless. I did give her a hug that was probably a little longer than it should have been. That'll happen when you're facing your own mortality.

I arrived at Vest around 11:15. There had been a party across the street and the parking lot was half full. That came as no surprise. Taylor had told me the lot was used on occasion for spill-over from the club across the street. It actually made me feel a bit more comfortable to have some people around, but within a half hour nearly everyone had left. I had parked near the basin at the top of the hill. I got out of the car, put on a jacket and an old John Deere hat I kept in the car, and got out. I moved up the fence toward the north side because I felt like I could see more of the facility there. Suddenly, a little past midnight, the gate mysteriously opened. I looked around, saw nothing and walked in. I headed towards the recycling basin. The gate to that facility was open too. Someone was setting me up. The basin had more water than the last time I had seen it. It looked about half full but it was still a long way down. I leaned on the U-bolt devices set to keep anyone from falling in. They seemed pretty secure, but the second one I touched moved slightly. The pool was dotted with pipes and big suction hoses. It had a small safety ladder attached to the wall used, I guess, for bringing those hoses up from the very bottom of the pool.

I noticed the retaining wall on the north side of the basin was lower than the south. If it was a clock I was at six o'clock. I decided to move to the south or twelve o'clock side to have the high ground, though it really wasn't that much higher. I sat the cap and the shoe at the three o'clock position. It dawned on me that I was now farther away from the gate entrance, but I still liked the slight extra protection the retaining wall gave me. I sat down on the ground to give myself as low a profile as possible, checked my gun, sat a box of extra cartridges down beside me, and waited. It began to rain. Really rain. The kind of rain that made you wish you were at home in front of a roaring fire sipping a hot cider, rain. I was soon drenched. Thunder and lightning provided my only company. I slipped my gun and cartridges into my jacket pocket and moved back against the fence that separated the basin from the rest of the complex. It gave me a sense of security, but it did nothing to stop the soaking.

Over the next few minutes the thunder got louder and the lightning got closer. The strength of the storm was causing some power outages. In the distance, I could hear the occasional transformer blow out. Hardly any traffic was moving, but headlights appeared on Oaklawn, the street to the north of the water works. The vehicle drove by and looked to be turning on Beatties Ford when it suddenly did a U-turn to come back to the north gate. Someone got out of a black SUV, the kind I saw at Mindy's, and walked over to the gate. I couldn't see if they did something, or said something into the intercom but the gate opened and the SUV slowly rolled in.

I stood up, backlit by the lightning as much as any artificial source. They still didn't see me at first. A door opened and someone got pushed out into the parking lot. It was Beetle, and he looked to be in some pain. One of the guys grabbed him by the arm to pull him up. Another person got out of the other side of the SUV and approached the inner gate near the water basin. I decided to make my presence known. I hollered as loud as I could, "Beetle, are you ok?" partly for them to know I was here and partly hoping someone else would hear shouting. I heard nothing, but it looked like he nodded. In the darkness and the rain it was becoming increasingly difficult to make out anything more than a few feet in front of you.

"He's fine," someone shouted. I guessed it was Alphonzo, though I had no way of knowing it.

Taking charge, I replied, "Ok, this is how we're going to play this. Come up to this basin. I laid out your stuff on the far side. You send Beetle up the other side. Everybody goes nice and slow. I get Beetle and you get what you want and we both leave happy."

There was a momentary conversation between the two kidnappers. One of them loudly asked "What all you got on that wall?"

"I got what you asked for. Now send me Beetle."

"The cap, the wallet, and the money?" shouted a disembodied voice. I truly could not see more than ten feet in front of me and I hoped it was the same for them.

"Just go over there and get it. It's too damn cold and wet out here to be screwing around," I said loudly and got an affirmative from one member of the group who said, "He's got that right." The three entered the enclosure. It looked like they were holding Beetle up. "OK," said the voice I thought must be Alphonzo. "I'm gonna send Lewis over to check on what you said was over there."

"Not unless you start sending Beetle first. I'm not playing games and I'm packin' heat." Packing heat! Where the hell did that come from? Here I was facing death and the best I could come up with was some cliché from a Turner Classic movie. Christ, just let me get back home in one piece, preferably with a live Beetle Whitmore.

Beetle looked disoriented but it was too dark to really tell. He slowly began to move towards me at the top of the basin. His kidnapper, Lewis, moved more rapidly and soon was at the spot where I had put the incriminating evidence. "What do you see?" shouted Alphonzo.

"I can't see shit. Wait a minute," he said as he pulled out and opened his phone to get some light."

"Are you fucking crazy?" screamed Alphonzo, "You're gonna stand out like a hunderd watt light bulb. If he can see you, he can shoot you."

Damn, he was right. I had been watching Beetle and hadn't even pulled the gun out of my pocket. The light went out and I sensed I had missed my best opportunity to even the odds. Beetle stumbled over to me and I had to catch him. He had been beaten up pretty badly.

"I didn't tell 'em nothing, C.W."

"I know, Beetle, you're very brave."

"No," he whispered, "I just didn't know anything to tell them."

Alphonzo spoke again, "What do you see, Lewis?"

"I can't see a damn thing, you fool. You told me to put out the light." At that exact moment a flash of lightning danced horizontally across the sky right behind Lewis. "Wait a minute," he cried, "I see a cap and a shoe. There's some money in the shoe. I don't see no wallet, Zo."

"What the hell kind of game are you playing!" shouted Alphonzo.

"I'm not playing any kind of game. It should be inside the shoe. He must have dropped it when he picked it up." I hoped my game would keep them guessing for a moment or two and maybe, just maybe, Zo would go over to help him. That would leave an open path for me and Beetle to run for the gate. I knew you should never count on a Biggs plan working. Another bolt of lightning flashed across the sky and a clap of thunder signaled the storm's return. Things got really crazy after that, or maybe more crazy. I'm not sure about the sequence of events but I'll try to give it to you as best as I remember.

The rain was pelting down in large drops that felt like tiny pieces of gravel against our already soaked skin. Zo had joined Lewis at about the five o'clock position on my basin clock and Beetle and I were at about the ten. We definitely were higher than they were by a couple of feet, and the retaining wall provided a little safety. Alphonzo and Lewis were not happy with what they had found, or rather hadn't found. A huge flash of lightning hit behind us. Suddenly the old transformer at the plant blew circuits and spit out sparks. As the last lights in the plant parking lot went out, I looked back across the pool and saw Lewis and Zo pulling out what I could only assume were weapons. I pushed Beetle down to the ground, easy to do since he was standing only because I was holding him up and followed him down. A fraction of a second later, I saw flashes but heard only the barest of sounds. Beetle had been correct on his earlier guess. They had been using silencers. The bullets hitting the brick just above my head were easy to hear and far too close for comfort.

I pulled out my old .38. I knew I had little chance at hitting them but the noise might worry them and, more importantly, might be heard by someone who could alert the police. However, the thunder following the earlier lightning bolt covered up any sound made by my little pea shooter. It did have the effect of sending the bad guys down to the ground. A lightning flash occurred again; instantaneously I saw new gun flashes.

"OOOW," cried Beetle, "I've been hit!"

Hit? How the hell could that happen? I was basically sitting on top of him. "That's not possible, Beetle. They would have had to shoot through me."

"I tell you, I'm hit and I'm bleeding on the back of my neck."

I took my hand and touched the back of his head. He wasn't hallucinating, it was sticky and bloody. Then it dawned on me, he had been hit by a ricochet from a piece of brick from the wall behind us. My notion of higher ground didn't seem to be panning out. I moved away from Beetle, telling him to keep his head down. I fired three quick shots over the wall without looking. One of them sounded like it hit something and another pinged the fence or the wall on the other side.

"Jesus!" screamed Lewis, "he almost got me. I got a hole in my damn jacket."

"Yeah, he's a pretty good shot," replied Alphonzo. "He shot Tiny Bill in the ankle up at Mindy's." Ah, the wonders of my lucky shot had come back to save my bacon again.

"You could have fucking told me that before I got into this. I thought you told me it was going to be an easy $5000 bucks." Five Thousand! What the hell did L.J. tell these guys?

"Shut the hell up," hollered Zo, "and keep shooting." Two more shots flew through the air.

"OWWW," Beetle said again, "They've shot me in my arm."

I whispered to Beetle, "Will you get quiet? How did that happen?"

"I raised up to see what was going on," murmured Beetle, "And they hit me in the shoulder." Beetle had to be the unluckiest guy I had ever met.

"Stay down, Beetle! Dig a hole if you have to, but keep your damn head below this retaining wall!" I rose up and fired another shot. It was low and to the right but somebody must have been moving that way because I heard a body flop to the ground. They were trying to move back to the entrance. I told Beetle to start crawling that way. I couldn't afford to have our exit route closed off. Suddenly all of us paused as the first real light other than the flashes of our guns came up on the site. A large car, it looked long enough to be a limo, pulled in the Oaklawn entrance with its high beams on. I was blinded, and I hoped that was true for the pair across the basin as well.

The driver popped out of the stretch limo and came to the other side. He opened up the back door. Out came the largest man I had ever seen in my life. It was obviously Big Ed. Calling him a whale may have been a misnomer, bear-like fit better. He wasn't as big as a Grizzly but he was bigger than the black bear I once saw as a child. The rain had begun to slow down but lightning illuminated the small mountain that moved up the hill. I was surprised at the grace and speed of the man ambling through the gate. His chauffeur couldn't keep up with him.

"Jesus, look at the size of that guy, Beetle!" I spluttered. Beetle rose up and I pushed his face down in the grass again.

"How can I look with you planting my head in the ground?" he muttered.

Another shot rang out and I flattened down right next to Beetle. By now the giant was at the inner gate and for the first time I noticed he was holding what looked like a rifle, but he surprised me. He pointed it towards Lewis and Alphonzo and said in a powerful voice, "What are you two jerkoffs doing? What the hell is going on?" He had reached the area where the ladder led down into the basin and leaned up against the U-bolt bar set as protection against the unwary water engineer. He held up the rifle pointed it towards me and Beetle and said "And who the hell are you shooting at?"

Unfortunately, I heard that about a millisecond too late. Another lightning bolt flashed and from what I saw, he was about to shoot with that assault weapon. Without really looking, I fired my gun towards him. As I did I saw that the supposed 'Kalashnikov' was really a large curved cane. The bullet pinged off the U-Bolt. Then slowly, like some great ship slipping below the waves, Big Ed Malekola fell into the basin. It could have been my shot, it could have been Big Ed's size and weight. It could have been a weakened connection at the base of the U-bolt he was leaning against, but whatever it was, it led to the biggest belly flop in the history of Charlotte.

Ed fell face down and spread-eagle at least fifteen feet. The collision with the water sent up a spray at least that high. Almost simultaneously I heard a police siren in the background and lights began flicker back both on the street and in the plant's parking lot. Lewis and Alphonzo sprang up, took one look down at their commander's body, and ran like hell. The chauffeur came in to the enclosure and hollered to his boss, "Mister Ed, are you okay?" and again, "Are you okay?" There was no answer. The sirens were getting louder, the lights were getting brighter and Ed's driver suddenly decided this was no place for him. He scurried to the limousine, did a great three point turn, squealed the tires, and headed out.

I got up and looked at Beetle. He looked at me and half smiled. I walked over to the basin. Big Ed was not moving. "Geez, Beetle, I think he's either drowning or out cold." I thought for just a half second and then I did the stupidest, or bravest, thing I have ever done in my life. I jumped in.

Life-Saving 101 or When All Else Fails, Just Fake It

The rain had nearly stopped and the lightning and thunder was lessening by the minute. Lights in the parking lot were starting to get stronger as they flickered on, but the water was still damn cold and I was deep enough in the basin that barely any light was reaching me. I had jumped in and managed to miss pipes, but I had gone in so fast I was still wearing my jacket. It weighed me down for a second and I went under. I pulled back to the surface and stripped it off me, wrapped it around my gun, and screamed up to Beetle. "Beetle, catch, there's a gun inside. For God's sake don't use it unless you have to." Beetle still had enough of his old baseball skills to catch my poor throw.

I moved towards Big Ed. He was not moving, but the water didn't seem to be discolored with blood. I had to assume he had just knocked himself out when he hit the pool so hard. But he was still face down in the water. Have you ever tried to roll a 450 pound dead weight over on his back? That was a rhetorical question. I knew I had to do something fast. I reached out and caught the ladder. Both of us were very close to its position. At least I could steer him over to the ladder. Now what? You remember that game Twister. It dawned on me that if I could get his left arm and left leg inside a rung of the ladder, I might could get enough traction to push him far enough to get his head out of the water. In about ten seconds, though it seemed a lot longer, I managed to get his arm and leg up on a rung above the water. I still couldn't flip him but now his head was tilted slightly out of the water. It didn't look like he was breathing. I began to beat on his chest. Breathing into his mouth just didn't seem kosher.

Nothing seemed to be happening and I was getting tired and cold very fast. One last bolt hit near the parking lot. It wasn't nearly as strong as some of the others, but it hit a light pole and must have skipped down to the iron bars and chain fence that

211

surrounded the basin. I'm not sure of the electrical formulas, but being inside a metal basin in a twenty foot deep pool and holding onto an aluminum ladder is not conducive to safely surviving a thunderstorm. However, in this case it was just what the Samoan doctor ordered. Big Ed jumped, took a deep gasp and opened his eyes. Startled, he began to struggle to get out of the little snare I had set up to keep him above water. His head dipped down below the water again and he pulled his arm and leg out of the rungs. The effort seemed to wake him even more and he came back up almost immediately.

"Ed, Ed can you hear me? Are you ok? Can you breathe?" I shouted.

He didn't speak, but he gagged and I was inundated and spewed with vomit and water. In a way I had my answer, I also knew what Big Ed had for dinner.

"What the hell is going on and who the hell are you?" he spluttered.

"I'm the guy who just saved your life, you ungrateful bastard." Ordinarily I would have been scared to death, but getting shot at and almost electrocuted will give you a strong burst of courage, at least for a minute or two.

Big Ed eyed me, then gasped, "God, I hurt. And where are those two sons of bitches you were shooting at?" I got a good look at him, His face was black and blue and he had been bleeding from the nose. He didn't give me a chance to answer continuing, "My ribs hurt, God, my whole body hurts." He seemed about to faint. I wasn't sure I had enough strength to pull him back up. I told him, "Grab the ladder! Wait, let me grab it first." I reached out, touched it, and felt nothing, "OK, go ahead."

He grabbed the rung, looked back at me and said "There is no way I can make it up that ladder. Who are you?"

"My name is C.W. Biggs. I was sent to bring that guy home," pointing up at Beetle, "but your two goons thought he had seen a murder and kidnapped him. I met them here to ransom him but they had a different idea. They shot at me and you showed up."

Sirens were now on top of us and lights reflected on the water.

"Those lousy sons of bitches. When I get a hold of them, they're dead men. God, the cops are going to be all over me. Listen, for what it's worth, I didn't know anything about this until late this evening when some guy called up and said my guys were planning a hit. I came here to stop them. I don't need any trouble with the cops."

"That guy wouldn't happen to be a fella by the name of LJ."

"Yeah, I think so." God bless him, I thought. He could have my old Dodge and the spare tire and even my Wal-Mart CD player.

He breathed hard again, "Man, I hurt! Listen, can you help me get out of here."

"I'll help you get out but I'm a private eye and I'm going to tell them what I know. They say you're pretty good at getting out of jams, so I'll only say what I know about Alonzo and Lewis. But if they ask me who was behind all this, I'm going to say it was you. You can do the fancy footwork from there."

"No, I wasn't talking about that, I meant just help me get out of this damn well."

"Oh, uh, okay." I wasn't sure how to take that. Big Ed seemed like a decent guy. I had to do some thinking about this. Fortunately, the police and fire department ended our discussion and began to take over the process.

It was a very detailed process. Big Ed was too hurt and too big to get up the small ladder in the basin. The emergency workers and fire department took twenty minutes to figure out how to get him out. It basically took a big horse collar and a pulley to pull him up the side. I stayed in the water the whole time to help get the collar over him and lift him up. In the meantime, they began treating Beetle for his gunshot wounds. The rescue workers asked me if I wanted to climb up the ladder, I said if it was all the same with them I didn't mind going up the same way as Big Ed. So the last fish pulled from the water was me.

The cops began taking statements and finding evidence. I told them what I knew and admitted I didn't know what part Big Ed played in the process. They were not happy with that. There were more than a few gleeful detectives absolutely convinced that they had finally netted the biggest prize of the new century. I couldn't hear everything Big Ed said but I sensed he had sold Lewis and Zo down the proverbial river. Once again my bacon was saved when I saw Officer Robb and a Detective Murphy from my other adventure with the Charlotte police at Mindy's. They were able to confirm most of my story, although they were intrigued by how I had found Beetle and let him get away. Officer Robb also made it clear that I was as naïve as I seemed. Ordinarily that might have bothered me, but in this case, it helped and I was grateful.

After a half hour, one of the EMTs wrapped Beetle up in a blanket, packed him into an ambulance and sent him to the hospital to tend to his wounds. I told him I would follow and asked which hospital. They told me they were headed to University Center. As they turned on the siren and left, I headed to the old Dodge, but I ran into a bit of a hiccup. The Dodge was bleeding. Oil was pouring out from under the engine. I opened the hood and saw a hole through the block. I wasn't going anywhere, and to add insult to injury judging from where I was during the firefight and the angle of the shot, it looked like I had applied the coup de grace to the old chariot. Well, if she had to go, it was better that a member of the family put her out of her misery.

That only left one problem. How was I to get to the hospital and then home. I was a bit nervous about calling Uncle Barry this late. It was past two. I had already intruded too much on his hospitality. Even worse, I realized I had sent Beetle to the hospital with my jacket and wallet. Maybe Officer Robb would once again come to my rescue and give me a ride, but he said the storm had left calls coming from all over Charlotte and he needed to be on his way. He looked over at the other ambulance that had been called for Ed Malekola. He asked the driver if I could go to the hospital with them.

"Now officer," said the EMT, "you know that's against the rules. I can't transport anyone who isn't injured."

Officer Robb punched me in the shoulder.

"OOOW," I gasped, but I caught on really fast and quickly began complaining about my sudden injuries. I really did hurt and was sniffling from my half hour in the basin's pool.

The EMT gave both of us an exasperated look. "Hmm, well I'm not even sure he can fit in. Aren't one of you going to the hospital?"

"I'm sure there'll be someone waiting for you when you get there. We don't have enough to arrest him yet," pointing to Big Ed lying on the gurney, "but we will soon."

Big Ed took off his oxygen mask and wheezed. "He can ride with me, I want to talk with him and I'm not going anywhere. I haven't done anything wrong."

The EMT took one look at the massive form in the back of his ambulance, rolled his eyes and said "Damn, ok, let's just go. I'll be glad when this shift is over."

Now it was my turn to look a little worried, being in the same ambulance with Big Ed put me in between a rock and a...., well you know what I mean. But with police cars leaving at a very fast pace, and the rain starting to fall again, I decided that I could put up with this huge man a little longer and that is how I got to go to the hospital with Charlotte's most wanted. My mama would be so proud.

I originally got into the front seat, but Ed asked for me to come to the back. I climbed over and sat on a first aid bin. There wasn't a lot of room with me, the EMT and Ed in the back. Ed took off his oxygen mask to look my way.

"Why?" he asked.

"I'm sorry, were you asking me?"

"Yeah, Why?"

"Why what, why am I a P.I? Why am I in Charlotte?"

Ed took another breath from the oxygen mask and said, "No, you know what the hell I mean. Why did you jump in the water to save me? You could have been on the front page of the *Observer* if you'd just sat there and let me drown."

It was a good question and the truth of the matter was I didn't have a good answer.

"I'm not sure. Maybe it was my upbringing, give credit to my mother. Maybe it was because I realized in that last second that you had that crazy cane instead of a rifle."

He smiled at that, "You weren't the first to be fooled by my crutch cane." He stopped long enough to wheeze again, "I've found that once you have established a reputation fear and respect can do just as good a job as intimidation and violence."

I laughed. "It worked for me. As dark as it was, I was sure it was an assault rifle. I guess I also wasn't sure I hadn't shot you. I can't have it going around I shoot unarmed men."

"You didn't shoot me!"

"I know that now, but I did shoot towards you, and then you fell. That's when I realized you weren't holding a rifle. By the way, that has to be the biggest splash I have ever seen." Almost as soon as I said that I wished I had bit my tongue, but he surprised me again when he laughed, "Yeah, I wouldn't mind having a video of that myself now that I know I'm going to be all right."

"Are you going to be all right, Big Ed? It looks to me like the police are licking their chops to charge you with something, and I'm not going to cut you any slack. I nearly got killed because of your bunch and you've got to bear some of the responsibility for having that bunch of cutthroats for your gang."

"I understand that, and I appreciate what you did for me when all my boys had left me. I won't forget it."

I wasn't exactly sure how to take that until he said, "I kind of like you, Biggs."

"Thanks, Mr. Malekola. And I, uh, uh, admire your, uh, uh, toughness." Toughness??? Geez, I was tongue-tied in the back of an ambulance with a master criminal and I admired his toughness? I might as well ask if I can be his bitch when they put us in the same cell at the Mecklenburg County Jail.

We arrived at the hospital, and to my astonishment there was Beetle in the waiting room handcuffed to a hospital security officer.

"Beetle," I shouted, "what the hell have you done to get arrested?"

"C.W., I'm glad you got here, tell them this isn't my gun," pointing at an evidence bag holding my old .38. I had forgotten I had tossed it up to Beetle when I hit the water. How it got by the Charlotte cops was another matter. I told him to give me my jacket. I pulled out my wallet and my P.I. identification. It took me a little while to convince the security guy but I think he was glad to get the squirming Beetle away from him. They finished fixing up Beetle, he wasn't exactly in critical condition and I went to an ATM, got some money and called for a taxi.

We were headed out the doors when Big Ed called me over. He was now surrounded by a coterie of investigators accompanied by an army of well-dressed lawyers. I assumed they were Ed's defense team. Once again, he was moving at least as fast as the authorities. Ed held up his hand for me to shake it. I thought about the consequences of refusing and decided to shake. He pulled me down with a vice-like grip and whispered, "I won't forget you Biggs, I won't forget." I tried to look at the declaration as positive, thanked him and scooted out the exit. The dawn was breaking-a Sunday, a day for prayer, rest, and reflection. The clouds were lifting and I was alive. Considering what I had been through in the last twelve hours it was looking like it was shaking up as a very good day for the Biggs.

Getting Out of Town

Beetle and I were hungry, so we stopped at a Waffle House and grabbed a bite to eat. I even fed the taxi driver with about the last of the money I had placed in my account from Len. It occurred to me that my next phone conversation with him was not going to be overly friendly, but I did have his brother back in one piece. Well, almost one piece.

We got back to the house in Oakdale around 6 AM and both of us hit the sack without a shower or shave. I was sleeping on the couch when Barry woke me up around noon. I kinda filled him in on what happened and why there might be blood on Marian's fancy sheets. I told him I knew my presence was starting to be a burden. He shrugged and said it's what family did. I said that this was going above and beyond and I intended to get out of Charlotte as fast as I could round up some transportation. I was getting very nervous about the family.

"Barry," I asked, "have you seen anything suspicious in the last couple of days?"

"Suspicious in what way?" he responded.

"Oh, I don't know. Any strangers or strange cars in the neighborhood?"

"Not that I know of, but I'll ask some of the neighbors. This is a kind of secluded neighborhood."

He was right about that. Oakdale was one of the older communities on the west side and unless you knew your way around the short side roads you could get lost real fast. Many of the folks on his street had been his neighbors for twenty years. He felt sure they would report something unusual to him. Still, I was uncomfortable. The faster I could get out of here the better for the Oakdale Biggs. That, however, was going to require an infusion of money from Len Whitmore and that required calling him. Two hours later, I couldn't come up with any more excuses to avoid the call,

219

and Beetle was still asleep. I thought that might be good. I needed to give Len the closest thing to the unvarnished truth before Beetle gave his version. Damn lawyers.

"Hello, Len. Glad I got up with you on this beautiful Sunday afternoon."

"Hello, C.W. What's going on? You sound unnaturally happy."

"Why do you say that?" I said, too defensively.

"Because the last time you called you sounded like this and you were hiding something."

"No, No, I've got nothing to hide. Things are just going great."

"All right, C.W., let's move on. I thought you all would be back by now."

"Well, we've run into a little bit of a problem."

Suddenly Len's voice bristled. "What kind of problem?"

"Uh, do you want the good news or the bad news first?"

"I want the bad news."

"Oh, are you sure? I kinda thought you'd want the good news first."

"C.W. just tell me the bad news. What the hell is going on?"

"We've got a transportation problem."

"I'm not surprised," Len interrupted, "I thought your car was on the brink of breaking down when you left here. But why not use Beetle's?"

"Uh, Beetle's car is missing."

"I thought you got it out of the tow garage."

"Well, we did, but it went missing again."

"What do you mean it went missing again? Did it just drive off into the sunset? Did Beetle leave it at a bar?"

"Uh, no, Beetle thinks it might be at the bottom of Lake Norman."

"WHAT?" Len shouted, "PUT BEETLE ON THE LINE RIGHT NOW!"

"Well, he's still sleeping."

"At two o'clock in the afternoon? Is he drunk?"

"No, no, it's nothing like that. I think it's the Percocet the doctor gave him after he stitched him up, and he took another about 6 AM."

"STITCHED UP! WHY WAS HE STITCHED UP?"

"Jeez, Len. You don't have to holler. It was after he got shot."

"HE GOT SHOT!"

"I told you, Len. You don't have to holler. I can hear. It was a clean wound, no broken bones."

"How did he get shot?"

"He got shot after I ransomed him, which is why I need more money. That and the transportation costs."

RANSOMED?! DID YOU SAY RANSOMED?"

"Yeah, after he was kidnapped."

"KIDNAPPED, DID YOU SAY KIDNAPPED?"

"Well, I think he was kidnapped, now that you mentioned it, Beetle didn't say. He might just have gone off with them for a drink."

"C.W., Are you drunk?"

"No, I rarely drink, but I wish I had a Sun Drop about now." Aunt Marian walked across the kitchen and whispered "I'll check the fridge."

"C.W., explain to me what's going on! Who shot him?"

"A guy named 'Zo. At least I think it was 'Zo. It could have been Lewis. But based on the angle, I think it was 'Zo."

"And who the hell is 'Zo?"

"Zo's part of Big Ed Malekola's gang."

"Big Ed's mixed up in this?"

"No, I don't think so. At least, that's what he told me after I rescued him from drowning."

"YOU RESCUED BIG ED???"

"Yeah. It seemed like the right thing to do at the time."

"The right thing….C.W. are you crazy???"

"No, if you'd just let me explain from the start, I'd could do this better. I wanted to tell you Beetle was ok right from the start, but you messed up my presentation."

"Sorry, I didn't know I had interrupted the power point," Len said sarcastically.

Finally, I began to tell the story the way I wanted to tell it. It took about thirty minutes and was punctuated often by some choice phrases from Len like, *"You were lucky as hell,"* or, *"Amazing"*, or his personal favorite *"You stupid idiots"*. Slowly I got my version in and he realized I was telling the truth. He probably was also very glad that none of this had come out in the newspaper or on TV yet. After he mumbled something about he wasn't wasting money any on more cars, he agreed to send me some money. Since we had already killed two, I could understand where he was coming from. He said he would have two tickets waiting for me at the Amtrak train station. We'd be on the train at noon Monday and Len would be waiting for us in Cary. That was slick Len for you. He knew there'd be less chance of the press or seeing someone we knew in Cary as opposed to Raleigh. Beetle had gotten up by now and I put him on the phone with his brother.   They didn't talk long and I didn't ask questions. I figured the two had enough on their minds. I know I did.

We ate a quiet meal at home that evening. Marian had fixed beef stew and mashed potatoes. Beetle ate like a man possessed, but Marian seemed to appreciate it. Beetle and I said the least we could do was clean up after dinner and we were nearly through when the phone rang. Sandy got to it and I heard her ask, "Who?" at least twice. She looked over at me, and I realized the person on the phone was asking for me.

I whispered "Tell them I left for Green Top this evening." She started to talk, then turned back to us saying, "He hung up." I felt a cold chill go up and down my spine. I exchanged a look with Barry. He caught on and said, "Nobody is going out tonight. In fact, I think we all should turn in early." I smiled and nodded. No one objected. Everyone was now on pins and needles.

Barry and I sat up all night. He had an old .22 rifle and I had my trusty pistol. I spent most of the night cleaning and re-cleaning it. Every time a car would come down the road we'd head to pre-arranged positions at windows facing the front. There were several cars that travelled up and down the road that night, but only one slowed down. It was about 3 AM and an SUV slowed to a crawl. Barry and I looked at each other in anguish, but just as we opened the windows, it sped up and didn't come back. Less than a minute later we saw what had spooked them. A police car drove by, slowed for just a second, and went on down the road after the SUV. Nothing else happened except I went to sleep about dawn. Marian woke me up for breakfast and Beetle and I began to pack shortly afterwards.

I gave a call to the Charlotte police to clear me getting on the train with a gun and confirming the inevitable return for us to give depositions before the grand jury that would be called. They didn't have an awful lot of information for us, but continued to pursue any information I could give on Big Ed. I told them what I had said before and Beetle admitted that he had not seen or heard of Big Ed's involvement until the incident at Vest. They were irked that the conversation I had that night seemed legitimate. The investigators were convinced this would be a golden opportunity to send Ed away for a long time.

Barry said he would drive us to the train station, but I was still concerned about last night. I decided we'd go by taxi but I wanted to be sure no one was following us or Barry. He pulled his car into the garage. Me and Beetle got into the back seat and down on the floorboard. We were going to have the taxi meet us up at a convenience store on Old 16. I had Barry go there in a roundabout way, and even then we played like we were in some bad spy movie. Barry drove up and down Belhaven until we saw the taxi pull in. Barry pulled up beside the car. We spilled out, jumped into the taxi, ducked down again, and told the taxi where to go. Barry didn't even slow down. I kept a running conversation with the driver asking if he saw anybody following us. He asked if a school bus counted. Funny guy. We arrived at the Amtrak station about a half hour early and ran for the ticket office. The tickets were there and we headed to the platform to board.

Now the fun began. On the platform waiting for us was Big Ed in a wheelchair, surrounded by about ten guys that were at least as beefy as the Panthers offensive line. I know my mouth was gaping. All I saw for our side was one plain clothes man talking to an Amtrak official. I didn't even see a sidearm. Great. My peashooter versus at least eleven guns. The *Observer* might get its headline yet: TWO RUBES RUBBED OUT BY SAMOAN ARMY. I tried to look straight ahead as the Charlotte detective called me over. I pushed Beetle ahead of me and told him to get on the train. The detective handed over some papers to the Amtrak agent and introduced us. He wanted to look at the gun. I showed it to him and he laughed, not a reassuring move with Ed's gang watching my every move. I looked back over my shoulder and Big Ed was staring at me. At first he said nothing but gave me thumbs up and held up one finger. I wasn't sure how to take that. Was it that now we were even or was it saying that I only had one day left in my brief life? I sure was hoping it was the former. Just as I started to step on the train Ed took off his oxygen mask and called,

"C.W., you got no car?" I turned and grimly nodded.

"What kind of cars do you like?"

What a strange question, but I answered anyway. "I don't know, Pontiac Trans Am, Dodge Chargers, you know American muscle cars."

It seemed to satisfy him and I hurried onto the train, got Beetle settled and looked out the window. None of the gang was there. For some reason that was not reassuring.

Nothing happened on the ride home. Beetle slept, and I may have nodded off myself. We reached Cary about mid-afternoon and Len was waiting for us. He did not look happy but he was smart enough not to ask many questions until we were well on the way back to Green Top.

"Ok," started Len. "Where do we stand and what do I have to do?" Len was always good at cutting to the chase.

"Both of us have to report back to Charlotte," I began. "The DA down there will give us a call."

"Any idea when that will be?"

"I don't know. It could be six weeks, it could be six months. I guess it depends on if they catch the two guys, maybe three, who did this."

"Two guys? What about Big Ed?" Beetle and I looked at each other, "Well, there's a problem there, sort of," I said.

"Explain."

"Neither Beetle or me are sure we can connect Ed to the kidnapping. In fact, we believe he may have helped us."

"I don't believe it."

"Yeah, the Charlotte detectives weren't exactly happy with our answers either."

Len mused on that a moment. "I might be able to use your cooperation and the situation Bradley was in to our advantage."

"Bradley, who's Bradley?" Beetle gave me a hard stare. "OH, oh yeah, Bradley. Sorry," I said as diplomatically as I could.

Len continued, "I think it could impress Judge McKendall."

Beetle spoke up, "Judge McKendall? I like Judge McKendall. He's nice to me."

"Yeah, I know," said the younger, smarter Whitmore. "That's why I got you on the docket for next Friday before he leaves for vacation. I think I might get you off with an extensive probation and a house monitor stay." And that's exactly what happened. It's good to have a friend in high places (or a brother.)

Surprise, Surprise, Surprise

The next six weeks Bradley and I waited for a call to return to Charlotte and a visit to the Grand Jury. While we waited, we practiced our stories. We didn't change anything but it wasn't exactly what you're supposed to do. I finally heard from Len that they had only caught one suspect, the one they called Tiny Bill. Now that kind of put me in a bit of a quandary. You may remember I had taken a lucky shot at Tiny Bill up at Mindy's and hit him. I had shot first and although the way the gang had acted proved they were up to no good, it could be argued that I had started the melee with that first shot. It was the way the old film noir detectives always acted, but it wasn't exactly part of the licensure program for a private investigator in North Carolina. I was nervous as to how this might play out. Then the strangest thing happened.

I was sitting at my desk one morning, going through the internet to see if I could find a bail pickup that could earn me some money, when the phone rang. An assistant district attorney from Charlotte was calling. I can't remember his name, probably because his news left me stunned and bewildered. Tiny Bill had pled guilty to aiding and abetting a kidnapping and was going to get at least 20 years. Bill had told the district attorney Big Ed had nothing to do with Beetle's kidnapping and beating. It was all between him, Alphonzo and Lewis. So Big Ed seemed to be off the hook. But here came the real shocker. Big Ed had pleaded guilty to having knowledge of the kidnapping but not reporting it to the police until after the fact and accepted a sentence of nine to thirteen months to be spent at Central Prison. Lewis and Alphonzo were still missing.

"So, Mr. Biggs, I guess your and Mr. Whitmore's testimony will not be necessary," said the assistant D.A. "The city of Charlotte and county of Mecklenburg want to thank you for your actions and courage." There was silence on the other end. "Mr. Biggs, Mr. Biggs.....are you still there?"

"Oh, uh, yeah, uh, thank you."

"Oh, by the way, I have a message for you from our star Medical Examiner. She says the blood in the shoe did match Ubaldo Echevaria. It seems Mr. Echevaria was a courier for the Mexicali cartel and had rarely been up in the States, so she had to really do some research to find him. We are pretty sure Mr. Echevaria was up here to check the possibility of setting up an operation for the cartel and we're also pretty sure he is no longer a living member of the gang. But until we find a body we can't do a whole lot."

"Oh, well I can understand."

"Anyway, she said to tell you 'nice work' and, how did she put it, 'not as dumb as you look,' Mr. Biggs. She said to come by and see her the next time you were in Charlotte."

"Wow, really?"

"Yeah, I'm a bit shocked myself, if I were you I'd take her up on that. She doesn't usually have much to do with, ahem, people in your line of work. Well, anyway, thanks again. Goodbye."

What in the world was going on? I didn't know whether I was more surprised about Big Ed's confession or my dream Medical Examiner acknowledging that I lived. I spent most of the rest of the day in a fog and it continued for several days afterwards. I just couldn't wrap my head around it all. About a week later Len called and congratulated me on avoiding facing a grand jury. I questioned him about why Big Ed would accept prison when he had done everything he could to stay out of Central Prison for so many years before.

"Maybe," Len began, "he cut a deal to avoid more investigations. It certainly wouldn't be the first time. Or maybe the DA in Charlotte was just glad to get him off the streets for any period of time, no matter how short. There is one other possibility."

"What else is a possibility?" I pushed him for an answer, I wasn't satisfied with his first suggestions.

"Maybe it has something to do with that Cartel courier Beetle may have seen shot." That was interesting. Len was now conceding Beetle did see a murder. "It wouldn't be the first time that a big shot on our crime scene accepted a short stay at a protected facility while the Latino cartels stopped looking for him. In any case, be glad you got out of there with your skin. There was a reward for convicting Big Ed, although by the time it gets cut up into all the claims, I doubt you'll get more than $500."

That didn't bother me. I had made more on this case than any other since Mr. Cline's nice present. However, I was still pondering the situation that led to Big Ed accepting his fate. Several weeks went by before a small news article appeared on one of the internet press outlets I often checked. It reported that Ed Malekola had begun his sentence at Central Prison in Raleigh. My curiosity got the best of me, and a week or two later I sent to letter to him. It basically asked why, what had occurred and what did our last meeting mean to him, (hinting ever so carefully on whether I should always be watching my back.) I didn't hear anything for three or four months. One day while I was napping, er, checking my mail at the backroom at the old bus station, there was a knock on the door.

I opened the door to a tall, well-dressed, muscular black man who I vaguely remembered from the group on the train station platform. I invited him in. It seemed the right thing to do since most of the garage and all of the beauty salon patrons were watching.

"C. W. Biggs," he began.

"Yes."

"I have a message for you from Ed Malekola. He asked that you read it right away."

That didn't sound reassuring, but I decided a refusal might not be well received.

"I'll be outside, in case you have an answer," he finished.

229

I looked at the letter for a few minutes, holding it up to the light to see if there was any strange powder at the bottom of the envelope. Seeing nothing, I tore it open and began to read.

C.W.,

You asked some interesting questions and I've thought long and hard about my answers. I don't have much else to do and yet despite my deliberations I'm not sure I have any answers for either myself or you.

I do believe you may have saved my life. I'd like to know more on why you think you jumped in. Perhaps you can write again. Maybe I accepted the sentence because I just needed some time to think and what could be a better and safer place than Central Prison, although I admit my reputation may have made that easier.

By the way, you may have saved my life twice. The doctors here said I was a walking heart attack and put me on a strict diet. I've already lost 50 pounds. Soon I won't make nearly as big a splash the next time you see me jump in a pool. Ed still showed a sense of humor, I took that as a good sign.

I think the law also thought my being in jail would cause a split, or fight, in my organization but I've actually been able to run it quite well from inside here. I didn't need to let the authorities know that, which is why I sneaked this letter out to be personally handed to you. However, my near brush with death has made me consider what will happen to my investment should something happen to me when I move on. So I've been trying out a couple of successors. The leading candidate is the one who brought you this letter and he has something for you waiting outside which should answer your question about what I asked you at the train station. Enjoy!

Ed Malekola

PS-That friend of yours, LJ, tried to hit me up for $500 for that old car you had. I told him to get lost.

Poor LJ, he can't seem to catch a break. I got up and started out to the parking area. There was a crowd around something but they parted for me when Ed's assistant called me over. It was a cherry red 1987 Pontiac Firebird, 305 cubic inches with a golden firebird painted on the hood. It looked to be in mint condition. The message deliverer tossed me the keys and started to walk away.

"Wait," I cried, "What is this?"

"Big Ed said to tell you thanks, and give you the keys."

"This is for me? I can't pay for this."

"Oh, it's all paid for. The papers are in the dash pocket. All you got to do is drive it."

"But, but, I ...."

"You're not turning down Big Ed's gift are you?"

"Well, no, not exactly. It's just this is kind of showy for my line of business."

"I told Ed, I told Ed, I said 'if he's a smart as you say, he ain't going to take a car that announces your business five minutes before you arrive.' So, you want me to take it back?"

"Uh, yeah, uh, no, let me think about this. Tell Ed I am very appreciative. I just, I just...."

The tall black man smiled, "I understand, I'll tell him you're going to test it out and you can go from there." A black SUV suddenly appeared and he got in, waved at me, and left.

I really needed a car but I was looking for a Toyota, like a 2002 Camry, gray or some inconspicuous color. I just couldn't see myself doing surveillance in a Trans Am. I'd stick out like a sore thumb or a would-be pimp. Nope, I had to sell it and get something more sensible. I'll write Ed and explain. Maybe say something more about my reasons for jumping in that pool that night. He'll understand, I hope. But not right away. I'll write him in a week or two and start seeing what I can get for this collector's item. Who knows, I might be able to get a 2004 model, and maybe a bigger air conditioner for my little compartment. First, though, I'm going to take this jalopy out for a spin. Maybe go to Ramseur one afternoon. I could stop and stay a night at a bed and breakfast. I know the owner. I think she might just be delighted.

Biographic Notes

Steve 'Doc' Underwood is a native of Charlotte and taught in the Lee County Schools in Sanford, North Carolina for thirty-three years. He and his family live in Sanford. This is his first book since his dissertation, so this is the first book that somebody may read. He hopes his former students enjoy it as much as they enjoyed his classes. If you like the book, please like him on the Facebook Author page, Steve 'Doc' Underwood.

Jared Terrell is a teacher and graphic illustrator from Pittsboro, North Carolina. He lives there with his wife, Julia and sons, Nathan and Ruben.

www.ingramcontent.com/pod-product-compliance
Lightning Source LLC
Chambersburg PA
CBHW070610130626
46556CB00001B/332